# AOIFE

By

# Katherine Pathak

For Rakesh, Shona and Jamie
With Love

All rights reserved. No part of this publication may be reproduced in any form or by any means – graphic, electronic, or mechanical, including photocopying, recording, taping or information storage and retrieval systems – without prior permission in writing of the author and publishers.

© 2013, Katherine Pathak, all rights reserved.
© Cover Image, Anne Currie, 2013, all rights reserved.

**THE GARANSAY PRESS**

This is a work of fiction. Names, characters, businesses, places, events and incidents are either the products of the author's imagination or used in a fictitious manner. Any resemblance to actual persons, living or dead, or actual events is purely coincidental.

The moral rights of the author have been asserted.

My thanks go to Avril Paton for kindly granting her permission for reference to be made in this book to her painting, 'Windows in the West'.

References to the 'Aoife's Chariot' myth in this novel come from the following texts, with some changes having been made to the original story for fictional purposes:

Kuno Meyer (ed), 'Tochmarc Emire la Coinculaind' Halle an der Saale, Max Niemeyer volume 3, 1901, pp. 229-263

Kuno Meyer (ed. & trans.), "The Death of Conla"1, 1904, pp. 113-121

Kuno Meyer (trans), 'The Wooing of Emer' 1, *Archaeological Review*, London, volume 1, 1888, pp. 68-75; 150-155; 231-235; 298-307

Rolleston, T.W. (1986). *'Celtic Myths and Legends'*. London: Gresham. p. 192

**THE GARANSAY PRESS**

# PROLOGUE
## July 1982

As the Secretary of the Garansay Society of Hill Walkers, Isabel felt obliged to take part in at least a couple of their outings a year. On this sunny and warmish July afternoon, it seemed like a pleasure as well as a duty. The group of eight walkers had already completed a short hike along the stony path leading away from the outhouses of Lower Kilduggan Farm. They had now reached the first stile, which took them into a pretty wild flower meadow just beyond the boundaries of Isabel's land.

At this point, Isabel stopped to take her breath. Turning to gaze out across the Kilbrannan Sound, she could just identify the outline of the impressive mountains of Jura through the hazy cloud. Isabel Nichols had not often taken the time to admire this remarkable view during the summer months. Not since Gus had died and left her with the farm, the boarding house and three children to support single-handed.

Beyond the shimmering sea, she surveyed the rolling hills of Kintyre, which appeared deceptively close in the clear morning sunshine, as if she were looking at them through Gus's old, battered binoculars.

# 4

'There'll be freshly baked scones and my plum jam waiting for us, when we get back down to the farmhouse!' Isabel shouted encouragingly to the group just up ahead of her, as they started to steadily climb the long, narrow path which ran through the wild meadow.

Appreciative noises were made by way of a reply and a few walking sticks lifted in acknowledgement. Billy McKinley, the retired school master, fell into step beside Isabel. They lapsed into a familiar exchange about the shoddy treatment of Garansay by the Council on the mainland. The rhythm of their words matched the gentle pace of their footfall on the path, helping them to make good progress on this steep section of the climb.

The views from the peak of Ben Mhor would be worth the effort. There was a very pleasant loch, just at the foot of the last ascent that would provide a perfect spot for their picnic lunch. Just ahead of Isabel was Susan Dickson, who ran the general store in Port Kilross, which lay on the eastern side of Garansay.

Port Kilross was the largest village on the Island and known to all local residents as simply, 'The Port'. It was rare to see Susan away from her post behind the counter, particularly during the height of the tourist season. Her husband had given her the day off and brought in a local lad to help him man the shop.

'Will Jimmy be alright without you?' Isabel called ahead.

'Aye, but I don't think I'll be getting another break for a good long while!' Susan shouted back, as she picked up her pace.

Susan Dickson was actually a cousin of Isabel's on her mother's side. A few years younger than her, she was trim, fair-haired and pretty. Susie was always to be found manning the till of the shop. Jimmy was a quiet man, more comfortable in his stock room and negotiating with the skippers of the fishing boats than in making small talk with the tourists and locals.

Susan's children, Alison and Davy, were of a similar age to Allan and Imogen. They came over with Susan whenever she visited. It was a bone of contention with Jimmy that his eldest daughter would never help out in the store. She seemed to have grander plans for herself. Alison was struggling to get a place at art school and spent most of her time sketching. A visit to Lower Kilduggan on a sunny day like this would suit her very well, thought Isabel.

The path was following the course of the burn now and after swinging around to the left for a short while, it suddenly became very rocky, with some sections requiring the walkers to perform an undignified scramble over the steep outcrops of slate and scree. After tackling a couple of these, the group were ready to stop for a drink. Isabel lowered herself onto a smooth rock by the side of the path and took some sips from her plastic water bottle. Billy McKinley sat on the adjacent stone and raised his flask in a silent toast to the impressive view.

# 6

'Let me carry your bottle in my rucksack Isabel,' Billy offered, as they stood up to resume their climb. 'It must be making your bag heavy.'

Normally, Isabel would have declined such a gesture, seeing it as kind, but also a little patronising. However, the heat and the strenuous nature of the walk made her tempted to agree.

'If you don't mind Billy, I'll take you up on that.' She handed the bottle of water to her companion which he slipped into a side pocket of his walking rucksack.

The remainder of the hike proved to be less arduous. The group only stopped once more when Alec Ginley spotted a golden eagle, hovering on an air current a few yards away from them. They passed around his binoculars and photographs were taken of the glorious bird against the vertical backdrop of the steep mountainside, made purple by a thick blanket of wild heather.

When they reached the pebble beach surrounding the loch, at the foot of Ben Mhor, Isabel felt almost giddy with tiredness. As the group searched for a dry spot to sit and eat, Isabel suddenly noticed the absence of a familiar weight on her right shoulder.

'Where's my bag?' she exclaimed, and instinctively felt her back and shoulders for the missing appendage. Billy walked over from the other side of the beach, sensing Isabel's panicky mood.

'Is everything okay?' he asked cheerily.

Isabel paused from her frantic search to look up at the retired teacher. 'I haven't got my bag, Billy,' she replied, trying her best to sound calm.

'Well,' he said, 'when do you last remember having it?'

Isabel thought carefully. She had looked at the eagle with Alec's binoculars, when he had passed them around to each member of the group. She hadn't taken a photograph, or reached into her satchel for anything else that she could recall.

'I don't remember having it with me since... yes, that's it, I took my drink out of my bag, down at the bend in the burn, by the big slate rock. You remember Billy - you offered to take the bottle for me.'

Billy reached into the side pocket of his rucksack and pulled it out. 'Well, at least we've got your water,' he added with a raise of his eyebrows.

Isabel had to take a deep breath to try and calm her rising frustration. 'I must have left it there - when I didn't put my bottle back into the bag.'

Billy's face fell at the implication of Isabel's words so she quickly added, 'och, it's not your fault, you were only being helpful.'

The rest of the group had gathered around them by this point and were quietly listening to their exchange.

'We can always re-trace our path when we climb back down,' suggested Susan Dickson. 'It should be perfectly safe in the meantime.'

Of course, this was the most logical course of action and Isabel had no desire to spoil the day for the rest of the group. She also had no intention of leaving the bag unattended down there for so long.

'I am going to go back for it.' Isabel made this statement in a tone that challenged contradiction. Inevitably, Billy offered to accompany her in the search. Isabel knew her friend was keen to reach the peak of Ben Mhor and was offering out of an outdated sense of chivalry. She firmly but kindly refused, wishing that she had done so earlier.

'I will meet you at the farmhouse later,' Isabel called out as she gathered her remaining belongings and started walking over the ridge. She strode purposefully downwards, watching her footing carefully, as she was exceeding her usual pace. Suddenly, heavy steps could be heard, approaching quickly from behind. Isabel turned to see her cousin, Susan Dickson, marching towards her.

'Slow down a minute, I'm coming with you,' she shouted.

Isabel did not reply but smiled at her cousin as she fell into stride next to her. They continued their descent in companionable silence. As they re-trod their route, the women scanned the path for a glimpse of the bag. Isabel described the satchel to Susan as medium sized, made of battered black leather and with a silver buckle that fastened at the front. Susan had found a long, gnarled stick that she was using to beat the heather at the side of the path, in case the bag had somehow slipped into the thick, coarse undergrowth.

Finally, the two women reached the precipitous outcrops of granite which marked the steepest section of the climb. The place at which they had stopped for their rest-break was not as obvious as Isabel had thought it would be.

'There were two, smooth rocks positioned next to one another,' she told her cousin as they clambered down a rough section of loose scree. 'The boulders were large enough to sit on. I must have put my bag down next to the one on the left hand side.'

Isabel squinted her eyes against the brightness of the lowering sun. Suddenly, a memory returned to her mind's eye. 'I had just put some pieces of slate into my bag for Imogen,' Isabel went on, 'because she likes to skim stones in the sea, but there are never any flat ones down on the shore.' Isabel then looked intently at the path ahead, trying to identify any familiar features.

'So we must have stopped close to the slate path, the one that runs off to the left and then straight towards the second stile,' Susan said, continuing Isabel's train of thought.

When the two women reached the larger boulders they got down on their hands and knees. Susan poked her stick into the gorse and heather bushes that colonized this stage of the route. Isabel was trying not to allow the panic that was rising within her chest to completely overcome her.

'This is the last group of rocks on the path. Beyond this point there is only the meadow and then we are practically back at the farmhouse. My bag can't possibly be anywhere beyond this point.' She gazed longingly at Susan for some kind of solution.

'We've looked everywhere. Are you sure you even brought it up the hillside with you? Maybe it's back on the table in the kitchen and we'll see it as soon as we open the back door...' Susan's words trailed off as she saw the expression on her older cousin's face.

Isabel was staring ahead at the outline of the farmhouse which had just become visible beyond the tall flowers and grasses of the wild meadow. The woman's trademark composure had gone. She took hold of Susan's upper arms. 'It's up here somewhere on this hillside. I clearly remember bringing it out of the farmhouse with me this morning.' Her words became an urgent demand, 'I can't go back down without that bag.'

Susan did not know how to reply, so she simply removed Isabel's hands, picked up her twisted beating stick and solemnly continued the search.

## October 2012

## Chapter 1

If you have lived near the sea as a child, you will always be drawn to the water, in all the forms that it takes. I have certainly observed this tendency in my own mother, who always had a fascination for the marine landscapes created by rivers, estuaries and reservoirs as well as by the ocean.

In the two decades that my mother spent travelling alone, after the death of my father, her preference was always for a holiday resort by the sea. She was undeterred by the prospect of travelling by herself and the extremes of weather which can often terrorize the coastline never appeared to daunt her. I have myself chosen to live by the sea and no doubt my children will display a similar prejudice in later life. But for now I am returning to the Island of Garansay, where I spent my childhood, to visit my mother's farm that faces the water and to organise the material remains of her long life.

The landscape outside the window gradually alters as my train carriage passes parallel to the dramatic coastline of Northumberland. We will soon pass over the widest section of the River Tweed at Berwick and then across the border into Scotland where the track will switch its course, for a time, inland.

## 12

This stretch, just before we reach the border, is the most attractive of the entire route, as the landscape that surrounds us is sparsely populated with only the occasional glimpse of a ruined castle to indicate the chequered history of this long disputed territory. The change of scenery as we cross the border, particularly the sudden appearance of the imposing concrete structure of the Torness Nuclear Power Station, seems to challenge my memories about Mum. At heart, she was a practical woman. Mum loved the countryside around her, but would rarely have taken the time to contemplate it. Isabel had always been a working woman. The environment in which she lived was inseparably connected to the way she earned her livelihood, as it was for all of the farming folk on Garansay.

We make a prolonged stop at Edinburgh Waverley Station, where a significant number of passengers alight. But it is as the train finally judders and lurches towards the extremities of Glasgow Central Station that I force my mind to switch to more prosaic matters. It has fallen to me to sort out my mother's affairs following her unexpected death. I will need to clear out the farmhouse and consider the future of the business, such as it is.

I have left Bridie and the boys with Hugh. On the whole, the children have taken Isabel's death very well. Despite her age, we were all surprised by the news that she had passed away. Mum was still very active. My eldest son, Ewan, has come home for the weekend from college and Kath and Gerry have set up camp in the guest room while I'm away. Hugh's parents are always good like that and it helps the kids are so close to them.

Hugh is Kath and Gerry's only child and they dote on our children. In contrast to Hugh's parents, I was always nervous about leaving Ewan, Ian and Bridie with my mother. She loved them, of course, but she was not used to devoting time purely to youngsters. When we were growing up at Lower Kilduggan, Mum and Dad were always grafting. Dad would be out on the farm and Isabel would be making beds and baking for the boarders.

My brothers and I were expected to entertain ourselves, so we disappeared up the glen and didn't come back until tea time. Or, if the weather was really dreich, I would sit in my box room under the sloping roof and read books. When I had finished my own I read Mum's books - the Georgette Heyers and the Jean Plaidys.

Isabel found it difficult to relate to her grandchildren, who demanded constant attention and accepted as a right that trips and entertainment should be provided for them with no expectation of anything in return. My older brothers and I were all required to help out on the farm as kids. Michael got the worst of it. My father was training up his eldest son to take over Lower Kilduggan Farm when he had gone. This tactic proved wholly unsuccessful and Michael is now an inventive Glasgow based architect.

As I queue to climb aboard the ferry to Garansay, with my ticket in hand and bags slung across shoulders and dragged on tiny wheels behind me, I imagine how my father must have first made this journey. Not on a ferry, but aboard his naval warship. I don't know much about Dad's childhood but he must have been very attracted by the peace and open space of Garansay after his youth in a crowded tenement building in Glasgow. Which did he fall in love with first I wondered, my mother, or the island where he was posted?

The crossing is calm. I use the time to finally read through the notes that my mother's Glasgow solicitors have sent me. Mr Galloway, of Galloway, Son and McGrath has been very thorough. My mother has bequeathed the farmhouse and the three acres of land that still remain to her three children. Her car, a ten year old hatchback, and the contents of the farmhouse and outhouses have also been left to me and my two brothers. Isabel's savings will be divided equally between us. Mr Galloway had warned that the money would need to go towards the renovation of the property, if we chose to keep the bequest rather than sell up the whole place in its current condition.

This is one of the decisions that Michael and Allan are hoping can be made whilst I am here. Allan has promised he will make it over at some point to help with the clearing of the house. But Michael was very clear that he is leaving the decisions up to me and will not be returning to Garansay in the immediate future. To be fair to him, it was my older brother who arranged the funeral and out of all of us, he had seen Mum the most regularly in recent years.

I pack up the notes into a paper file and place it in my satchel as the tannoy announces the ferry will shortly be arriving at Port Kilross. I stand out on deck to watch the stunning panorama of Kilross Bay become gradually larger as we glide towards the harbour. As it comes into view, I notice that the top of Ben Ardroch, the largest mountain on Garansay, is under cloud but the vista is still a breath-taking one.

Despite the cloud cover, I can just see the outline of the 'sleeping warrior'. This is the name Garansay residents give to the jagged contours of the mountains that lie to the north-east. The hills stand imposingly behind the string of little fishing villages which populate the eastern coast of the island. When all of the peaks are visible, and you look at them in the right way, you can see the profile of a giant reclining medieval warrior, known as Goyfut.

The evening light is giving the hills and water a soft golden glow. I cannot shake the prickling feeling of anticipation that this view always provokes in me, even though I know it is not appropriate to the purpose of this particular visit.

Mr Galloway has arranged for Mum's car to be brought down to the harbour. As I descend the passenger walkway I see my second cousin, Davy Dickson, leaning against the black car with his hands in his pockets, watching me approach.

We played together sometimes as children. His mother, Aunty Susie, would leave Davy and Alison at the farm in the summer holidays whilst she was running the shop. It was the busiest time of the year at the boarding house so Mum kept a distant eye on us whilst we played on the hillside or swam in the freezing cold burn.

'It's good to see you,' I call out as I get closer.

'You're looking well, Imogen,' Davy says as he reaches for my bags with sleeveless arms that seem impervious to the October chill.

'I really appreciate this.' I help him to make a space for the luggage in the untidy boot. 'I know how busy you and Fiona must be in the shop.'

'It's really no bother. Alison gave me a lift to Lower Kilduggan to pick up the car. She's left you a few essentials in the fridge and on the kitchen table. You should be all set up for a couple of days at least.'

Davy stands up straight from his labours and I take the opportunity to fully examine his appearance. He too looks well. He is more filled out than when I last saw him, but still has a boyish look. Davy is tall and wiry, with the sandy blond hair and light blue eyes of his mother.

'Have you still got a key to the farm?' he enquires.

'Yes I have. Tell Alison I'll pop over to the cottage and see her over the next few days.' I climb into the car and adjust the front seat position.

Davy hands me a scruffy key ring through the open driver's window.

As I turn the key in the ignition, he leans into the window and adds sombrely, 'we're very sorry about your mother. She was a good lady.' Then he stands back and lightly taps on the roof, a wordless gesture to bid me a safe journey back to my childhood home. I join the traffic that is slowly creeping off the ferry and take the right fork, driving off along the Glenrannoch road in the direction of the north of the island. Davy strides back towards the village shop, mounts the stone steps and then pauses at the door. He briefly turns his head to look towards the hills that separate Kilross from the more exposed and rugged 'north end'. Just as quickly, he turns back, picks up one of the empty grocery pallets sitting at the front of the shop and disappears into the building.

## Chapter 2

My heart is pounding in my ears. It takes me a few seconds to recall where I am. I'm in my mother's bedroom at Lower Kilduggan Farm and it is still dark. Disorientated, I swing round to the side of the bed and slip my feet into a pair of slippers, giving me a reassuring sense of normality. Then the noise that woke me up comes again - the unmistakeable crunch of gravel outside.

Trying to breathe away my escalating panic I move over to the bay window and pull back the heavy curtain. The courtyard outside is empty and quite clearly lit by moonlight. I sense a movement down by the side of Mum's pottery shed, at the foot of the burn. As I look more closely, two startled eyes turn towards me and glow brightly in the pale light. Four legs make a bolt for it, back up the hillside.

It was most likely a red deer. I scan the outhouses up to the skyline to check there is no other, more sinister nocturnal intruder on the farm. All appears to be clear. I pull the curtains shut and go back over and sit down on the edge of Isabel's grand double bed, with her hand crocheted floral eiderdown scrunched up at the bottom.

This was the bed that Mother had slept in, alone, for the thirty years she had been without my father. Although, I merely assume she slept alone. I do know Isabel had a man friend at one time,

Kenneth he was called. He was a gently spoken golfer who was a regular when Lower Kilduggan was a boarding house and who developed a close friendship with mother over the years. I was busy with my babies at that time so I'm afraid I didn't show a great deal of interest in the relationship. After a couple of years the friendship just fizzled out. Kenneth stopped coming to Garansay and I didn't probe Mum on the reasons why.

I smile to myself at the thought of the deer. I should have known really. I have forgotten what it's like to live on a farm. Far from being a peaceful life, the countryside is full of noises. Not least the howling, swirling winds that become deafening at night, particularly as the north wind comes in off the Kilbrannan Sound. These are the gales that toss the ferries in the winter months and smash the crockery in the ships' galleys. For the time being, the weather is very still and the farmhouse is now perfectly quiet.

I look at the clock on Mum's bedside table. It is quarter to five. Too tense and full of thoughts to go back to sleep, I pull on Isabel's stripy cotton dressing gown and go down to the kitchen. It is just starting to get light.

The farm was built so the kitchen and living room both have windows that face the sea. Only the bathrooms and a couple of bedrooms face the grassy slope of the hillside at the rear of the house. My old box room and the bedroom that Michael and Allan shared were at the back of the house. This was so the guestrooms could all have a sea view. Down here in the kitchen you can only catch a glimpse of the Kilbrannan Sound beyond the manmade features that have been constructed over the years, like the outhouses and animal sheds which encircle the gravelled courtyard.

I fill up the kettle and place it onto the stove. I cut myself a slice of the fruitcake that Alison Dickson left yesterday and sit down at the table to eat, suddenly famished. Although exhausted, I had made a start last night on sorting out Mother's books and papers. There are already two cardboard boxes in front of the larder to show for my labours.

Isabel's papers contained the usual detritus of the farm's business: the tax returns and the receipts for machinery long since sold on or scrapped. Mum had been an efficient business woman and wound up the farm when she accrued a decent pension. Then she threw herself into other interests, like her pottery making and the Walking Society. She also liked to travel, alone and sometimes with her single friends.

Isabel had got quite good at the pottery. She made bowls and plates with pretty designs depicting local scenes. The pottery shed was converted into a workshop and her pots still line the shelves and tables in there. Her wheel and kiln are housed at the back. During the summer season, Mum would open up the shed to visitors, selling her creations and allowing the children to have a go at turning their own pots.

Lower Kilduggan had been becoming busy again. Mum started thinking about providing coffees and teas and maybe taking on a student to help her out. But in the event, it didn't come to this. One day in late September, she was found by her friend Mae, who was picking her up for their weekly shopping trip to 'The Port'. When Mum didn't answer the door, Mae came around to the kitchen window. She saw Isabel slumped over the table, her breakfast tea cup on its side and the beige liquid spreading out like an inhuman hand, dripping slowly onto the stone floor below. Mae knew where the spare key was kept; under the large stone by the back door, so she rushed in and tried to revive her. Isabel was already gone. Her heart just gave out. Not a painful, gripping heart attack the doctor informed us, more like a switch going off. There would have been no pain, he said.

Suddenly, the memory of a distant summer spent here at the farm comes into my head. It is a recollection from very early in my childhood. There had been a heat wave, which was very unusual for Garansay and is probably why the memory had lodged itself somewhere in my brain. This makes me think it might have been the hot summer of 1976, but that couldn't be the case, because Dad was still alive and the boys were very young. I was just a toddler.

We were down on the Kilduggan shore. The boys were playing football whilst I was paddling in the water. I was holding up my white cotton dress which was getting wet around the fringes and shrieking with delight as the cascade of surf cooled my legs. I remember sensing there was no one with us. We were alone on the beach. Without warning, a bigger wave came and it knocked me backwards into the water. I tried to put my hands down to stop myself. The sand was loose and shifting and I couldn't get a grip. The wave then sucked me forwards, deeper into the sea. My eyes were open and there were bubbles all around me, but the force of the water was preventing me from floating back to the surface. My chest was bursting with the desperate need to breathe.

I felt a painful and hard grip on my upper arms, as if I were being pulled backwards by a force greater than that of the wave. Lifting my head above the water I coughed and gasped frantically for air. Then I was lying face down on the wet sand. Mum was gently hitting my back to help me bring up the seawater in my lungs. Once my breathing had steadied, Mum scooped me into her arms and rocked me gently. In her eyes I saw desperate relief and love.

Michael and Allan were standing a few feet away from us, their mouths open in shock. They were totally still and silent. Mum led us back up to the farmhouse and no one said anything. I didn't even get told off for playing too close to the water. I could feel Michael's relief by the evenness of his breathing as he walked next to me. He instinctively knew that this time it wasn't him who was to blame. It had not been his responsibility to look after me.

We all knew that somebody else should have been with us on the beach. It was a very long time ago and perhaps I am mixing up memories, superimposing two separate events, like a doctored photograph. But somehow, I know that the person who should have been there, who had set out with us that morning with beach bags and packed lunches and who had reprimanded the dog for running in and out of our legs, but had then inexplicably vanished - was Dad.

The kettle has been cheerfully whistling for a couple of minutes now. I lift it onto the back ring of the stove. I set out the teapot which is one of Isabel's creations, beautifully glazed in greens and blues with sheep frolicking around its middle. I pop in a couple of tea bags and pour on the steaming water. Performing this ritual tugs my thoughts back to the present. Perhaps it takes a person's death to make you truly examine your relationship with them. I can reluctantly accept that Mum had not always been distant from us. There was a time when we were the centre of her universe. She fought battles for us and protected us.

I stand at the kitchen window and sip my scalding hot tea, surveying the landscape of the farm, which is beginning to be illuminated by a weak autumn sun rising over Ben Keir to the east. With a sense of determination, I take my steaming cup across the hallway into the study. I set it down and cast my eyes over the tightly packed shelves.

Two wedding photos are positioned on the window sill. One is of Hugh and me. It's a carefully posed shot. My thick dark hair is coiled up on top of my head and the skirts of the dress are fanned out on the ground. Hugh is grinning at me like a Cheshire cat.

The photo sitting next to it is more formal and dated. It is of Michael and Miriam. At least Mum finally decided to take down the shot of Allan and his ex-wife Suz. It had become an acute embarrassment whenever he and his new partner, Abigail, came to stay. Mum was either oblivious to the effect or she didn't much care. Somebody must have had a word with her. Michael probably, he was good like that.

I turn my attention back to the shelves, lifting down the shoeboxes and the lever arch files. I pull out the battered brown leather chair that Artie, our border terrier, used to curl up in when the sun was spilling in through the window. Artie is long gone now so I can safely sit myself down at the desk. I take a tissue out of a cardboard dispenser and wipe away the thin layer of dust which has settled on the scratched wooden surface. Then I slowly and methodically lift over the files and with an awakened sense of curiosity, begin my task.

## Chapter 3

Alison Dickson's cottage is situated at the top of a long grassy bank. It stands back from the coastal road which runs along the eastern side of Garansay. The small white-washed stone dwelling is in the hamlet of Gilstone. From here there are lovely views across the Firth of Clyde to the Ayrshire coast. If you stand at the end of the tiny pier, where children dive into the tropically clear water at the height of summer, you can see as far as the Cumbraes or even Bute.

Gilstone is a popular village for summer visitors. It has also been adopted by the wave of artists and sculptors who have come to Garansay over the last twenty years. The little harbour and the nineteenth century stone cottages have provided painters with ample inspiration. There are at least three new galleries along the main street.

I park outside the Sea-Shell Tearoom, which is not yet open. The shop front is painted a light blue colour and the window and door are bedecked with hanging shells.

Walking up the long, straight path to Alba Cottage, I look at the hills that form the dramatic backdrop to the tiny terrace which sits in their shadow. These mountains are my favourite view on the island. The two peaks of Ben Keir and Ben Mhor are connected by a dipping 'saddle' of rocks. This unusual formation is popularly known on the island as 'Bealach nan Aoife', which has been anglicised to 'Aoife's Chariot'.

I first learnt about the origins of this name from our English teacher at Kilross Primary School, when we were studying the Celtic myths and legends. The myth centres around an ancient warrior-maiden named Aoife. Although the story is chronicled in the 'Ulster Cycle' of Irish mythology, it is recorded there that she lived to the west of a land named 'Alba', meaning Scotland. Because of the closeness of the Isle of Garansay to the Northern Irish coast, Aoife is believed to have been from here. Or, I should add, that this is how Mr McKinley introduced us to the tale of 'Aoife's Chariot'. He spun the yarn with such a grand solemnity that each one of us in his class believed every single word of it was true.

One rain lashed day, invaders come to Garansay by boat and the warrior-maiden Aoife is forced to defend her island. The army of men are led by the mighty Irish hero called Cu Chulainn. The fighting between the invaders and the islanders continues for five days. Finally, the Irish hero finds himself fighting hand-to-hand with Queen Aoife. In the heat of combat, the warrior-maiden shatters Cu Chullainn's sword and is poised to slay him. Just before she delivers the fatal blow, Cu Chullainn tells the maiden that her precious chariot and horses have been driven off the cliffs by his men.

When Aoife turns to look, he quickly overpowers her and slings her over his shoulder. Cu Chulainn puts a knife to the maiden's throat and when she pleads for her life he agrees to spare it upon three conditions: she must give him undisputed access to the Island, spend the night with him, and bear him a son.

When Cu Chullainn returns to his Irish home, Aoife is pregnant. The Irishman has given her a gold ring to give to her child when it is born. He tells her that when the boy is 12 years old he must come to Ireland. But the warrior makes her swear that when he does, the boy will not reveal his true identity to anyone.

In another of the Ulster sagas, the boy who Aoife named Connla, comes to Ireland as instructed. By now he is a great soldier. However, the boy steadfastly refuses to identify himself, as his mother had directed him, and Cu Chullainn fights and slays him. When the Irish hero bends down to lift the boy's body in victory, he recognises the gold ring upon his finger. It is too late. He has killed his only son.

I was mesmerized by this tale when Mr McKinley told it to his spellbound class in primary six. From that moment onwards, I have clearly seen the silhouette of Aoife's war chariot in the shapes made by the mountains above this spot. The tale has been firmly imprinted on my brain ever since. I am sure the mythical story surrounding this glen must have contributed to Alison's decision to set up home here. For an artist, the significance of the place would have been too much to resist.

Alison Dickson is already standing in the doorway, leaning casually against the frame, when

I reach the cottage. She brushes her lips against my cheek and takes the bunch of wild flowers I hold out to her.

'They're lovely, Imogen, thank you.' She carries the rustic bouquet along the narrow corridor that leads into a kitchen at the back of the cottage. I glance in at the sitting room as we pass. Alison has converted it into a studio and her colourfully rendered canvases are propped up against every free surface. It is a mild, fresh morning and Alison has the paint chipped French doors standing open onto the small courtyard garden that sits at the foot of the path up to Aoife's Chariot.

Alison makes coffee for us both and we brave the chill to sit at the palazzo table outside to drink it. Alison is about ten years older than I am. She is more a contemporary of Michael's than of Allan and me. However, I note that she is still beautiful, as she sits opposite me in the morning sunshine, wrapped in a dark blue woollen cardigan and with her white blond hair falling dead straight to her shoulders. She has very clear green eyes and is as slim as lifelong smokers tend to be. Alison looks every bit her fifty two years, but she has a playful manner which makes her as attractive as a teenager.

We talk about Mum's funeral and the people who attended that we hadn't seen for decades. My old friend asks about Hugh and the children and I enquire about her job at the hotel.

I tell Alison that I want to find out more about the history of Kilduggan Farm before I decide what we are going to do with it, trying to steer the conversation to the topic I am keen to discuss. I lift out some of the papers that I unearthed over the weekend and place them on the garden table. The impractical structure wobbles as I unfold and lay out the family tree that Mum had started compiling back in the early nineties.

Mum had pretty much completed the Stewart line of the family, including the American branch who were descendants of Isabel's uncle, William Stewart. I remember Mum writing letters to her newly discovered cousins, the Walkers, of Boston, Massachusetts at around this time.

But I found there were gaps in the tree and am hoping that Alison can help me to complete it. There aren't many entries for the Piries, who belong to my maternal grandmother's side of the family. Isabel's mother, Elizabeth Pirie, married my grandfather, Donald Stewart, in 1920 and Isabel came along five years later.

Mum was an only child. She had inherited Lower Kilduggan Farm from her father in the fifties. Mum has quite a lot of documentation about her father's family, who had lived on Garansay for as long as there are printed records. Donald fought in the Great War and Mum had photocopied records from his regiment, The Argyll and Sutherland Highlanders.

Elizabeth Pirie, on the other hand, I know much less about. She was also born on Garansay and had two sisters, Katherine and Peggy. Alison and Davy's mother was the daughter of Katherine Anderson (née Pirie). Beyond this, I have very little information about them.

'I was hoping you could help me to fill in this section of the tree,' I say, running my fingers down the lines made by Mother's black ink pen on the thick yellowing paper.

'Okay,' Alison replies hesitantly, whilst she peers carefully at the details Mum had recorded. 'I'm glad Isabel has got the birth dates for the three sisters, because I couldn't have told you that.'

'Yes,' I add, 'but I'm not sure Mum's got those right. The dates don't seem to tally, look.' I lean over and point to the entries. 'According to this, my grandmother was born in 1893 and her older sister Peggy - or Margaret, was born in 1890. Your grandmother, Katherine, was born in 1888 and married Alasdair Anderson in 1912.'

'That sounds about right.'

'But then *your* mum, Aunty Susie, wasn't born until 1932.' I state.

'Well, I can certainly verify that date,' Alison adds with a chuckle. She takes a cigarette out of the packet in her cardigan pocket and lights up.

'Doesn't that strike you as strange - that Katherine and Alasdair didn't have a child for twenty years after they got married? And Katherine must have been what, 44 years old when she had your Mum, which was pretty late to have your first child back in those days.'

'But not unheard of.' Alison takes a long drag on the cigarette and then tips her head back, blowing smoke towards the sky, which is gradually darkening as clouds blow in from the west. She sits back in her chair with a big grin on her face. Crossing her arms, with the smouldering cigarette carefully pointed outwards, Alison declares, 'you are right though.'

'What do you mean?'

'Well, there's actually a little mystery behind that.'

Intrigued, I sit forward taking a deep breath of Alison's second hand smoke, relishing the long forgotten nicotine kick that it provides.

Alison uses her free hand to trace the triptych of entries for the Pirie sisters and pauses to create a dramatic effect, before finally providing her explanation. 'Mum once told me that Katherine and Alasdair had got married just before World War One, so 1912 sounds about right. Anyway, within the same year, or maybe less than a year, if you catch my drift, they had a baby, a little girl called Aileen.'

'Mum hasn't got her in the tree. So Susie wasn't their first child after all? Did Aileen die young then?'

Alison holds up a hand as if to halt my barrage of questions. 'Uh, uh, let me finish, please!' She takes another drag of the cigarette and tosses it down to the paving stones to grind it out with her boot. She is enjoying telling me this story. I will just have to curb my curiosity and allow her to take it at her own pace.

'So, Alasdair returns from the trenches in 1919, a year after the end of the war, as he has been helping to keep the peace in Russia in the months following the Armistice. He then returns to Garansay and makes a reasonable living on the fishing boats. Alasdair and Katherine are a happy couple and Aileen does not die in infancy, but is a strong little girl who helps her mother to carry out seasonal work on the local farms.'

The fast moving clouds have now completely overlaid the sun and it has grown decidedly chilly in Alison's little courtyard. But we stay exactly where we are. Alison's voice becomes the only discernible sound within the surrounding glen.

'Then, in 1932, a baby arrives, another little girl whom they named Susan. Now Mum says that she can remember Aileen very well. She was a bonny, fair young woman and she recalls playing with her out in the fields when Katherine and Alasdair were busy working. However, when Mum was still very young, Aileen was taken ill - some sort of virus it must have been, and she died. Mum went to the funeral at Kilross Kirk and everything. Anyway, years later, when Mum was about to marry Dad, Katherine takes her aside and it all comes out. She tells Mum that her sister, Aileen, had actually been her birth mother. That she had got herself pregnant, no mention of who the father might be, and they had simply absorbed Mum into the family. She said they never lied to her about it. Mum had always just assumed that Katherine and Alasdair were her parents.' Alison sits back triumphantly in her seat.

'Why did you never tell me this before?' I ask after a few moments of silence.

'Well, you were never interested until now and Mum absolutely swore me to secrecy when she told me. I mean, no one would bat an eyelid now, but even when we were young, in the sixties and seventies, it would have been quite a scandal, especially on Garansay.'

'You're probably right, but I suspect it's not uncommon.' I start to carefully fold up the family tree, feeling a little uncomfortable about having probed so enthusiastically into someone else's family secrets.

'You might as well fill the facts into your tree now. Let's finally write Aileen back into the family history books,' Alison adds as an afterthought.

'Is that okay?'

'Sure, Davy and I know all about it and anyone born in the last half century isn't going to give two hoots!' She chuckles as we clear the table and bring our detritus into Alison's bijou kitchen. The clouds have begun to deposit large drops of rain. I just manage to get my papers inside before the heavens open in earnest.

I leave Alison's cottage with promises that we will get together again before I leave the Island. I walk back to the car, in the steady rain, quietly considering all of the information that Alison has given me. It is not a particularly scandalous story, just a sad one really. What I am trying to comprehend is why Mum had not added Aileen to the family tree. She must have known of her existence. They were practically contemporaries. Mum must also have known the truth about Aunty Susie's parentage, or at least suspected.

I am amazed Isabel had kept that information to herself for all of those years. Is it possible she had forgotten that Aileen ever existed? It doesn't seem likely. She must have *deliberately* left her name off.

## 34

I climb back into the car, already soaking after just a short walk and feel suddenly cross with myself, for having the arrogance to presume to know what Mum was thinking. Since returning to Garansay a few days ago, I have discovered that I don't really know any of these people – Mum, Aunty Susie or even Alison, quite as well as I thought that I did.

## Chapter 4

'I've never had you down as the investigative type, Mrs Croft, I'm impressed. I could have done with your services during my divorce,' Allan says with a good natured smirk before taking a long sip of his 70 shilling ale and sitting back luxuriantly in the velvet covered armchair.

'Yes, very funny. I feel pretty embarrassed about it to be honest. It's news to me that the Dicksons had any skeletons in the closet. I wish Mum had told us, then I would have been more prepared.'

'Maybe she was going to, but just... ran out of time, as it were.'

'Hmm.' I crunch on a handful of the complimentary nuts sitting in an oval shaped bowl on the table in front of me. The public bar of the Glenrannoch Hotel is filling up with locals and visitors who look as if they have come straight off the evening ferry. The Glenrannoch is the premier hotel on the Island and has been recently refurbished.

Allan has just arrived on the same ferry and we are stopping in Kilross for something to eat before driving back to Lower Kilduggan. Allan has flown up from Stansted Airport to Prestwick and is only planning to stay for a couple of nights before he has to get back to London. He works for a major city bank which has Scottish roots. He started as a trainee there straight from school and has worked his way up ever since.

'Did Alison ever mention anything about this mysterious Aileen when you were both younger? You and her were as thick as thieves at one time,' I enquire.

'No, she did not. But then I don't have your interrogative skills, darling.' Allan is properly laughing now and I suspect he has had a few G&Ts on the plane. This trip probably counts as a holiday for him.

'Okay. I don't think I'm going to get any sense out of you this evening.' I sigh and stand up with the single card menu in my hand. 'I'm going to the bar to order.'

As I carefully relay our food choices to the young Polish bartender, I notice a group of well-groomed middle aged men standing on the opposite side of the semi-circular bar. One of them, who looks to be about my age, with thick, greying wavy hair and a deliberately smart-casual styled appearance, is staring across at me. I keep focused on placing my order. Paying for the food, I try not to glance in his direction. Despite this obvious attempt at evasion, the man has squeezed himself out of the group and is striding over to intercept my path.

'Excuse me,' he asks in a broad local accent. 'I'm very sorry to bother you, but are you Imogen Nichols by any chance?'

'Well, it's Imogen Croft now, but I am, yes.'

The man holds out his hand. 'I'm Colin Walmsley,' he states. 'From Loch Crannox Farm?'

'Ah, of course.' I smile in recognition as the penny drops. 'You're Kitty and Malc's son. How are your parents keeping?' I ask with genuine interest.

'Aye, Mum's no' bad thanks. She's in a nice wee nursing home in Gilstone. I manage to take her out for a drive and an afternoon tea once a week. She's still able to get around the village. Unfortunately, Dad passed away about three years back.'

'I am really sorry to hear that.'

'And please accept my condolences. I saw quite a lot of your Mum in recent years, since I took over running the farm. She had some great ideas for the future of Lower Kilduggan.' he clears his throat. 'It wasn't her time yet.'

I nod in silent agreement. Colin reaches into his wallet and produces a card. 'Please take my business card, it's got my mobile and office number on there. It would be great to catch up on old times.' He pauses, looking a little unsure of himself. 'And Imogen, I may also have a business proposition for you - and your brothers, of course.'

'Okay,' I reply, taken slightly off guard. 'I will be in touch.'

Colin lightly squeezes my arm and strides back to the group of men by the bar. I hear his pals send up a muted cheer when he re-joins them. Glancing over my shoulder, I see a couple of the blokes give him a slap on the back. Colin appears to be happily joining in with this horseplay. However, I can't help but think that Colin's friends have misinterpreted his motives, which are far more prosaic than what they have in mind.

I turn back towards Allan, who has drained his glass of 70 shilling and is watching me approach our corner table from the depths of the all-enveloping armchair. His eyes are positively sparkling.

'My dear Mrs Croft,' he declares rather loudly as I step into earshot, 'what *are* you up to now?'

This time we both laugh, so noisily that the men standing by the bar look over at us with puzzled expressions on their faces. We are still giggling stupidly when the young Polish waiter brings over our food.

\*

When we returned yesterday evening, Allan helped me to sort through the boxes that had come down from the attic. He is currently fast asleep in one of the old guestrooms. We stayed up late, drinking coffee and talking about Mum as we sorted through the ancient photograph albums. Allan then set up his work laptop so I could chat to Hugh. My brother slipped off to bed whilst I talked to my husband into the wee small hours.

After we had recovered from our mild hysteria last night in the Glenrannoch, I told Allan that Colin Walmsley is probably interested in buying Mum's land, and potentially, the farmhouse as well. We have a good idea of what the property should fetch in the current market. Allan certainly feels it is a foregone conclusion that we will sell up. He is primarily interested in getting a good price and in ensuring that the land will be well used in the future.

The Walmsleys own the neighbouring farm and their land borders ours over about two acres. In fact, Malcolm Walmsley bought five acres of land from Mum maybe twenty years ago, when she was scaling back production on the farm. Colin has obviously taken over the family business and this is to his credit. Neither I nor my brothers wanted to take up that mantle and now it looks as if Lower Kilduggan will pass out of the hands of the descendants of the Stewart clan.

If I remember rightly, the Walmsleys have a modern and well-equipped operation down in Glen Crannox. They have been specialising in some interesting breeds of cattle in recent years, hardy animals that are happy grazing on the exposed bog and heathland that predominates in the exposed north western side of Garansay. They have a very good operation going at Loch Crannox, with a healthy attitude to animal welfare that would make me feel quite confident about them taking over Kilduggan.

Kitty and Malc were also good friends with Mum for a long time, although they were busy working farmers during most of those years, so they saw each other only sporadically. Mum and Kitty had both been pregnant at the same time in the mid-sixties. Mum with Allan, and Kitty with Colin's older sister, Sandra. I seem to remember a story about them having to travel together on a local fishing boat over to Kintyre, so they could be picked up by ambulance to be taken to the closest maternity hospital.

Many Island women simply give birth at home, with assistance from local doctors and midwives. However, both Mum and Kitty had experienced some late complications - high blood pressure or a baby who had refused to turn, I can't remember which. This was a bit unexpected for Mum, who had given birth to Michael at home, with the doctor only arriving after the event to give the new arrival a clean bill of health.

But second time around it didn't prove quite so straightforward. The heavily pregnant women had to endure a choppy voyage huddled in the cab of a small fishing boat, holding on for dear life, trying to ignore the stench of fish and diesel. They returned to Garansay a few weeks later with two bonny, healthy, bouncing babies. This shared experience had left the women with a strong bond. Kitty was very supportive of Mum in the days and months after Dad died.

One of those 'bouncing babies' is currently fast asleep upstairs. I am up and about as we have a local firm here at the moment creating a drainage ditch around the farmhouse. They are also laying some water pipes down the steep bank that runs adjacent to the public footpath behind the house. Mum had booked the work months ago and the contractor, Danny Monroe, called me up a few days back, sheepishly asking whether we still wanted the job done, as he had just spotted it in their diary.

I am very glad he did, because the work is pretty essential. With the frequency of high intensity rainfall in the last two years, water has been rushing out of the overflowing burn and straight down the hill towards the farm. Our surveyor's report indicated the farmhouse was starting to show evidence of damp, and that the disused cellar was filling with water during the periods of heaviest rain. So Monroe and Son began work yesterday.

The weather is still fair and I've decided to take advantage of my early start to take a walk up to Loch Crannox, which lies about six hundred feet below the peak of Ben Mhor. There is a pretty pebble beach on the western side of the loch and it is one of the loveliest experiences on Garansay, to sit on a beach that is over a thousand feet above sea-level. In summer, walkers take their costumes and towels so they can cool off after the strenuous climb by taking a dip in the absolutely still and clear waters of the loch.

I leave the breakfast things out on the kitchen table for Allan, scrawling a note to let him know where I am going and propping it up against a jar of Dundee marmalade, certain to be one of his first requirements once he has dragged himself downstairs.

As I step out of the kitchen door I can see two sailing boats taking advantage of the perfect conditions out on the Kilbrannan Sound. The public footpath to Loch Crannox and Ben Mhor runs across our property. It starts down at the road and then takes a left turn through the courtyard and along a gravel path that ends at the first stile. It carries on up a steep incline, with the wild meadow over to your right and a field that is laid to pasture on the left. I spot Danny and the young lad who is helping him. They are using a mini-digger to shift the soil in a series of marked out trenches. Both are wearing ear protectors. Danny raises his hand as I pass. I wonder how on earth Allan can be sleeping through this racket.

It proves to be a lovely walk. I need to take off my jacket before even reaching the second stile because it is so warm. I try to enjoy the solitude and the fantastic views that become progressively more spectacular as the gradient increases. I had forgotten how demanding the walk can be in places, where the large granite rocks jut out over the path and you have to climb them using the hand and foot holds that have been created by years of human use. However, it does not take me long to reach the summit. The first view of the crystal waters of the loch are worth all of my efforts.

The water is quite still except for the tiny ripples on the surface which resemble the butter-cream icing that Bridie pipes onto her cupcakes. I stand down by the water's edge and skim a couple of flat pieces of slate across the surface, deliberately disrupting the beautiful symmetry of these miniature waves. I think about the many times we had climbed up to this beach as children. Once we had swum in the loch, we scampered back down the hillside. We would remove our sandals and our scruffy pumps in order to scramble down the burn, sliding on the smooth rocks, the cold water making our feet numb and impervious to the sharpness of the stones and shingle.

The hike back to Lower Kilduggan doesn't take long. When I step up onto the final stile, I get my first view of the farmhouse. In the distance, Danny has stopped digging and he and the young lad are sitting on a bench in the garden, eating their sandwiches. When I get within sight of them, Danny waves his hand and gestures for me to come over.

'How are you getting on?' I ask.

'Aye, we're making good progress, Mrs Croft. But I wanted to show you something - if you've got the time.' Danny places his remaining sandwiches on the wooden bench behind him. His assistant continues to eat his lunch, seemingly engrossed in a crumpled newspaper perched on his lap. He has shown no apparent interest in my arrival.

Danny leads me along the path to the edge of the wild flower meadow. There is a newly dug trench here which houses a pipe that runs out of the hillside and drains into the ditch. Danny reaches into the gap between the pipe and the muddy dugout, retrieving a black object that is battered and dirty.

'I just wanted to check with you before I threw this onto the skip. Young Nial found it when we were digging the outlet for the pipe into the meadow bank.' Danny hands the object over to me. 'It's pretty beaten up and filthy, but the lad thought it might be something that someone was wanting back.'

It is a black leather bag of some description. I turn it over and note it has a tarnished silver buckle at the front and, although caked in mud, it is a very good quality piece of workmanship, possibly even hand made.

'I'm happy to get rid of it for you,' Danny adds good-naturedly. 'It's just that when I opened the bag up, I noticed the label that's sewn inside. It says that it's a Fraser-Mackintosh. Now, an old aunty of mine used to be a machinist in their workshop in Glasgow back in the seventies. I happen to know for a fact that their stuff is not cheap. They make every single bag by hand, you know, and they've used the same pattern for over eighty years. There doesn't seem to be much wrong with it. If you clean it up and maybe replace the buckle, it'll do you fine. Why anyone would want to bury it, I've got no idea.'

I have been lost in my own thoughts during this tale, as something about the bag is tugging at the fringes of my memory. As I turn it over in my hands I am trying to release the recollection, unsure as to whether it is something from the recent or the long distant past.

'Sorry Danny, what do you mean?' I ask, jerked back to the here and now by what this well-meaning man has just said.

'Well, Mrs Croft, I may not have made myself totally clear. You see, Nial and I have excavated a five foot trench alongside this meadow. As we dug the outlet for the pipe here by hand, we found the bag amongst the debris. So I would estimate that it had been buried not far from where the edge of the meadow meets the path. It was maybe three or four feet below the surface - at about the depth you might bury a small animal, you know, like a pet.'

I am not sure if it is my post-walk chill, now that I have cooled down and am standing in the blustering westerly wind without my jacket. But hearing those words from Danny has left me suddenly cold. I instinctively hug my arms around my body and involuntarily shudder.

## Chapter 5

I have cleaned and polished the satchel that Danny Monroe dug out of the hillside. The buckle still works perfectly well and I have left the bag, hung by its strap, on the back of one of the heavy oak chairs in the kitchen of the farmhouse. When I was able to look properly, it appeared that the thing was completely empty.

I am amazed that Artie hadn't dug the satchel up at some point and presented it to us as a well chewed and slime coated offering, as he had done with a dozen half buried broken toy cars and limbless dolls over the years. But perhaps it hasn't been buried that long, I am no expert and it's difficult to tell.

I had shown the bag to Allan as soon as I returned to the farmhouse after my walk. As I came through the back door, he had been sitting at the kitchen table eating croissants coated in butter and marmalade, pouring himself a large mug of coffee from the glass *cafétiere.* He was, at least, fully dressed for the day, even though breakfast time for him had morphed into an unusually high fat and sugar filled lunch.

Allan had joked about my peculiar new interest in landfill as I encouraged him to look at the dirty object. However, he obliged me by examining the bag closely. He looked inside at the label and even tried the buckle. Then, he turned his back to me, in order to wash his hands at the butler sink.

Allan said he'd never seen the satchel before, lamenting how it was a shame anyone deemed it acceptable to discard it in such a fashion. He made a joke about how many years it would have taken to degrade and that perhaps recycling and 'green issues' couldn't have been quite so fashionable at the time the object was placed there.

Allan's jocularity hadn't fooled me. I saw the shadow which passed across his face when he first noticed me standing in the doorway with it. I knew then that Allan recognised the bag. That even from a distance of several feet and irrespective of the state it was in, it had triggered an immediate response, just as it had done for me, as soon as Danny Monroe pulled it out of its damp, muddy tomb.

Despite his tardiness in getting started, Allan was making up for lost time. He had sorted through a number of the rooms in the house and was filling a wheelbarrow in the front garden with rubbish, ready to go on the skip. We were double-checking with each other what items we wanted to keep and trying to second guess Michael by selecting the articles we felt would be of value to him. Allan was doing a great job. However, I was starting to experience the stirrings of long suppressed sibling irritation, finding I needed a break from his relentless joviality, which was beginning to feel a little false.

I've taken the car for a drive over to Kilross with the stated purpose of doing some grocery shopping. Wandering around the Kilross General Store, I pick out a loaf of the bread that comes in fresh from the local bakery each morning. I select a couple of freshly caught, filleted pieces of cod and decide to serve it simply - pan-fried with a parsley butter sauce, potatoes and wilted curly kale. I lift down a bottle of Chenin Blanc that looks like a tipple Allan will find bearable and head to the counter.

Fiona Dickson is busy serving a small line of customers. I stand obediently in the queue and watch her at work. She is a fresh faced and athletically built woman who must now be in her mid-forties. Her face has on only a hint of make-up, yet she is rosy cheeked and youthful, not pretty exactly, but handsome and very well preserved.

Fiona is pre-occupied, but we manage to snatch a few words whilst she processes my bag of shopping. I glean that Davy is over on the mainland visiting his parents, Aunty Susie and Uncle Jimmy, who now live in a retirement bungalow in Largs. We don't get an opportunity to chat any further but I ask Fiona for a recommendation of somewhere quiet in Kilross where I can get a decent coffee and preferably a good view.

She suggests the 'Boat House', which is a little café right down by the beach, where the owners have cashed in on the new trend on Garansay of recreational watersports. They hire out kayaks and windsurfing equipment and take paying groups for speed boat trips around the bay. Fiona says it is mobbed in summer, but today it's beautifully peaceful and the café looks straight out onto the water.

I sit at a table by the window, ordering a coffee from a young lad who seems to be manning the café single-handed. I assume there must be someone else working out in the kitchens, but cannot see any sign of them. When my coffee arrives the young waiter sits at one of the other tables, engrossed in the infinite amusements of his mobile phone. I feel confident to call Hugh from here without fear of interruption or causing irritation to others.

I am lucky and catch my husband when he has just returned to his office after giving an afternoon of lectures. I hurriedly tell him about the progress of the work on the farmhouse and Danny's discovery of the bag. Because my husband is a Professor of Psychology, he is quite happy to discuss my brother's reaction to this event.

'What I don't understand is why Allan didn't say straight away that he recognised the bag. Essentially, he lied to me.'

Hugh takes a sip of his coffee, ruminating on my words. 'Can you be absolutely sure that he did? You may have misinterpreted his response.'

'Hugh. I recognised that bag as soon as I saw it. It took me a few minutes to remember the exact circumstances, as it was a very long time ago. But there is no way that Allan could have forgotten. Mum was so upset about losing it. It was one of the most memorable events of our childhood,' I reply decisively.

'The event was memorable and significant to *you*, darling. It may not have been so to Allan. You may have been more sensitive to your mother's distress. Or perhaps he simply doesn't wish to resurrect unpleasant events.'

'I am more inclined to think it's the latter. Allan has been keen to try and keep the mood light these last few days. He has been reluctant to broach any difficult issues.'

'That is a perfectly natural. The man is dealing with the loss of his mother in his own way - through inappropriate humour and the consumption of alcohol.'

I laugh at this and ask Hugh if the children are managing okay without me. He explains they are perfectly happy and I'm absolutely fine to stay a little longer to tie up loose ends. I promise to phone the kids at bedtime. Then Hugh adds as an afterthought, 'of course, another reason why Allan might have lied about recognising your mother's bag is because it was he who buried it there.'

'I did have that thought myself.'

With promises I will take care and not go jumping to any wild conclusions, we ring off. Glancing at my watch, it becomes clear I'd better get a move on. I leave the correct change on the table and make my way to the car. There is one more thing to do before I head back to the farm.

I drive halfway along the Glenrannoch Road, swing into a turning on the left and park up on the grass verge. I get out and walk to the little wooden gate which marks the entrance to the Kilross graveyard. The gravestones are irregularly positioned up a steep bank that leads off a dirt track. You have to be quite careful of your footing, even when you are following the main path which runs straight up the slope.

Most of Mum's family were laid to rest in this cemetery at one time or another. The new plots have been added to a strip of land to the east side of the hill. I reach Mum's grave quite quickly. The ground here is freshly turned but we are still waiting for the headstone to be completed before it can be laid, so it looks a little stark. I place a selection of meadow flowers onto the moist earth before sidestepping along the bank, leaning into the hillside in order to keep my balance, purposefully heading towards the grave of my grandfather, Donald Stewart, which I know is about halfway along this line.

Donald passed away in 1952 and my grandmother, Elizabeth, was also buried here. Her name was added to the headstone when she died in 1968. I am intending to seek out the resting place of the other two Pirie sisters. I scan the row of headstones that runs behind my grandparents' plot until spotting the one I am looking for.

It is a smaller stone slab which bears the name of Katherine Anderson, buried here with her husband, Alasdair. These are Aunty Susie's grandparents. I am surprised to find that this gravestone is in fairly good condition. The carved memorial for Katherine reads: Katherine Anderson, 1888-1975 dearly beloved wife, mother and grandmother.

I inspect the nearby plots, looking for an older and possibly smaller one. I shift along the path a little in order to continue my search and then climb up a few feet, being careful to step respectfully between the graves. I cannot see any other Pirie headstones. I find this puzzling. Alison definitely said that Aileen's funeral had been at Kilross Kirk. I would have thought she would have been buried up here with the rest of the Pirie clan. I have no more time to look as the light is fading and I need to make a move back to Lower Kilduggan before Allan decides he's been totally abandoned.

I shuffle crablike along the bank, clambering my way down the footholds of the main path. This scramble brings me to the section of the churchyard with the oldest graves. The foliage here has been allowed to go to seed.

With the light nearly gone and my eyes resolutely scanning the ground, I spot something that catches my interest. A small stone cherub is peeking out of the long grass at the foot of a larger stone obelisk. Stopping instinctively, I pull back the greenery to search out the inscription. The stone has been weathered by time and the moss needs to be cleared with my fingertips in order to read it.

The faintly visible lettering indicates this is the final resting place of Margaret Pirie, née Salter, who died in 1918 and her husband, Robert Pirie, who died in 1922. I deduce from the dates that these must be my great-grandparents. I run my hand along the jagged stonework, following the rough surface to the bottom of the slab where there is some additional writing, which appears to be more recent. It is partially obscured by the stone cherub. I shift the ornament forward in order to reveal the newer engraving which reads:

Here Lies
Aileen Marianne Anderson
1912-1937
Beloved Daughter and Granddaughter

The acorn is not formed
That yet shall grow a tree,
Whose branch shall lull to rest the babe
That oft shall sing of thee.

## Chapter 6

By the time I return to Lower Kilduggan, it is almost dark. Approaching the turning for the farm, I can see the dipped headlight beam of another car. It appears to have stopped in the entrance to the driveway. I slow down and flash my lights. In response, the car pulls out of the drive, turns to the right and then speeds away towards the north eastern side of the island.

Entering the house, I am surprised to find the place in darkness. 'Hi Allan, I'm back!'

I turn on the main light in the kitchen and start to rapidly unpack the shopping. When there is no reply, I walk out into the hallway and throw all the switches in order to inject some cheeriness into the place. The hall is now filled with cardboard boxes. The pictures have been removed from the walls and stacked up along the skirting boards.

'I'm in here!' Allan calls from the sitting room.

He is seated at the far end of the sofa, swilling what remains of a whisky dram around the bottom of a glass tumbler. Something moves me to go over to him, sit down and gently rest my head on his shoulder. He squeezes my hand.

'Stay here,' I say quietly. 'I'll let you know when I've finished the dinner.'

*

Allan took the early ferry this morning. I drove him to Kilross, just as the overnight rain was clearing and the sun began to rise over Ben Ardroch. Allan has decided to take a trip to Fort William to visit his ex-wife, Suzanne, and their kids, before he takes a flight back to London. This is unusual. The children usually come down to stay with him.

Suz moved back to Scotland to be nearer her family. Despite the distance, relations are good between her and Allan. Alice and Robin stay with Allan and Abigail quite often and sometimes they visit us too.

My brother was married to Suz for nearly twenty years and I am still very fond of my ex sister-in-law. She will always be my children's 'aunty'. Suz was much better at remembering their birthdays than Allan ever was. Things started to go wrong after they moved down to London with Allan's job in the late nineties. The kids were in school all day and Allan was working very long hours, socialising a fair bit with clients.

The couple have always been cagey about what happened during that period, but we suspected at the time Suz had become involved with somebody else. Absolutely no one blamed her for this, except Allan, of course. We all knew she was lonely and homesick. I don't think it was anything serious. Whatever had been going on soon ended and Suz gave Allan an ultimatum. She wanted to return to Scotland with the children. She couldn't wait any longer for him to get to the right point in his career.

Allan refused to leave London. Suz moved back to her Mum's with the kids. For some reason, he just couldn't find it in his heart to forgive her.

I wonder if Allan had been remembering the summers we used to spend up here at the farm with Mum, maybe ten or fifteen years ago. Suz and I would pass the whole summer break on Garansay. Allan and Hugh might come and join us for a week or two. The youngsters usually ran off to the beach whilst we reclined on sun loungers on the front lawn. Bridie sat in her bouncer and the adults drank chilled white wine and cans of beer. Mum would be in her huge straw hat, sipping G&Ts until the sun went down.

Hugh and Allan smoked cigars at the bottom of the garden after dinner and argued about politics. The subject was often Tony Blair, and the unfettered freedom he seemed to be giving to city traders and the banks. Then, later on, it was the Iraq war. Hugh would become angry and animated, cleverly countering Allan's arguments with a barrage of statistics. Afterwards, my husband would become morose, as the effects of the alcohol and nicotine kicked in.

Allan and Suz were happy then. I used to think they were happier in their marriage than I was. Suz was always lightly tanned in her t-shirt and shorts, her shoulder length curls a honey blonde colour and her creamy complexion a perfect complement to Allan's dark looks. He used to hold her to him in a proprietorial way. If you walked into a room in which they had been alone, you would find them in some kind of embrace. It was awkward and made you feel like backing out in order to give space to their unique and grand passion.

It used to make me question my own relationship. Why weren't Hugh and I like that? Was that how it was supposed to be? But I don't ask those questions now. I still can't explain what happened to the powerful love Allan and Suz once had, but it certainly did not go the distance. It burnt itself out. Allan wouldn't give up his job to preserve it and Suz couldn't overcome her boredom at spending a few years away from what was familiar to her in order to hold on to it. So it couldn't really have been love, could it?

I have laid out Mum's family tree in the centre of the kitchen table. Around it I've placed piles of letters and documents. I am trying to create a separate area for each branch of the family.

After some on-line searching, I discovered that the words on Aileen Anderson's gravestone are an extract from a poem by Charles Spence, who was a Scottish poet popular at the end of the nineteenth Century. The poem was entitled, 'The Lost Love' and would probably have been recognisable to most people at the time it was inscribed for Aileen. I dimly recall studying Spence at university. He was certainly not as well known as Burns but he had other strings to his bow. Aptly, he was also a very talented stone mason and some of his creations can still be found in various museums around the country.

The choice of verse just seemed so perfect. The words suggest that Aileen was very much loved.

There is an acknowledgement that the baby Susan was hers and that one day the child would know of it and Aileen would be remembered. It makes me deeply sad to think that Aileen's identity actually became an embarrassment to the family, a secret to be kept in order to avoid social stigma. It feels unnecessary and to reflect the attitudes of an age which is thankfully long past.

I glance back at the family tree. Donald and Elizabeth Stewart inherited the title to this property in the 20s and continued to work the farm into the early 1950s. Mum played an active role in helping to run the place. It was my grandmother, Lizzie, who had the idea of taking summer guests at the farmhouse after the end of the Second World War, when money was very tight. This change of direction for the farm corresponded with the period when Dad had come onto the scene. His naval warship, HMS Ramillies, was stationed on the Clyde for a time. He met Mum when he was on leave in Kilross in 1941. But their relationship didn't really start until Dad had been demobilised in 1946 and returned to Garansay to find her again.

I thought this story was very romantic when it was told to me as a child, although the events described never really seemed to tally with what I knew of Dad's personality. He had always seemed to be so fiercely practical and unimaginative. But the facts speak for themselves. Dad gave up the life he previously had, one that involved exciting international travel, to come and live with Mum on this remote edge of a Scottish island, taking on the bleak and sometimes treacherous winters in order to farm this isolated piece of hillside.

I would like to know more about Aileen, but for the moment remain satisfied with having found the site of her grave and being able to set the family tree in order by adding her name to it.

I think again about my Dad coming here to Lower Kilduggan. The Nichols had no links to Garansay that I know of, yet Dad took the job of running the farm very seriously. He trained up his own sons to take over when he retired, particularly Michael, whom he obviously envisaged as his successor. Dad solemnly shouldered the duty of managing the place, desperately trying to ensure that it stayed within the family, just as if it was he and not Mum who had possessed the birthright to it.

## Chapter 7

The unseasonably late spell of fair and sunny weather appears to be breaking. Almost overnight the dense woodland that separates the north and south of the Island has turned to deep shades of orange and reddish brown.

Some Islanders, however, are still clinging to the vestiges of the high season and today the dairy farmers of the south are holding their annual show. It should stay dry for it, but the temperature has noticeably dropped. A generous scattering of fallen leaves on the meandering country road that leads to the village of Calderburn, on the southern tip of the Island, signposts the impending arrival of winter.

The village is busy for the show. I have to drive around for a while before finally locating a parking space at the rear of the village hall. Coming to the south of Garansay is like visiting a different island. The mountains, heath and moorland that characterise the landscape of the north-west are replaced by rolling emerald hills, secluded bays and sandy beaches. The features of the coast here are reminiscent of the cliffs and coves of North Devon and Cornwall and this part of the Island attracts many English tourists, to whom this style of landscape seems to appeal. The climate here also benefits from the mildness of the Gulf Stream and is sheltered by the Mull of Kintyre that lies across the water at the confluence of the Atlantic Ocean, the North Channel and the Kilbrannan Sound.

The result of this geographical circumstance is that the weather in the south is less extreme. The undulating hills are covered by lushly green pasture, ideal for grazing. This means the agricultural production of the 'south-end' is dominated by dairy farming. Here in Calderburn there is a factory and farm shop which makes the Island's own range of award winning cheeses.

Several fields have been given over to displays of farm vehicles. Rows of colourful stalls present an extensive range of local produce and craftsmanship. I have arranged to meet Alison in the tea-tent at eleven so have an hour or so to wander around the show. I stop and browse at a handmade jewellery stall, finding a junky bead bracelet in an unusual shade of blue and orange that I'm sure Kathleen would love. As I wait to be served, the woman next to me is talking expansively with the stall-holder.

I have a sudden feeling I recognise the voice, which is softly spoken south of England, but with a faint hint of Scots. When the lady has finished her conversation, she turns around and I get a clear view of her face. She is in her late fifties, expertly made-up with her hair styled in a neat, brown bob.

'Jenny Marsh?' I ask with surprise, after my brain has successfully connected the voice to the evenly pretty features.

'Yes?' she replies, but I can see the recognition is not mutual.

'You probably won't remember me,' I explain. 'My name is Imogen Nichols. I'm Michael's sister. It's been such a long time, but I was sure it was you.'

Jenny smiles as she makes the link. 'Oh my goodness,' she says. 'You are so very like Michael, I should have known straight away.'

Jenny had been my elder brother's girlfriend for a few years when they were both teenagers. Jenny's father owned one of the hotels in Kilross. Her family were English, but Jenny had lived in Scotland since she was a baby.

We find a seat and Jenny tells me that she comes back to Garansay every few years. Her children have left home now and she and her husband sometimes come over to the Island for a weekend. They live in Stirlingshire so it is not too far for them to travel. Jenny seems genuinely saddened when I tell her about Mum's death. She remembers spending a lot of time up at the farm with us back in the mid-seventies.

'I was quite heartbroken when Michael went off to university.' Jenny looks down at her hands and absentmindedly twists the sparkling eternity ring on her wedding finger. 'He said we couldn't hope to keep being boyfriend and girlfriend if we were living apart. He said long distance relationships never work.' She shifts her gaze up from her lap. 'He was letting me down gently, I know, but it did make me angry at the time. It seemed as if he was telling me how it was, like I had no say in the decision. I desperately wanted to argue with him and persuade him. He never gave me the chance.'

'There would have been no point,' I say, but not unkindly. 'You knew Michael back then. He was very stubborn when he had made up his mind about something.'

'That's right. Isn't it funny that it should still make me cross after all these years? I wouldn't swap the life I've had for anything. But there was something about Michael. The other girls all adored him and for a few years it was me who had him. That was a very good feeling. He did love me too - for a time.'

'I know he did.' I want to take hold of her hand but Jenny will only see this as condescending and I wouldn't blame her. She has obviously had a very good life and doesn't need my pity.

'How is he now?' Jenny adds politely and I sense it is a difficult question for her to ask.

'He is very well. Michael's firm has just designed the new Scottish National Theatre building in St Enoch Square. He has a lovely daughter called Sarah who is 27 years old and works as a lawyer. Sadly, Michael's wife, Miriam, died ten years ago from cancer. Michael was devastated and there has never been anyone else.'

'Och, I am really sorry to hear that.' It is she who takes my hand and gives it a squeeze. I don't doubt the sincerity of Jenny's words but I sense she has been battling with some conflicting emotions during this conversation. It might be my imagination, but I am convinced that when I mentioned Miriam's death, Jenny's body relaxed just a fraction and her face became a little less strained. I think she was relieved. It seems incredible that after all this time Jenny could still find it so painful to think of Michael with someone else.

I find myself wanting to part company with her as quickly as possible. My meeting with Alison, for which I am already late, is the perfect excuse. I slide my hand out of hers and promise to pass on her regards to Michael. As she pecks me on the cheek and slowly walks away, carefully placing her expensive high heeled shoes on the flattest sections of the pot-holed field, I sincerely hope that our paths will not be crossing again.

I hurry towards the tea-tent which is located in a large white marquee in the centre of the main field. I am about twenty minutes late to meet Alison. The tent is full of people but I can't see her anywhere. I walk outside to give her a call on my mobile.

The beer tent is in another marquee opposite this one and that is where I spot her. She is standing outside with a bottle of lager in one hand and a cigarette in the other. She is with a group who look like the artists and artisan types from Gilstone. Relieved that she has not been waiting alone, I make my way over to the merry cluster of drinkers.

'Hi, sorry I'm late. I bumped into an old friend of Michael's who I haven't seen for years. It was difficult to get away.'

Some of the people in the group turn to me and smile. Alison refuses to make eye contact for several seconds before finally acknowledging my presence.

'Oh, okay,' she says, a little dismissively, flicking ash from her cigarette onto the grass.

'Shall I get a drink here?' I ask. 'Or do you want to go for something to eat?'

Alison turns towards me and shrugs her shoulders in a noncommittal gesture. She takes a swig from the bottle in order to indicate that she is not finished here yet. I start to feel irritated with her. It is fairly obvious this is not the first drink she's had this morning.

'Right,' I say, losing my patience with the situation. 'I'll be in the tea-tent when you are ready. At this time of the day I'm afraid that I can't stomach anything stronger than an espresso.'

I spin away from the party of drinkers, only managing to take a few steps before a hand grips my arm and roughly turns me back round. The unexpected movement knocks me off balance. I have to right myself in order to face the person who is preventing my departure.

Although she has a slight frame and is a good few inches shorter than I am, Alison's eyes are blazing with anger and her close physical presence is very intimidating.

'Don't you dare talk down to me,' she hisses. 'You absolutely take the piss, you do - sauntering up, twenty minutes late and then having the gall to look down your nose at me for having a drink with my mates.' She backs off a little, now some of her anger has been vented.

Not wishing to inflame the situation further, I evaluate whether or not it is worth replying. As it is, our exchange has silenced the beer tent. The occupants of which have gathered outside to watch our altercation, as if it were a piece of street theatre, laid on as part of the entrance fee.

'I am genuinely sorry if you think I was judging you. Perhaps we could just go inside the tent, have a coffee and talk about this?' My face is burning with embarrassment.

Alison lets out an unpleasant laugh. 'Trying to sober me up are you? You've always been the sensible one. You know what? We were not at all surprised when we found out you'd become a schoolteacher.' she chuckles. 'Could there ever have been a job more suited to you?'

Embarrassment has given way to anger. My brain is working hard to process the meaning of these words. Just who, exactly, does she mean by 'we'?

Alison is not finished. 'Mooning around the hillsides, pretending you were 'Eustacia Vye', leading the boys on and then giving them the cold shoulder - just when they thought they'd finally got a look in,' she spits out.

'Sod off Alison - you're pissed,' I bark back. But before I have the chance to turn and storm off, Alison jettisons the contents of her beer bottle at my face. The tepid liquid drips slowly down the front of my blouse.

It is her who gets to walk away. Out of immediate necessity, I hunt in my bag for a hankie. The huddled groups of onlookers are shuffling back into the beer tent, now that the show is over.

Presently, an arm is slipped around my shoulders and a large handkerchief shoved into my hand. 'Come with me,' says a broad local accent, quietly voiced in my ear. 'My car is parked in the next field.'

It is Colin Walmsley. I say absolutely nothing but allow him to lead me out of the main showground, through a gate and into the field the organisers have taken over as a makeshift car park.

As soon as he has closed the driver's door on us I burst into tears. He sits in silence next to me for a couple of minutes, until I have regained my composure.

'I am so sorry,' I say with feeling. 'I can assure you nothing like that has *ever* happened to me before.'

'No - I can see that,' Colin says with a perceptiveness that is unexpected.

'I have no idea why Alison was so angry with me. I simply cannot explain what has just happened.'

'This is a small island in many ways, Imogen. There are certain facts that you may not be aware of.'

'What do you mean?'

'It is well known that Alison Dickson enjoys a drink or two and that Davy has been having difficulties with her of late.'

'What kind of difficulties?'

'Well, everyone on Garansay knows everyone else pretty much, so when Alison gets the worse for wear in a pub in Calderburn, someone in the bar gives her brother a call to come and pick her up,' Colin explains. 'This has been happening more and more often recently, in different bars, in different parts of the island.'

'I had no idea.'

'Aye, well you wouldn't do.' Colin adds, 'she's no' a bad person, but she can be hard to handle when she's had a few. It might take a couple of folk to help Davy get her home to her cottage.'

'Have you ever helped her to do that?' I enquire, starting to get the picture.

'Aye, a couple of times. But it's Davy who I'm pals with, not his sister.'

'Look, I'm really sorry to have dragged you away from the show. But I am really grateful to you for getting me out of there.' I pause before adding, 'did you see the whole thing?'

'Aye, pretty much,' he states without elaboration.

'Were you in the beer tent?' I enquire, making an assumption based on the fact that the only time I have seen Colin in the last quarter century was in a hotel bar.

'No. I was having tea and scones with Mum.'

'Oh, God.' I place my head in my hands, jerking it back up again as a thought hits me. 'Where is she now?'

'It's okay, she was here with a group from the nursing home so I took her back to join them. They will give her a lift on the mini bus. I'll call later to check she got home alright.'

Colin looks across at my mortified expression and starts to laugh. 'Sorry,' he says. 'It's just that you've no need to be so embarrassed. You've forgotten what it's like to live in Scotland. We have that sort of 'set to' all the time up here you know. It's like water off a duck's back to those guys in the beer tent!'

I start to laugh a little myself, although I know he is just being kind. I pat my front to check my blouse is sufficiently dry to return to my own car. 'I will wash the hankie before I return it to you,' I say, 'and I'll definitely call you about the farm.'

Colin waves his hand dismissively at this, as if to suggest that I shouldn't be thinking about that for now.

As I pull the handle on the door, ready to climb out, Colin clears his throat and adds, 'If you don't mind me asking, who is 'Eustacia Vye'?'

'Ah,' I say and sit back in the seat for a moment. 'She is a Thomas Hardy character from 'The Return of the Native' and she happens to be one of my all-time favourite literary heroines. So I actually took that part as a compliment. You should read it.'

'I might well do that,' Colin says.

I climb down from the 4x4 and make my way back towards the showground with my head held a little higher. Now that my embarrassment and anger has faded, it has been replaced by questions. Alison's mood seemed to have changed significantly since I'd last seen her at the cottage. Sure, I had asked some probing questions about her family, but she seemed okay with that at the time. I walk past a display of noisy milking machinery, lost in my own thoughts.

The other person whose mood seemed to have altered in the last few days was Allan. I had put this down to him being at Kilduggan and brooding about Mum. However, after today's undignified events, I am wondering if those two occurrences are connected.

About an hour ago I was feeling that perhaps I had overstayed my welcome in Garansay and should simply organise the sale of Lower Kilduggan and go home. But now I am seeing things differently. There are still some questions to be answered here and I'm not going to slink off with my tail between my legs. For better or worse I'm going to find out exactly what is going on before making any rash decisions about the future of Mum's farm.

## Chapter 8

Contrary to yesterday afternoon's resolution, I am preparing to leave Garansay, albeit just for one day. After returning to Kilduggan last night, I poured myself a dram of Mum's whisky, sat back in the armchair in the sitting room and considered all of the happenings of the last few days. I came to the conclusion that the event which had precipitated Allan's change of mood was the discovery of Mum's satchel up on the hillside. I also formed a hunch, with very little evidence to back it up, that it was this discovery which had somehow led to Alison's drunken outburst outside the dairy show beer tent.

Driving home yesterday afternoon, in the failing light, I was reminded of the car that I'd seen parked at the entrance to the farm on the evening before Allan left. I had assumed at the time it had merely stopped in order to turn around or to watch the sun setting over the Kilbrannan Sound. This was not an uncommon occurrence, especially during the tourist season, and I thought nothing more of it. I am now wondering if the car had been leaving Lower Kilduggan.

Allan said absolutely nothing to me about having had a visitor that day. I suspect now it may have been Alison who was driving away from the farm. It seems implausible, but I cannot think of anyone else that Allan might have been in contact with while he was on Garansay. But then to my knowledge, apart from at Mum's funeral, Allan has had no contact with Alison Dickson for the best part of thirty years.

There was a time, however, when Alison and Allan had been very close. It is the memory of that friendship which keeps circling around in my head. I am not saying they were ever girlfriend and boyfriend. In fact, Alison is a little older than Allan - maybe four or five years - which made the difference between being a child and an adult back then. Alison also acted older than her years. She had been smoking cigarettes for as long as I can remember and hanging around with the summer visitors who could get her into the hotel bars when she was underage - young men in their twenties mostly. Allan was immature for his age, a bit gawky and awkward looking. It was Michael who I always thought Alison had her eye on.

What had united Allan and Alison during those years were certain shared characteristics. They both had a mischievous and slightly provocative nature. One summer, when Alison and Davy were spending the day at the farm, the five of us climbed up the hillside to the loch. It was hot and we were splashing our feet in the shallows where the water met the pebble beach. Alison suddenly dared us to go skinny dipping in the loch. This had seemed completely unnecessary to me as none of us were much concerned about getting our shorts and t-shirts wet. They would have dried soon enough in the sun. But Alison was persistent. She kept going on and on at us to do it. Allan and Davy stripped off straight away and chased each other into the loch, screaming as the cold water enveloped them.

Michael and I refused to get undressed. I remember being so relieved that Michael was there; steadfast, sensible and unbending, all of the character traits which also made him unbearably infuriating at times. Alison just laughed at us, blithely removing her shorts and cotton blouse. Leaving on her bra and pants, she climbed onto a tall, smooth rock at the far end of the shore. Without a moment's hesitation, she dived into the sparkling water below.

Michael and I sat sulkily up on the grass bank, watching whilst the others splashed and laughed in the water for what felt like hours. When they'd finally had enough, the trio came bounding out of the loch, shaking themselves dry like shaggy dogs. As they pulled on their clothes, Allan gave Michael and me a look of pure contempt, as if we had confirmed to him that we were as rigid and inhibited as he had always suspected us to be.

Davy was inclined to follow Alison's lead without question. He was a quiet, intelligent boy and I always liked him, but his Mum repeatedly instructed her children that Alison was to be in charge when she was not around. However unwise this delegation of authority happened to be, Davy had always obeyed his mum. Allan was a more difficult boy to control, as our mother found out to her cost in the years after Dad died.

There was a time during his childhood and adolescence when Allan would take part in anything he identified as exciting or, even better, illicit. Within our very limited group of friends, it was Alison who was the most likely to provide Allan with the type of fun he was craving. Because Michael was so much older than us, he was more like a father-figure than an older brother at times. Mum leant on Michael a lot to help out with the farm and in bringing up Allan and me.

Perhaps I am being unfairly selective in my recollections. Allan could also be warm and hilariously good humoured, even in the bleakest of circumstances. When Michael's wife died over a decade ago, Allan was an absolute rock. He was a great practical help when Michael was totally incapable of doing anything for the first few months. Terrible as it was, that experience brought us all closer together as a family. I could finally identify the common characteristics that bound us as siblings. It almost came as a relief to know we could understand and support each other in this way, as for such a long time Michael and Allan had seemed so fundamentally different. It upsets me to think Allan might return in any way to being the boy that he was back then, before time and bitter experience had mellowed him.

Hugh told me once, that if you want to understand a person, you must look at what they *do* rather than what they *say*. He suggested that most people are not always truthful, even to themselves. Our actions are the closest insight we can get into what really makes us tick. This theory has encouraged me to consider Allan's actions over the past few days. His first instinct after being confronted by the discovery of Mum's bag was to go and see Suz and the kids. It is a long shot, but I've decided to pay a visit to my ex sister-in-law, in the hope that I might find some answers there myself.

If Suz was surprised when I told her I was coming to visit for lunch, her reaction did not show it. I told her it was a stop off for me during a short tour around the Highlands. She didn't seem to question this explanation, but then Suz wouldn't really expect me to be lying to her.

The train journey from Queen's Street to Fort William is less attractive than the more northerly section of the West Highland Railway, but it is still an interesting one. We rattle alongside the desolate beauty of Rannoch Moor. As we approach our destination, there is a splendid view from the Spean Bridge across to Caol. This coastal village marks the westerly origin of the remarkable Caledonian Canal, which provided an essential shipping route between the east and west coasts of Scotland.

Suzanne Hunter lives in a modern semi-detached house about twenty minutes' drive from the town centre. Alice has just moved in with her boyfriend, but is often back at home. Her mother hasn't had the heart to clear out her room just yet. Robin is the same age as Ewan and now in his second year at St Andrews. Hearing Suz say that Alice has moved out of home makes it even more surprising that Allan came to visit, as he couldn't have been coming to see the kids.

Suz has made us a lovely lunch of leek and potato soup, homemade bread and a selection of local cheeses she picked up from one of the delis in town. I am touched that she has gone to all of this effort on my behalf. She is eager to hear my news from home and when Alice drops in during her lunch break I repeat the information all over again with exactly the same enthusiasm. After we finish our dessert of chocolate cake and coffee, Alice has to return to the office. She informs us that she is already late, so we share a rushed farewell.

When we are left on our own again, I decide to broach the subject of Allan's visit. 'It must be a bit of a surprise,' I say, as Suz lays down a freshly brewed pot of tea on the dining room table, 'to see two Nichols in the space of one week.'

Suz busies herself, cutting up what looks like homemade gingerbread into neat and even slices, carefully placing them in a fan shape on the plate. 'No, not really. I think I know why you are here.'

Taken aback by this response, I remain silent, allowing her to elaborate.

'I take it that Allan has spoken to you.' She delivers these words as a statement rather than a question.

Now, I've read plenty of detective fiction in my time and know that I should play along with this misconception in order to elicit more information from her. In real life, I suspect this will prove to be too difficult a trick to pull off, so opt for a more honest approach instead. 'He hasn't spoken to me since he left Garansay. But I know that something is wrong and that is why I'm here.'

'That's pretty typical. He promised me he'd speak to you straight away.' Suz takes a sip of tea and licks her lips, as if her mouth has gone dry.

'Why don't you fill me in? Then I can be prepared when he finally does. I swear I won't let on you've spoken to me.'

'You don't have to make that promise. It's your right to know and I should have told you years ago. It's just that when Allan first confided in me we were very much in love, it was him and me against the world, you know? Then, in recent years, I've simply been too dependent on him – financially, I mean. Allan has just helped Alice and Dan to put down the deposit on their flat. They wouldn't have had a hope of getting the mortgage otherwise, and he pays Robin's rent in Halls at St Andrews. In fact, I've got less freedom to question Allan now than I did when we were still married.' Suz's face looks strained. I lean across the table and place my hand over hers. She visibly relaxes and lets out a sigh of resignation before she begins. 'I just want to say first off - try not to be too hard on Allan. He might be a grade 'A' idiot sometimes but he loves you and Michael and he certainly loved your mum. He cried like a baby when he was here the other night, but he would never let you see him like that.'

I nod my head, to show I have taken this on board, noting to myself what a complicated relationship Allan and Suz still have.

'Okay. There was a summer holiday, when you and I had taken the kids to your mum's place for a few weeks. This was one of the early trips - so it was sometime in the mid-nineties, when the children were really small and Ian and Bridie probably weren't born yet. Allan came up to stay for a week, but Hugh couldn't get away, so it was just us.'

'I remember the year. Hugh had a lecture tour as his first book had only just come out.'

'That was it. Well, we were all drinking one evening, when the kids were in bed. We were seated around the kitchen table and Isabel had the twelve year old single malt out. I remember that you made some innocent comment about your mum losing her bag years before, and what a fuss everyone had made about it. I think you were imagining we would all laugh and perhaps say how silly it was, but nobody did.'

'No, they didn't. I changed the subject pretty quickly, if I remember rightly.'

'Allan was acting in an odd way for the rest of the evening. He drank a lot and then slipped outside for a smoke when it got dark. I went out to join him, took one of his cigarettes and lit up. He led me a little way down the garden, so we were out of earshot of the house, and that's when he told me.'

I sit forward in my seat, but stay absolutely silent.

'He started by describing the day that your mum lost her bag. I don't know if you recall much about it. Allan said you were about twelve years old at the time?'

I nod.

'Allan told me he was seventeen. It was the early 80s and he was going through a bit of a rebellious phase. He said that Michael was off the island studying for his first degree, before he had decided upon Architecture. With Michael gone, Allan was determined not be viewed as his replacement, you know, the responsible one who was a substitute for your father. Sorry, but that's the way Allan put it.' Suz takes another sip of tea.

I sit there wishing I'd brought some kind of recording device, or even a note-pad. I haven't been very well prepared.

'On the day Isabel lost her bag, Alison and Davy were at the farm too. If you remember, your mum and Susie Dickson had gone on an organised walk up to Ben Mvor. Alison came along with her mother because she was desperate to get out of helping her Dad in the shop. She was trying to get into the Glasgow School of Art at the time, so she told her Dad she was going up to the farm to make some sketches for her portfolio.'

'I remember. It was the summer break but Davy and I had some kind of holiday club. The minibus picked us up from the road end and we were on the beach all day, rock pooling and stuff. We got dropped back at the farm at tea-time. It turned out to be a really hot day.'

'Allan only mentioned Alison being at Lower Kilduggan, so that makes sense. Anyhow, your mum left Allan with instructions that he was to mow the lawns whilst she was gone. It was a busy time at the guest house so she asked him to hang out the sheets on the big washing line that hung across the bottom of the meadow bank, where they weren't in full view of the boarders.

Allan says he mowed the lawns, front and back. During this time, Alison had been in the kitchen, where she'd laid out her sketch pad and charcoals. When he finished, he was hot and wanted to go for a shower. He asked Alison if she would hang out the washing for him and she agreed. Allan took a shower upstairs and came down maybe twenty five minutes later.

Alison was standing in the kitchen doorway looking very pleased with herself. She took his hand and led him out of the door, across the courtyard and into one of the animal sheds. Allan and Alison had done this before, so he didn't think too much of it. He imagined that Alison maybe had some booze stashed in there for him on this occasion, so he was very keen to follow her lead.'

'Hang on. What do you mean when you say that they had done this before?' I interrupt.

Suz shifts in her seat. 'They'd been sneaking off to the sheds whenever Alison was over at the farm. Every so often she would get the bus and meet him somewhere else - like down on the beach or up the hillside.' Suz clears her throat. 'They would smoke, sometimes drink, but mostly they were just having sex.'

'Wait a minute.' I put up my hand as if to stem the flow of information. 'Alison must have been about twenty two years old at that time. Are you absolutely certain they were sleeping together?'

'Yes, I am sure. It's the main reason why Allan never told anyone about what happened. He assures me it only started after he'd turned seventeen. He'd filled out a bit and suddenly Alison started to show an interest in him. Previously she only had eyes for Michael. Allan was flattered, of course, and he was a teenage boy, so you can imagine what his motivation was.'

I am starting to feel a deep sense of anger growing inside me, at myself largely, for being so incredibly naïve.

'So, Alison led Allan into the barn. He moved towards her, to indicate that he wanted to, you know, fool around a bit. Alison kissed him for a while but then gently pushed him away and said she had something to show him. Allan thought this would be alcohol or fags, so he sat back and laughed. That was when Alison pulled your mum's satchel out from behind a stack of hay. Allan stopped laughing when he saw it and started to get worried. He didn't like the look on Alison's face as she held it up in front of him. Which he said was like, I don't know, triumph, maybe.

Alison told him she'd found it, up on the hillside, after she had hung the washing out on the line in the meadow. She'd gone further up the hill, beyond the first stile, to have a cigarette. Alison saw something silver, shimmering in the sunlight. She went over to it and that's when she found the bag. It was sitting next to a rock by the footpath. Without thinking about it - or so she told Allan – she grabbed it and ran back down to the sheds to find somewhere to stash it.

Sitting on the dirty floor of that cow shed, she persuaded Allan it would be a great joke just to hide it for a few days. They would wait for the dust to settle and then return the bag. Leave it on the kitchen table or something. She said the adults would be really freaked out and it would be hilarious.'

'Alison was an adult too,' I can't help but add. 'They never did put the bag back, because Mum never found it. So how did it end up buried on the hillside?' I am full of questions but this one seems like the most pertinent.

'They decided to split the loot, so to speak. Allan was to take the empty bag and Alison took the contents: the purse, some letters and a few other things that Allan only saw very briefly as they divided it all up between them. They thought this would mean that one of them couldn't bottle out at the last minute and put the bag back, because that would mean dropping the other one in it. So Alison stuffed the contents of Isabel's satchel into her rucksack. Allan rushed back to the farmhouse and hid the bag itself under a floorboard in the corner of his room.'

I am conscious of time ticking away and fear missing my train. However, I do not want to call things to an end, now I am so close to finding out the truth.

'But neither of them had counted on your mum's reaction after she discovered it was lost. Isabel and Susie returned from their walk early. Isabel had already noticed her satchel was missing. Allan had only just hidden it when your mum came storming into the house, looking through all the rooms and thundering about like a force of nature.

He just froze to the spot, finding himself unable to say anything at all. Alison was as cool as a cucumber. She went over to her mother and asked what she could do to help. They all searched, or feigned to search, for a little while and Isabel just collapsed into a chair, looking totally defeated. Then you and Davy arrived back. Susie took her children home soon afterwards. After the Dicksons drove away, Isabel sat at the kitchen table and wept. Allan was really frightened to see her like that, she had never cried in front of him before - not even when your dad died.'

'No. I remember it so well. Mum was devastated by the loss of the bag and she would never properly explain why. It had been a gift from Dad, years before, when they sold some calves for a good price. I always assumed that was the reason. But Allan was right, we had never seen Mum cry.' I shake my head, trying to understand this chain of events. 'Why didn't Allan just tell her then - when she was sitting there in tears?'

'He said that was his opportunity - when the three of you were around the table. But he couldn't bring himself to do it. He was terrified that if he confessed to your mum about the bag and Alison's part in its theft, she would tell everyone about them having sex in revenge. Allan was far more frightened of that happening. So he said nothing at all. It was the lesser of two evils to him.'

'But it was *Alison* who should have been ashamed of the relationship, not Allan,' I add with feeling.

'I don't believe Allan was thinking straight. To him, having sex with someone you shouldn't be was a worse crime than hiding a bag for a lark. So he decided to sit tight and ride it out. But your Mum's mood got worse. Allan said he actually thought she might be having some kind of breakdown.

In the early hours of the morning, after a sleepless night, Allan decided there was only one course of action open to him. He knew that if the bag just turned up after a few days, it would not simply be laughed off and forgotten about. The whole situation had turned serious, so he decided the only way to avoid exposure, for all of his crimes, was to get rid of the evidence.

He went to the tool shed, got a spade, and in the half-light, climbed up the meadow bank and dug a hole. He dug for ages until he thought it was deep enough. Allan rolled up the satchel, placed it inside and tipped the freshly removed earth back on top. He flattened it down with his boots, arranging the meadow flowers and grasses over the top. It was pretty overgrown at that time of year, but he was still amazed no one ever saw the newly turned soil. But they never did. He was back in his bed before breakfast time.' Suz takes a breather. Neither of us says a word.

'The next morning, Isabel was very quiet, but she just got on with her usual jobs. Allan slipped out as early as he could and caught the bus over to Kilross. It was the days before mobile phones, so he had to track Alison down. He waited on the beach until he saw her come out of the shop. He went over and told her they needed to talk urgently. Allan knew a few isolated spots where they had their secret meetings. They went down by the sand dunes, below the edge of the golf course. He told Alison there was no way they could blithely return the bag and its contents to his mother.

He told her that because of the way his mum was acting, there must have been something really important inside the bag. He demanded that Alison show him what she'd taken, thinking there might have been a lot of cash in the purse, or a cheque for a large amount, or something else of significant monetary value. Alison swore to him that there had been nothing important inside it, only some letters, receipts and stuff. A ten pound note and a bit of change had been in the purse. She actually gave the money to him, then and there.' Suz says this as if she would not have put it past her to have kept the cash too.

'What did Allan do with the money?' I ask, in the hope that Allan has redeemed himself somewhere in this sorry tale.

'He put it straight into your mum's tin when he got home. He thought she might notice but he took the risk. You see, he still didn't consider himself a thief. But that money was all Allan ever got back from the contents of the bag. Alison was angry with him for burying the satchel, so she said she'd burn the contents and then there would be no evidence left. Allan tried to argue against this. He was still convinced there must have been something important in there for Isabel to be acting so oddly. But Alison held all the cards. She just kept insisting it was junk and needed getting rid of. In the end, Allan just had to accept it.

He and Alison vowed they would never mention what they had done to anyone else, it would be their secret. Something good did come out of it all, as Allan never had any more encounters with Alison. He decided the fleeting pleasure he had derived from their liaisons was not worth the risk involved. He had already got himself well out of his depth by messing around with Alison Dickson.'

'Does Allan know if she did actually burn the contents of the bag?' I ask, trying to commit the main events to memory.

'He never said. I don't think he and Alison ever spoke about it again. Until a few days ago, of course, when the builders found the bag.'

'Which brings us back to the present day, so what happened?'

'Allan called me up out of the blue on Sunday night. He sounded really upset and said he wanted to come and see me. He needed to talk and I was the only person who would understand. Allan said very little on the phone, but arrived by taxi the following evening. I poured us both a drink. Once he'd taken a large sip of his, he announced that he wanted to talk about the bag they had stolen, all those years ago.

To be honest, it took me a while to remember the details, but it was obvious Allan felt as bad about it then as he had done thirty years ago. He told me how the satchel had been dug up and you'd brought it in to show him. He was convinced you knew it was him who had buried it. He thought that you were standing at the kitchen door, just waiting for him to confess. Yet again, he was too weak to do it.'

'He imagined that. I actually had no idea,' I correct.

'No, but Allan's guilt was making him paranoid. When you went out, later in the day, Allan called Alison Dickson on his mobile and told her to get over to Lower Kilduggan straight away.'

'How did Allan have her number - have they been in contact in the intervening years?'

'Allan swears they have not. He got her number from your Filofax. He found it sitting on your bedside table. He said Alison was pretty surprised to hear from him. She still got over there sharpish. Allan is not the weedy seventeen year old boy that he was back then and he was angry. He told Alison he was going to tell you and Michael everything about what happened with the bag *and* about his relationship with her.

He told her to be prepared for the fall out. Alison replied that it was alright for him because his parents were dead and would never find out. She actually suggested that discovering they had been having sex all those years ago might kill Susie and Jimmy. I told Allan that was crap - she was trying to frighten him. But Allan was pretty shaken up. It made him have second thoughts.'

'I can see it would complicate things.'

'In the end, they were just shouting at each other, so Allan told her to leave and he would let her know what he had decided to do.

I told Allan he had to tell you and Michael everything, for his own sake as much as anything else. That was when he started sobbing, I held him tight and he clung to me like a child. We spent the night just lying in each other's arms. Nothing happened, but I don't think Allan will tell Abigail. It didn't mean a thing, but if I were her, I wouldn't understand.'

'Allan hasn't said anything yet, so presumably Alison is still waiting to hear what her fate will be.'

I get up and start taking the dirty cups and plates into the adjoining kitchen area. I pluck up the courage to look at the kitchen clock above the cooker: it is just after four.

'Look, Suz, I'm really sorry but I've missed my train. I had a connection and there's no way I can make that now.'

'You must stay here, of course. Alice's room is freshly made up. To be honest, I could really do with the company. We'll go for a walk to clear our heads, buy a takeaway, watch a mindless DVD and try not to get quite so heavy.'

'That,' I say with some relief, 'sounds like a perfect plan.'

## Chapter 9

Suz gave me a lift to Fort William Railway Station to catch an early train to Glasgow. Although Suz did not ask me to, I have decided to keep her revelations to myself for the time being, largely because I would like the opportunity to think through the implications.

I've given myself a couple of hours in Glasgow to do some shopping and absorb a bit of normality before returning to Lower Kilduggan, a place that is becoming increasingly unknown to me, despite a childhood of living there.

There are a lot of questions that I would like to try and answer. On reflection, I am feeling less angry with Alison Dickson. She did not actually commit any crime by having a sexual relationship with Allan, as he was over the age of consent. If I am honest with myself, Allan would probably have been sleeping with someone during that time, even if it wasn't Alison. He was just going through that kind of phase. But what I am finding difficult to forgive is the deception about Mum's bag. A joke is one thing, but leaving Mum in that kind of distress is something else. I am pretty disappointed with Allan about that.

I certainly have some questions to ask Alison when I get back to Garansay. I want to know exactly what she found in Mum's bag and what she did with it. I'm certainly not going to let her fob me off. I will also get in touch with Colin Walmsley to discuss the sale of the farm. I feel a little uncomfortable about even staying one more night in the farmhouse on my own. It contains too many unhappy memories for me right now. It will take a little time for me to reclaim the happy times I had at the place.

Usually, I would have arranged to meet up with Michael whilst here in Glasgow, as his offices are just around the corner. On this occasion, I'm not sure what I would say to him. Michael has had enough unhappiness in his life. It has only been in recent years that he and Allan have built up a strong brotherly bond, despite the differences in their character. I don't feel inclined to damage that fragile relationship over something that happened thirty years ago.

I return to Garansay with a heaviness of heart that I did not possess the last time I disembarked here. The beauty of the mountains on this clear autumn day does lift my spirits and allows me to gain some perspective on my worries. I imagine how the hills have stood here for thousands of years, through various ages of man. This landscape has borne witness to the weaknesses and follies of human beings over so many generations, yet has remained aloof and unaffected. This is something I used to think about a great deal as a child, sitting at my desk, snatching a look out of the classroom window when Mr McKinley's back was turned, at the outline of Ben Ardroch, looming over the village. It gave me a certain comfort to know that whatever our actions - good or bad, they would soon be long forgotten. The material landscape would outlive us all.

I pick up the car from the harbour. Eddie Gow, who helps to bring the boats in and was at School with me, has kept an eye on it.

Crawling up the gravel drive to Lower Kilduggan Farm, getting used to the handling of Mum's old car again, I immediately notice that something is wrong. The kitchen door has a broken pane of glass. It has been smashed inwards by a large rock which is now lying on the stone floor inside. I know I should not be touching anything, but feel a burning need to see what damage has been done. I go to the car, put on a pair of gloves that are lying on the back seat and enter the house through the front door, which appears to be undamaged.

The house had been almost emptied after Allan and I cleared it out a week ago. Someone has tipped over the cardboard boxes in the hall. The contents are lying strewn across the carpet. I move quickly through the rooms. The sitting room seems pretty much as it was but the boxes in the study have also been knocked over and papers lie everywhere. I feel an overwhelming desire to weep at the mess and automatically tap the bag at my side where I had placed Mum's family tree and all the important documents such as birth certificates for safe keeping.

It is hard to tell in all this disorder if anything is missing. There was certainly not much cash in the house and all of Mum's bank and credit cards were stopped over a month ago. I rack my brain to try and think of anything valuable that had been left here. There wasn't much, maybe just the Rennie Mackintosh lamp that was in one of the boxes in the hall. I hurry out to have a look. It takes me a few minutes, but then I find it - wrapped up in newspaper and lying in the corner, under the coat stand where it rolled after the box was upturned. It seems to be intact.

The whole thing appears like vandalism. There is obviously nothing here worth taking and anything that could have raised a few pounds has been left. I wonder if it might be kids, based on a newly acquired suspicion that some teenagers would do anything for their idea of a laugh.

I carefully go back out through the front door and fight the strong urge to start clearing up. I phone the police from the car and then, inexplicably, call Colin Walmsley. I suppose I feel as if he has some kind of stake in the farm, particularly now I'm fairly sure we will be selling the place to him.

The local police arrive twenty minutes later. Whilst one of them has a look around the house: taking photographs and dusting for fingerprints, the other officer asks me questions. He seems convinced it is local teenagers, as this kind of thing has happened before - although not this far out of Kilross, he does admit. The policeman tells me that it was lucky I wasn't here when it happened. He encourages me to contact our insurers and get the kitchen door fixed straight away, reassuring me the vandals are unlikely to come back, but that I shouldn't stay here until the back door has been properly secured.

Colin arrived after about half an hour. Since then, he has been solemnly observing the policemen following their protocols. The officers seem relieved there is a man here. They are happy to leave me with Colin once my statement has been signed and they've been assured my insurance company will be contacted. Colin looks very serious and asks if I'm okay. I explain that I'd been visiting a friend and was not at the farm when the break-in occurred.

'What did they take?' Colin asks as he examines the broken pane of glass.

'I'm not sure yet. It looks more like vandalism than theft. All of the boxes that were ready to be removed were tipped over. But the few things in them that were of any value weren't taken,' I say.

'I can sort out this glass for you.' Colin brushes out the debris with a thick sleeve pulled down to protect his hand and arm. 'I've got a man back at the farm who can replace it and make sure it is secure by tonight.'

'Thank you. I've got a lot of clearing up to do.'

'I'll give Bill a call, then come and give you a hand,' he says in a reassuring, matter-of-fact way.

Once we were both busy righting the boxes and placing the contents back inside, it didn't take us long to tidy things up. The biggest job was clearing up all the broken glass.

'Bill will get rid of it for you,' Colin adds when we have finished brushing away the last of the glass fragments.

'What is weird is that if someone had come along wanting to break into the farmhouse a few days ago it would have been easy. They would have been able to pick up the key from under that rock by the back door. Mum had kept it there for as long as I can remember. There are dozens of locals who knew about it. Security has never been such an important issue out here. I only removed the key after having that run in with Alison and was feeling a bit jumpy.'

'Maybe someone came along and picked up the rock, expecting to find the key. When it wasn't there, they got frustrated and threw it through the glass instead.'

'Perhaps, but they must have then climbed in through the top panel of the door because the lock wasn't forced. That is most likely to be kids,' I suggest, eyeing up the size of the aperture which is no more than three foot square. 'What is really puzzling me,' I go on, 'is that this happened on the one night I wasn't here. It seems like one hell of a coincidence.'

'Did you tell anyone you were going to be away?'

'I didn't even know I was going to be away overnight myself until I missed my train. I did ask Eddie Gow to keep an eye on the car for me - although I certainly don't think that he would be involved.'

'No, but plenty of people could have seen you get onto the ferry. Eddie might have mentioned it to someone - either at the harbour or down at the pub. I'm afraid that unless you leave the Island in a rowing boat by the light of the moon, someone on Garansay is going to know your movements.'

'But that suggests this was a planned break-in. I really don't like the idea of that.' I shudder.

Colin asks me where I am planning to stay tonight. He adds that I'm welcome to sleep in a spare room at Loch Crannox Farm. I thank him for his offer, but inform him I have decided to pack up my things and spend the night at a hotel in Kilross, in order to get an early ferry home tomorrow.

'I think that is a very good idea,' Colin says, 'and I want you to promise me you won't make any decisions about the farm just yet. I am still keen to buy it but I don't want that to happen under these circumstances. You need to go back home and take some time. I will keep an eye on the place for you. Bill can fix up some security lights and someone will come by and check on it every day.'

'Thanks,' I say, happy to agree to this sensible advice. But I still have another favour to ask of my neighbour. 'Colin. I have no right to ask you this and please feel free to say no. I need to go and speak to Alison Dickson about something before I leave. Would you come with me? Even if you just sit in the car I would feel a lot better.'

'Yes, okay, as long as you promise that afterwards you will leave things to me and go straight back home,' Colin states.

'I promise.'

We sit in silence on the drive over to Gilstone. This isn't one of the days Alison works at the hotel, so we should find her at home. Colin parks his jeep up on the verge at the bottom of Alison's front garden. From there he has a clear view of the cottage.

'Imogen!' Colin calls out as I climb down from the seat, 'be careful.'

I stride up the long pathway towards the cottage. Drawing closer, I notice the front door is ajar. I still use the knocker, feeling increasingly nervous about the reception I am going to get. When there is no reply I take a deep breath and call out, 'Alison! It's Imogen.' I wait a few minutes and then push the door open to see if there are any signs of life inside.

The cottage is totally silent. I can detect the smell of both stale and freshly smoked cigarettes, so assume that Alison must be around somewhere. I walk down the long corridor to the kitchen, which is dark because of the lack of natural light. I glance in at the sitting room as I pass and see that Alison has been working on a canvas that is propped up against an easel in the centre of the room.

Reaching the kitchen, I feel a growing sense of foreboding. There is a half empty bottle of gin on the counter and an open packet of ibuprofen tablets next to it. The packet is almost empty but this doesn't really tell me much.

'Alison!' I shout, with more urgency this time, running upstairs and checking the two bedrooms and bathroom, all of which are untidy and smell vaguely unpleasant. Finding nothing, I suddenly have an idea of where she might have gone. I rush back out of the front door of the cottage and down the path towards Colin's car.

Colin is already out of the driver's seat before I reach him. When he gets within earshot I shout, 'Alison's not in the house. She's been drinking and has taken some pills. I think she might have gone up the hillside.'

We both run through the cottage. Colin says nothing but is silently taking in the chaotic state of the place. When we get to the bottom of the little garden I observe that the gate leading up to Aoife's Chariot is standing open. Colin and I stride quickly up the steep path.

It is many years since I have taken this route up to the hills, usually starting the ascent from the western side. However, I do remember that as the path levels off and we reach the foot of Ben Keir, there is a small loch. It is not as large as Loch Crannox and is not particularly deep, but there has been heavy rainfall over night, so the terrain will be very boggy and the loch will be full.

I stop to catch my breath when we reach the top of the hill. The rain has started to come on again and Colin is striding on ahead of me, shouting out Alison's name as he looks wildly around him.

That is when we both see her.

The loch in front of us has flooded its banks. The peat stained water is spreading out over the surrounding vegetation. Our feet are sinking fast into the saturated soil as we stand, momentarily frozen to the spot.

Alison is lying spread eagled in the centre of the swollen loch. She is face down in the water and very still. She appears to be wearing nothing but her bra and pants. I can't see the rest of her clothing anywhere nearby. After a couple of seconds, Colin makes his way across the bog and then wades through the water itself to reach her. He hauls her up by the arms and turns her over, dragging her body back onto drier land. Even at its deepest, the water is never higher than Colin's thighs.

Colin places Alison down in front of me. Her blond hair has been darkened by the water and her bloated face is almost unrecognisable. I quickly take off my jacket and put it over her, instinctively taking hold of her hands and starting to rub, in a futile effort to get some warmth back into them. As if she was one of my children, coming back into the house after playing out in the snow.

Colin has knelt down next to her and is performing mouth-to-mouth resuscitation. His face is a mask of total concentration and he is pumping on her chest to a regular rhythm. I am transfixed by the paleness of Alison's skin and by the complex structure of veins that I can see through its translucent surface. Colin carries on for about ten minutes and I make no attempt to stop him. Then he sits back on his haunches and looks up towards the sky, like Ewan used to do when he was trying to see where the raindrops fell from.

The Emergency services get here quite quickly. Ultimately, this will be a job for the Glasgow police, who will start to arrive on the Island within the next few hours. Colin and I both have to give statements, for me, the second in one day. Someone at the police station in Kilross organises me a room for the night at a local hotel. Colin and I just have time to shake hands and say a brief farewell, before a policewoman puts me into the back of a patrol car, ready to drive me to my accommodation.

I will have to go back to Lower Kilduggan Farm tomorrow to pick up my things. But after that I am going to walk onto the ferry, go straight into the café, buy myself a highly sweetened cup of coffee and begin my long journey back home.

## PART TWO

### 2013
Chapter 10

It is a gorgeous June day. It started out hazy, with a humid and damp feel in the air. The clouds have now lifted and the sun is blazing across Coopers Creek so that you can see both Osea and Northey Islands perfectly clearly through our living room window. Our house was built in the 1970s. It doesn't have the charm of the white weatherboarded cottages that are common to this part of east Essex. The benefit of our modern house, is that it is designed to provide the best possible views out over the River Blackwater, as it lazily navigates its way around the two islands to reach its destination in the attractive town of Maldon, which lies a couple of miles along the coast.

Our house has been elevated in order to take advantage of the views, with the living room having been added on to the second floor, at the front of the property. It has a large window that runs the entire length of the room and it is from here that today you can see as far as the concrete pill boxes on Osea Island to the north-east of us.

We live in a small hamlet on the banks of the Blackwater, between Maylandsea and Mundon called Cooper's End. The landscape here is flat and interconnected by a network of meandering waterways and sluggish creeks. This area does not have the dramatic features of Garansay. There are no great peaks here. But the mud flats and the slow moving river have a bleak and peaceful beauty. When the wooden sailing barges pass along this route, with their reddish brown sails and gaily painted hulls, you can imagine that you have gone back in time by a hundred years. We never miss the 'Barge Match Day' that will take place later this month on the Quay at Maldon. Over twenty of the wonderfully restored Thames barges race each other across the estuary as part of a tradition that goes back to the end of the Victorian era.

Despite these local traditions, there are times when we can feel quite isolated out here by the water. We experience this particularly in winter when the road to Mundon gets sporadically cut off by snow or floods. However, as long as the cars are running well, we are only a ten minute drive from Maldon and the market town provides all of the amenities that we need. Ian and Bridie both attend the secondary school there, where they seem to be happy.

In fact, that is where I am meant to be heading now, to pick them both up. Whenever the weather is good like today my children want to go to the sailing club at Maylandsea after school and take out the Skipper that we have moored down there.

In the summer holidays we will make the trip every day and soon become sick of the journey back and forth. I will just have to make sure that all of their gear is in the boot before setting off, as I don't want to have to come back home again in between.

The traffic is heavy as I try to get close to the school at quarter to four, but once we have turned around and are heading back towards Mundon, on a quiet road that is off the main routes out of the town, there are hardly any other cars about. On a sunny late afternoon like this one the journey is really lovely. Bridie is chatting happily about her day at school and Ian has attached his MP3 player to his ears and is absorbed by his music and his thoughts.

There has been building work going on at Maylandsea Marina for as long as we have been living in the area. A collection of rusty old barges sits alongside the rotten carcasses of abandoned boats on the shoreline here and spoils the view. Despite this, the Marina still has its rustic charm and there is a relaxed and friendly atmosphere to the place that is sometimes lacking in its more polished counter-parts.

I help Bridie and Ian to bring the Skipper out from under its tarpaulin. Once they have put on their wetsuits and life jackets I help them to carry the boat down one of the small concrete jetties and push them off into the water. There are very few strong currents here and the wind is light enough to allow them to go out by themselves.

I sit down on the bank, below St Peter's Way, the coastal footpath that runs along the front of the boat club and was once the route for pilgrims making their way to the ancient chapel at Bradwell. Looking out at the water, I note how good it feels to be back into my old routines again. Returning from Garansay last autumn, it felt as if I'd been away for months rather than just a few days.

My perception of things had been altered by that trip and what I had discovered there. It took me a few weeks to adjust back into my old life. There was also the investigation into Alison Dickson's death that had dragged on, making it difficult to return comfortably to my previous existence.

The Strathclyde Police passed on their evidence to the Procurator Fiscal who then began his own enquiry. Colin Walmsley and I had to give detailed statements of what happened on the day that we found her. Thankfully, under the Scottish system, we did not have to testify at an Inquest.

The medical reports revealed Alison had very high levels of alcohol in her bloodstream and that she had taken a number of ibuprofen tablets, although not enough to kill her. I spent a few days at the time agonising over whether or not to inform the Procurator Fiscal about the altercation that Allan had with Alison a couple of days before her death. In the end, deciding that I had a duty to share the information, I wrote a long letter setting out every detail of the argument.

The case finally closed with the Procurator deciding that it was death by suicide, whilst the balance of Alison's mind was disturbed. There had been evidence supplied by some of the locals of Garansay, relating to Alison's recent drinking habits and her increasingly erratic behaviour in the months leading up to her death.

I don't believe that Aunty Susie and Uncle Jimmy found out about Alison's relationship with Allan all of those years ago. I am hopeful there was enough evidence to satisfy the authorities that Alison had taken her own life and therefore, no need to release all of the painful details. My heart goes out to Susie and Jimmy as no one should have to outlive their child - it's a tragedy at any age.

I have not had much contact with Allan since Alison's death. But we have spoken about Mum's bag. I told him that as far as I am concerned he is forgiven. I have also tried to persuade him that he must not blame himself for Alison's actions. The truth was always going to come out in the end.

I have a feeling, just a kind of hunch really, that Alison had something else on her mind in the weeks leading up to her death, not simply the silly mistakes she had made in her youth. Unlike with Allan, it never felt as if she experienced any guilt at having taken Mum's bag. What Alison was concerned about, was whether she was going to get found out.

Bridie and Ian are tacking across the creek and they seem to be having a race with the children on another boat. The other crew are some of the regulars from the boat club. I will give them another half an hour. Hugh should be back from the university a little earlier this evening and I promised to prepare something nice for us all.

I have kept in contact with Davy Dickson, writing to him a few times since Alison's death. He is beating himself up for not reading the warning signs of her increasingly heavy drinking. He says that he should have made her seek professional help. It makes me a little angry that Alison chose such a cowardly way out of her problems. She has caused an awful lot of pain for her family.

Davy did tell me something interesting in one of his letters. The Police and Procurator Fiscal's report showed that Alison had quite a substantial amount of savings in her bank account. She left no will, so eventually this money will go to Susie and Jimmy, who have promised to use it to help Davy and Fiona keep the shop going.

Davy said he was amazed to be informed that Alison had just a little under thirty thousand pounds in her bank account. I suggested maybe she was hoping to buy her cottage from the land owner and was saving for a deposit on a mortgage. Davy agreed this must have been the case. But I know what he means. Alison had only ever worked in the hotel in Gilstone, which did not pay much. Her paintings did sell, but would fetch perhaps a couple of hundred pounds each and certainly not thousands.

I check my watch and then walk down the jetty and wave my arms about to catch Ian's attention. Thankfully, they have passed the stage where they would simply have ignored me for another twenty minutes relishing the fact I was incapable of doing anything about it. Now they are a bit older they understand that if they are caught out by the tide, they will end up stranded on the mud flats for several hours at least.

We are all pretty tired when we return to the house. The kids retire to their respective rooms to assimilate themselves into their virtual worlds. After a couple of hours of fresh air and exercise, I certainly won't deny them that pleasure.

After I have prepared the casserole and placed it in the oven, Hugh arrives back from work. We embrace and share a brief kiss. I have been more affectionate with my husband since returning from Garansay last year and he has responded enthusiastically to this thawing of relations.

I know he has noticed a change in me in the past few months, not least because I have been concentrating less on my home tutoring business and spending more time researching my family and the history of Garansay. I might even consider writing a book about it. Hugh has had a couple of books on Psychology published himself, which he has to do in order to maintain his tenure at the university in Colchester, where he is a professor.

Hugh returns to the kitchen after saying hello to the kids. 'Oh, I nearly forgot,' he says. 'Ann Larwood from the History Department was talking to me at lunch today. I mentioned that you have been doing some research into your family tree. She suggested you try the Mitchell Library in Glasgow. Apparently, they have all the archives for the Scottish nationals and some of the local papers too. She is going to send you the link.'

'Thank you darling.' I lean in to brush my lips against his cheek. Hugh slips an arm around my waist and pulls me towards him. 'All of their records are online, Mrs. Croft. So you won't have an excuse to go running off across the border again.'

I laugh and playfully push him away. The light is fading now and the water below us reflects back a deep orange sheen as the sun dips below the eastern channel of the river. Hugh walks out to the living room and stands silently at the tall window, staring out across the creek. I take advantage of this rare moment of peace to organise the plates. I ask Hugh to gather up the troops for an infrequent coming together of the Croft family on a week night.

The evening light spilling onto the dining room table makes the scene look almost magical. Suddenly, I am gripped by the terrible feeling that this is all part of an enchanted spell, and it is one that is just about to break.

## Chapter 11

I always love the peace and quiet in the morning, just after Hugh has driven off to work, taking the children with him to drop at school on the way. Even though I still need to clear the devastation wrought by breakfast and the hasty preparation of three lunchboxes, I feel a great optimism about the day that lies ahead, having not yet had time to miss the kids or to feel the hours slipping away from me.

In the past few months I have found myself making better use of this free time. We've made some space for me in Hugh's study and bought a laptop computer upon which I can conduct and write up my research. The glorious sunshine of yesterday has been replaced by a sky full of thick, dark clouds. It is raining directly across the estuary at Goldhanger. So it is just a matter of time before it reaches here. This change in the weather gives me the perfect excuse to stay indoors and get on with my work.

Since returning from Garansay last year, I have finished my research into Mum's side of the family tree. This completed document is now carefully pinned up on the wall. With Hugh's assistance in places, I was able to access all of the necessary information from the 'Scotland's People' website.

The first records that I looked up were Aileen Anderson's birth and death certificates. Unfortunately, Aileen was born just after the 1911 census, so she was not mentioned in this, but there were other documents on the site relating to her.

In fact, Aileen's death certificate provided me with some interesting information. According to this, Aileen had died of tuberculosis in 1937. This discovery prompted me to find out a bit more about the disease. I wanted to know how she might have caught it and why she was the only person in her family to die from it.

One of Hugh's friends, Phil Morley, was able to help me out with this. He is a research chemist who completed his PhD thesis in bacterial diseases of the nineteenth and twentieth centuries a couple of years ago. Hugh invited him over for dinner last weekend. Over the starter he told me that TB was still a very common disease in Scotland right up to the fifties and sixties.

Babies are still routinely offered the TB vaccine 'north of the border' whereas this practice has been virtually phased out in England. Phil said tuberculosis is now a very rare disease in humans - in this part of the world anyway. The vaccinations help to maintain 'herd immunity' so we shouldn't become complacent about it, particularly as just over fifty years ago it was still a common cause of death in the UK. He told me that TB is a disease spread easily in overcrowded conditions and made worse by malnutrition.

The accepted medical recommendation in the past was that sufferers should be separated from other people in 'sanatoriums' or taken to places where the air was 'cleaner' in order to help the lungs to function better.

I asked Phil if Aileen could have contracted the disease from the farm animals she was working with, recalling that the young woman helped her mother with seasonal work on the local smallholdings. He suggested that in the present day, there is almost no risk to humans from animals that carry TB. In the 1930s it would have been quite a different story.

Today, with hygiene precautions and the routine pasteurisation of milk, it is extremely unlikely that bovine TB will spread to humans. For Aileen, however, it was fairly likely this was how she had contracted the disease. He said that thousands of people in Britain caught TB from drinking contaminated milk in the decades before the outbreak of World War Two, especially on small farms in rural areas where pasteurisation was less likely to have been adopted.

Later that evening, as we were getting ready for bed, I suddenly remembered what I had learnt in a History lesson about the Highland 'Blackhouses'.

These were the small circular stone structures used by the crofters of the Highlands of Scotland before the clearances had removed them from their homes. The cottages were built so that animals could be kept in the same building as the family, with only a small partition between them. Our teacher told us how the crofters had caught all kinds of diseases from living in such close proximity to their livestock. I wonder now if TB could have been one of them.

Thanks to Phil, I was pretty sure that Aileen contracted TB or 'consumption', as it had been referred to in the nineteenth Century, from her work on the farms of Garansay in the twenties and thirties. This new knowledge led me to have an idea. Perhaps the reason why she was so little remembered by her contemporaries was because she had been 'sent away' somewhere, as the medical advice of the time had recommended.

I did some online research, looking through the patient records of all the sanatoriums and hospitals in western Scotland that I could find on the internet. I was amazed to discover how many of these institutions had detailed records going back to the Victorian times.

Finally, I found her name. Aileen Anderson, aged twenty four, had been a patient at the Broomhill Hospital in Glasgow, or, more accurately, at the Lanfine Home for Tuberculosis Sufferers which had been added to the hospital in 1904. Aileen spent several months there from the autumn of 1936 until her death in January 1937.

Somehow, this explained to me why Mum may not have had any strong memories of Aileen. Perhaps she had been sickly for some months, maybe even bedridden. She could have been lying ill in the house, hardly ever being seen out and about on Garansay. Then, when Katherine and Alasdair could afford to, they had taken her over to the mainland for specialist treatment. Sadly, the poor girl never returned. By solving part of the mystery surrounding Aileen's death, I have concluded the Pirie section of the Stewart family tree.

We instructed our solicitors last month to begin the process of selling Lower Kilduggan Farm to the Walmsleys. Colin was as good as his word and has looked after the place for me whilst we came to a decision. Michael, Allan and I were all in agreement that the sale seemed to be the best way to settle Mum's affairs. Michael was particularly keen that Kilduggan should not become a cheaply built estate of modern houses that would inevitably become holiday homes. Colin has promised the land will become a part of his estate and will be used only for farming purposes.

With my Garansay interests temporarily on hold, I began to ask myself why I'd shown such little interest in Dad's side of the family. This apparent negligence inspired me to have another sift through the papers and documents that Allan and I packed up in boxes and had shipped to us a few weeks ago. I found almost nothing that gave me any clues about Dad's childhood or family background.

I was only five years old when Dad died and my memories of him are fairly vague. We have plenty of photographs, of course, and Michael remembers him very well. I know that Angus Nichols was a quiet man, tall and dark like all of his children. He had grown a moustache and let his hair become thick and wavy at the time of his death in the mid-seventies, as was the fashion back then.

I most certainly remember the day he died. The boys and I had finished school for the day. What sticks in my mind is Michael holding my hand whilst we waited for the bus to take us back to Kilduggan. The Headmaster, Mr Garvie, came running out of the main building to find us. He told us not to get on the bus, leading us back, in silence, to his office.

Mr Garvie spoke to Michael first. My brother emerged from the room several minutes later with an unreadable expression on his face. Then we all trooped back in. Michael sat me on his knee, wrapping his arms around my middle whilst the Headmaster explained, for the second time, what had happened to Dad.

Allan and I burst into tears and asked endless questions. It must have been terribly difficult for poor old Garvie. I remember that having Michael's strong arms around me had really helped. I hope it gave him comfort as well. In retrospect, someone should have been there to hold Allan too. It may have made things turn out differently in the weeks and months that followed.

Dad had been driving one of the old trucks down to the 'South End' of the Island. The police were never sure exactly what had occurred. They thought Dad had met a vehicle coming towards him, too fast probably, on one of the tight bends of the cliff top road that winds its way around the rocky headland at Fowler's Point.

There were skid marks on the tarmac which indicated the possibility that two vehicles had been present at the time of the accident. It seemed Dad had swerved to avoid something and then hadn't been able to regain control of the truck. He'd gone straight over the edge.

The policeman told Mum, pretty unhelpfully, that Dad had been unlucky to lose control at that particular place because it was the only section of the road where there was no barrier. A small hedge ran along the cliff edge but beyond that was a sheer drop onto the rocks and shingle below, maybe fifty or sixty feet down.

The other driver didn't come forward, so we never found out exactly what happened on that day. We have to assume there wasn't an opportunity to save Dad. It was the motorist who came along a few minutes later, travelling in the opposite direction, who heard the truck hit the rocks at the bottom of the cliff. He stopped and looked over, saw the wreckage and drove to the nearest farm to call for help. There were no mobile phones back then.

What I don't remember is the funeral. Mum always insisted we were there but I have no memory of it. I must ask Michael and Allan if they recollect anyone from Dad's family attending. Dad's sister had died a couple of years before but I do know he still had some brothers, nieces and nephews living in and around Glasgow at the time of his death.

The only aspect of Dad's background that I have much information about is his naval service during the war. This is mainly because of what Mum told me and the fact that Dad was really interested in naval history. This was the only element of his past that Dad was actually keen to discuss.

I do like to think it is from Dad that my kids get their love of messing about in boats. Ian, in particular, has always had a fascination with ships. He had a real interest in the Napoleonic Wars at one time and I remember him avidly reading the Patrick O'Brian books one summer holidays.

The only person who can provide me with any information about Dad's family is Michael. He was eighteen years old when our father died and had known him for his entire childhood. We have hardly ever spoken about him. I would have to tread carefully, as they had a difficult relationship. Dad was always really hard on Michael. Even at a very young age I seemed to be aware of that. Dad had high hopes for his eldest son and wanted him to learn the ways of farming and do the job in the way he had always done it.

As parents we can sometimes be harder on our eldest child. But with Michael and Dad it was something more than that. Dad was always too quick to blame him and placed too much responsibility on his shoulders too young. Who knows, maybe he saw something in Michael, a potential for greatness, that he did not see in Allan or me.

My thoughts are interrupted by the ringing of the phone in the hallway. It is Mrs Holmes, the mother of a boy who I have tutored on and off for the past few years. As soon as we have exchanged pleasantries she launches into a ten minute diatribe about the shortcomings of the very expensive private school Joshua attends. He is due to sit his GCSE English paper in a couple of days.

She would like me to spend a few hours with Joshua to get him prepared for the exam. I don't have a pressing reason to let her down so I say yes, even though it will mean spending the rest of today swotting up on the syllabus. Mrs Holmes and I agree on ten tomorrow morning.

Putting the phone down, I let out a sigh of resignation, realising that the freedom to pursue my inquiries has been temporarily curtailed. Instead, I go over to my half of the study and dig out the relevant files, knowing it will take me until it is time to fetch Bridie and Ian from school in order to get up to speed. The research will just have to wait.

# Chapter 12

Mrs Holmes arrives to pick Joshua up at twelve thirty. I have a job on my hands to persuade her he certainly does not require another tutoring session before he sits the paper. I tell her that he is now fully prepared. All he needs to do is read over his notes again and get a good night's sleep. Breathing a sigh of relief, I enthusiastically wave them off.

Mrs Holmes backs her tank-like 4x4 down the drive and zips away at a speed more appropriate to the fast lane of a motorway than the single track that connects our house to the Mundon road.

She very nearly has a head-on collision with Kath and Gerry's little car. Luckily, Hugh's Dad has seen the 4x4 rocketing towards them, already pulling their Fiesta well over to one side. Mrs Holmes barely slows at all as she passes within a hair's breadth of their wing mirror.

When they reach my open front door, Hugh's parents are complaining vociferously about the arrogance of 4x4 drivers on country roads. Kath is proclaiming disbelief at the fact Mrs Holmes actually had the gall to wave and beam at them as she went by.

Once this outpouring of frustration is over, Kathleen bustles into the kitchen and unpacks some home-made offerings that she's brought over for lunch. Gerry heads straight round to the back of the house, laying his gardening equipment out on the lawn.

Tuesday is the day that Gerry likes to come over and 'have a go' at our garden, which to his experienced eye is running the risk of becoming dangerously overgrown. Whilst he is busy outside, Kathleen and I have some lunch together and catch up on the week's news.

My father-in-law has been retired for about ten years. Before that he worked as a bank manager in one of the nearby towns. Hugh grew up in this part of Essex, although his Dad's family were from Scotland and that is how Hugh found himself at Edinburgh University. He was encouraged to stay with one of his aunties up there while he was studying, to help reduce the costs.

That is where Hugh and I first met, when I was a 'fresher' and he was completing his post-graduate studies. We both got jobs in the East Lothian area after we graduated, finding it was a lovely place to live and start a family. The area has great schools and a beautiful coastline.

Despite the attractiveness of the area, once the children came along Hugh started to miss having his parents around. They came to visit a lot, but it's an awfully long journey. I think that Kath and Gerry were planning to move nearer to us when Gerry retired, as whenever they visited we would take a drive through North Berwick to look at houses for sale. It seemed they had got as far as deciding upon their preferred retirement location.

As it turned out, it was us who moved to be closer to them. Hugh applied for a professorship at the University in Colchester. He got the job and we began to prepare for the big move. It took some time to adjust to living in an area about which I had very little knowledge. I had the children at home with me then and that is a great help when you are trying to settle into a new place. There are toddler groups and toy libraries to get involved with. When they start school you get automatically sucked into their social-life.

Kath and Gerry have become like my own family. Some people might think this a little strange, as it is usually the husband who gets absorbed into his wife's family once they have had children, usually because it gives them a quieter life. But Kath and Gerry offered me something different from the relationship I had with Mum. With Hugh's Mum and Dad I have seen what it is like to have parents who are always on your side. Selfishly, this is exactly what you need when your children are little and one or both of you are trying to build a career.

I help Kath to tidy the dishes away and then inform her that I will take Gerry's tray of quiches and coffee out to him because I want to pick his brains about something whilst they are here.

Gerry looks hot and bothered when I reach him and immediately regret not bringing out a glass of water as well. I tell him to take a break from cutting back one of the dwarf conifer trees that is now perhaps more dwarfed than was originally intended. We sit at the patio table and I set down his plate and cup.

'I have decided to find out more about what my father did in the war,' I say. 'I thought you might be able to help me understand a few things.'

'Of course my dear,' he replies, 'If I can.'

'I know that Dad was in the Royal Navy but I don't think he was ever promoted to any kind of rank. He came from a very humble background when he joined up and hadn't had much formal education.'

'Well,' says Gerry between sips of his coffee. 'He probably stayed as an ordinary seaman then. Although, as he was a volunteer at the very start of the conflict he may have found he became an able seaman or even a leading seaman by the time he reached the end of his service.'

'Dad certainly served for the entire duration of the war. He left the Navy in 1946 to come back to Garansay and find Mum.'

'There were many couples whose paths would never have crossed if it wasn't for the war.'

I decide to put up the parasol as the sun is burning down onto the patio and there is no hint of a breeze to provide any relief from the heat. At this moment, Kath comes out of the house to join us. She has brought a large jug of orange squash and some plastic beakers. It suddenly feels rather indulgent to be sitting out here in the brilliant sunshine whilst most people are at work or school.

'Dad was on the HMS Ramillies and I've had a look at its operational record online. It looks as if the Ramillies had a very long and successful service. Dad joined the crew at the start of the war. In the early months they were based down in

Plymouth but once they were called into action, the Ramillies was posted to dozens of places around the world. They went first to Gibraltar and the Med. They spent most of 1940 in New Zealand, Australia and Tasmania. It was in 1941 that the Ramillies returned to the Clyde, where it had been originally built, to act as part of a convoy protecting passenger ships passing along the river. It must have been during that time Dad met Mum,' I conclude.

'I seem to remember your mother telling me about first meeting Angus. He was on leave from the ship and promised he'd come back to visit her again, but she hadn't really believed him. Angus turned up a year later with all this 'tropical fruit', like bananas, oranges and even pineapples, which of course you couldn't get hold of for love nor money during the war,' Gerry adds.

'What kind of life would it have been do you think?'

'Oh, don't be fooled by the sound of those exotic locations. Life on board the battleships was tough. Bad weather and sickness were problems, and living in those close, claustrophobic conditions. Most of all it was damned dangerous. Your father was lucky his ship never went down - a large number of them did.'

'I think Dad's life back home had been tough too. He had at least three brothers and a sister that I know about and they all lived together in a tenement flat in one of the most deprived parts of Glasgow.'

'There was a terrible amount of poverty in most of the major cities before the war. Overcrowding and malnutrition meant that disease was rife. It wasn't until we had a decent health service that the common diseases got properly dealt with for the poorest. The kiddies always suffered the most. The deprived areas of the cities also bore the brunt of the bombing once it had started. It would have been a case of "out of the frying pan and into the fire" for your poor Dad,' says Gerry, who is fond of using an idiom to illustrate his point.

'I am starting to understand now why Dad decided to make his life on Garansay with Mum and why the farm became so important to him. I used to think he had given up an exciting life to be with her.'

'Don't you believe it - that farm was very likely the only chance he ever had of making a decent life for himself. I met a good few men like your father in my years working in the Bank. They'd managed to get themselves a job at the end of the war, when a few opportunities finally opened up for them.

This provided an escape from the slums of the East-End. Those men worked damned hard and often became very successful. But they were driven by the fear of slipping back into the poverty of their youth. The likes of us, with our comfortable lives, have no idea what those men experienced in the worst of the slums. Be in no doubt that your Dad would have been holding on tight to the life he had made with your Mum - be in no doubt at all.' Gerry says this with a forcefulness that is uncharacteristic.

I glance quickly at my watch and when Kath spots this reflex action she says, 'we'll go and pick up Bridie and Ian from school if you like. We haven't seen them for a while and can take them to Promenade Park for an ice-cream. You just get back to your research, darling. I think it's a very good thing to be finding out about your father after all these years. I think he would be very pleased to know that he is still so much in your thoughts.'

## Chapter 13

Isn't it odd how sometimes when you have been thinking about someone who you have had no contact with for some considerable time, you will suddenly receive a phone call or a letter from them. It is enough of a coincidence to make you start to believe in something, although I'm not sure what.

This morning at breakfast, I was vaguely conscious of the phone ringing but was too busy preparing sandwiches and checking the contents of schoolbags to take much notice. Just when it seemed as if I might get away with making a start on my toast, Bridie shouted from the hall.

'Mum! It's Uncle Michael!'

Taking a mug of tea with me, I hurried out to take the call. Michael was phoning from the airport, about to get on a flight to London. His firm were due to give a presentation to a building consortium at a hotel on The Strand today and he wanted to meet me for lunch.

It was short notice but I agreed, telling him I needed to sort out some childcare issues first, priming Kath and Gerry to pick the kids up from school and give them an early tea at their Victorian townhouse on one of the leafy roads between the High Street and the Hythe Quay in Maldon. Hugh will fetch them on his way back from work later.

It takes about forty minutes to reach central London from any of the mainline stations that lie within a few miles of where we live. Many people choose to commute using these routes every day. From Liverpool Street Station the underground deposits me at Charing Cross.

I have not been up to London since last summer and note how much quieter the tube carriage was today by comparison. Last year London was full of tourists and spectators for the Olympic Games. I had never known the city to be so busy. That August, Bridie and I had been coming back from seeing a matinee at the theatre. It was still early evening but we got stuck in a packed carriage that had been temporarily halted in a station.

The driver apologised for the delay, informing us that the train had been stopped in order to search for a missing five year old boy. A gasp went up from the passengers as we contemplated this awful scenario. My children are much older than that now but the thought of a little boy, lost on a busy underground station, with the exposed track and the long tunnels and the towering escalators was almost too much for us all to bear.

Bridie had been very upset and found it difficult to get to sleep that night. I kept telling her they must have found him otherwise it would have been all over the news by that evening. Eventually, this seemed to pacify her. But the experience has left me with a slight phobia about the underground, especially when it is stiflingly airless and rammed with people. I just keep picturing that terrified little child.

London is cool and breezy today. Outside of the rush-hour, it is pleasantly quiet. I am anticipating that Michael might be delayed so upon reaching the 'Thai Pot' I take a table next to the elaborate indoor water feature, ordering myself a glass of white wine and some prawn and sesame toast. For some reason I'm feeling nervous about this meeting, perhaps because my older brother doesn't yet know about Suz's revelations. I've never kept anything from him before.

To my surprise, he arrives within the next few minutes. I stand up to receive the kiss he places warmly on my cheek. Michael is now in his late fifties and his once jet black hair is almost entirely grey. He is tall and more finely featured than Allan and me. Today, he is formally dressed in what looks like a made-to-measure suit. I feel a little shabby by comparison in my loosely fitting navy blue cotton blouse, thin woollen cardigan and slacks. I have put on my high-heeled sandals but didn't have a lot of time to do my hair and make-up before leaving the house.

As if Michael has read my thoughts he says, 'you look lovely. You've lost some weight and it's given you that fragile look you used to have when you were a girl.'

'Thank you Michael. You always were a gentleman. How long have you got? Shall I order you a drink?'

'Actually, I've asked my junior to present the afternoon session for me so I've plenty of time. It will be good training for him and we are in two minds about whether or not we would take on this project if it's offered.' Michael shakes out his golden napkin.

I gesture to the demure and immaculately dressed waitress who rushes off to fetch another cold white wine. We discuss the progress of the sale of Lower Kilduggan and Michael tells me that his daughter, Sarah, has just announced she is getting married next summer, so he is going to need the money when it comes.

'I've got something to show you,' Michael says, in a sudden change of tack. 'It's the reason why I wanted to see you at such short notice.'

I feel my heart beat faster as Michael reaches into his briefcase and pulls out a small envelope that has already been opened. He places it carefully on the table, next to a platter of spring rolls and dim sum that has just been delivered.

'I want to explain a few things before I hand it over okay?' Michael says this slowly and carefully, as if preparing a child for bad news.

'Alright.'

'Just over two years ago I met Mum for lunch at my flat. She had brought some documents with her. I could tell she was a bit reluctant to show them to me and had to steel herself to do it, but finally she handed them over. The papers were all the official documents relating to our father, things like his birth certificate and his demobilisation papers. I couldn't imagine at the time why Mum was so wary of letting me see them.'

'Where are they now?' I interrupt, sensing this may be the start of a long story.

'They are in my safe back in Glasgow. You are welcome to see them whenever you like. Anyway,

Mum then asked me if I remembered Dad's sister, Aunty Mary.'

'And did you?'

'Only very vaguely. I recalled that she died a couple of years before Dad and he went over to the mainland for the funeral. I think it stuck in my head because we had heard so little about anyone from Dad's side of the family before that.'

'Why was Mum bringing her up all those years later?' I press.

'Well, she then told me Aunty Mary's husband had just passed away - that would have been in early 2011. She asked if I wanted to come with her to the funeral.'

'She never asked me!' I blurt out immaturely.

'I got the distinct impression she didn't want to go herself. The funeral was in Motherwell and she just wanted a bit of moral support. You know how she always looked to me to take on the responsible jobs after Dad died. It was the cross that I had to bear for being the eldest,' Michael explains.

I have drained my glass of wine and am feeling a pressing need for another one.

'So, I went along with her. It was a very depressing affair. It was a freezing cold February day. We were stood in a churchyard somewhere in Motherwell and suddenly here were all of these cousins that I never even knew we had.'

'Did you speak to them? What are their names?'

'It seems as if Aunty Mary had been married to a man called Eddie Galbraith at the time that she died in 1973. They had two boys, Alec and Andy, who are about ten years younger than me, I'd say.

They are both married and have their own children. There were two boys and two girls with them all at the funeral, but I forget what their names were.'

'Why did we never meet up with them as children? They were our cousins after all. What did Mum have to say about that?' I demand rather petulantly.

'Mum said Aunty Mary had her problems. She was a very heavy drinker and was a little unstable. Apparently, that was why she died so young, she had cirrhosis of the liver, Mum said. After Mary had died, Mum just lost touch with her family. She and Eddie had been practically separated at the time of her death anyway and Eddie didn't want much to do with Mary's family after she had gone.'

'That sounds plausible,' I say, still not convinced. 'So how did Mum know that Eddie had died? She must have been in contact with someone from Dad's family then.'

'Yes, it was Dad's younger brother, John Nichols, who wrote to Mum to tell her.' Michael leans forward in his seat. 'At the funeral I exchanged numbers and addresses with our two first cousins, Alec and Andy Galbraith. They both still live in Glasgow and I thought the least I could do was to send them a Christmas card. I hadn't had any meaningful contact with either of them since but then, last week, I received a letter from Andy, who is the younger of the two.'

'That letter there,' I say, tapping the envelope.

'That's right. He says he'd been meaning to write to me for months, but was worried about raking up the past and damaging his family's reputation, when the scandal was all so long forgotten. He said his girls deserved to be kept right out of it.'

'You're worrying me now.' I take a large slurp from my freshly filled glass.

'It didn't make easy reading for me either. Andy wrote me this letter,' Michael jabs his index finger at the innocent looking envelope, 'because he has been in a state ever since he read in the papers about Alison's suicide, back in October of last year.'

'How on earth can what happened to Alison Dickson have had anything to do with him?' I am now mightily regretting that second glass of wine as my stomach has tightened and I'm starting to feel sick.

'Andy was extremely distressed to read the particulars of Alison's death in the paper. He says that at first glance he thought it might be some kind of tasteless practical joke. Then he realised it was completely serious. You see, according to what Andy says in this letter, the way in which Alison Dickson died - up there on Aoife's Chariot - was identical, in every detail, to the way in which his mother had died - forty years ago.'

Michael lets these words settle between us. For a moment, despite being in the centre of this hectic city, the restaurant falls absolutely silent and all I can hear is my own heart, drumming out a fierce and deafening rhythm inside my head.

## Chapter 14

After absorbing this information, I excuse myself from the table and rush into the ornately decorated restrooms to retch into the toilet bowl. I have had too much to drink and too little to eat. But I also think this is my body's way of trying to reject what it has been told, in the only way that it knows how.

I feel as if all of the strands of my past are slowly but surely unravelling and have a dreadful sense that now the truth is beginning to come out, things are never going to be the same.

I wash out my mouth with tap water and look at my reflection in the gold inlaid mirror. I suddenly remember how, as a very young child, one of my teachers had nicknamed me 'Snow White' because of my pale skin, ebony black hair and rosy red lips. The soubriquet had stuck for a few years. I was even chosen to play the part in a Christmas performance. But then I got sick of the label and begged in vain for Mum to let me bleach my raven black hair.

I take a few deep breaths and ask the waitress for some water on the way back to my seat. Michael looks really concerned and clasps both my hands when I sit back down.

'You look as if you've seen a ghost, darling,' he says gently, 'I am truly sorry to have upset you with this. I should have kept it to my damned self.'

'No. I absolutely want to know about it. I had been doing some research of my own into Dad's family. I'm genuinely pleased to find out more about them. It's just that I can't understand all of these lies that Mum has told us. Maybe not lies exactly, but things that she has kept from us. I always thought we could trust her.'

'We could. Look, I think she must have had a good reason. When Miriam found out she was ill, we didn't tell Sarah straight away and there were plenty of aspects of her treatment that we kept from her. Sometimes we keep secrets from people in order to protect them and we should try to bear that in mind. You don't remember our father that well - you were very young when he died. Angus was not always an easy man to live with. I think Mum was trying to protect us from Dad's family. That's why she kept them at arm's length. There was nothing more sinister to it.'

'Okay, I can accept that. But what about Aunty Mary? What exactly happened to her?'

'I will give you Andy's letter and you can have a look. It won't tell you much. Reading between the lines, he seems to think we already know what happened so he doesn't go into any details. He is sharing his concerns with someone who he believes already knows all about it.'

'But we don't know anything about it at all,' I say in a defeated tone whilst intermittently taking large gulps of iced water.

Michael asks for the bill and once I am feeling a little better we take a walk down one of the tiny alleyways that leads us to the Embankment. We stroll next to the river and the fresh, warm breeze coming in off the water revives my spirits.

We watch the plethora of pleasure cruisers that are passing up and down this stretch of the Thames. Michael points out how much the City has changed since he was last here. He says it is so much more vibrant and tourist friendly and, like Glasgow, the service sector seems to be experiencing a boom time.

We walk as far as Temple Station and I inform my brother that I will get the underground from here. He embraces me carefully, as if I were made of cut glass. I tell him jokily that I'm not quite as fragile as he thinks. Striding away I briefly glance back and see that his smile has disappeared. I can tell Michael is troubled about having shown me the letter. I know he is going to brood about it and resolve to reassure him that I am big enough to face up to the truth - whatever that might prove to be.

\*

Closing the front door behind me I feel exhausted. All I want to do is fall into bed. But as I deposit my bag and keys in the hallway, Hugh comes striding out of the lounge, where he has no doubt been impatiently awaiting my return. He and Ian have argued. There has been a party organised by one of Ian's classmates which is due to follow on from the events of the 'Barge Match Day' next Saturday afternoon.

Ian and Bridie's school are sponsoring one of the barges at this year's event. They have both been helping to produce the decorative bunting and posters for the boat. The whole school has been buzzing with anticipation for weeks. The parents of the boy behind the party are well known at the sailing club. Hugh says there is bound to be no limit on the amount of alcohol available and Ian and his friends will be completely unsupervised.

All I can do for the time-being is to take a couple of paracetamol tablets and inform Hugh I will deal with it in the morning. My husband takes a breath then and notices my subdued mood and pallid appearance. He ushers me straight up to our bedroom, helping me into bed and fetching a large glass of water which he places on the bedside table.

This is the last I remember before waking up the next day to an eerie stillness in the house. I can hear nothing except for the pleasant chirping of the local starling population who come out in force at this time of year. I glance across at the clock and see it is half past nine. After a wave of panic has passed over me, I realise that Hugh must have left me to sleep whilst he got the kids ready for school. I am deeply grateful to him but have a suspicion he has given them money for the canteen rather than preparing the lunchboxes. This will mean that Ian buys all the wrong things and Bridie nothing at all.

Despite this niggling concern I feel considerably better after having had a decent night's rest and some serious rehydration. After showering and getting dressed I am overcome with hunger. I cut a thick slice of the lemon cake that Bridie made at cookery club a couple of days ago and take it with me into Hugh's study. Whilst powering up my laptop, I try to recall the name of the website Hugh's colleague had recommended for accessing the Scottish newspaper archives. Then, I remember that she told Hugh she would send me the link, so once online I check my e-mail inbox.

I haven't accessed my mail for a few days now so the inbox is quite full. After scrolling down for a bit I find the message I am looking for. 'Thank you very much, Ann Larwood,' I mutter to myself and double click on the link to the Mitchell Library archive.

I reach into my bag and take out the letter from Andy Galbraith, more to use it to check dates and the correct spelling of names rather than because it provides me with any concrete information. All I could gather from reading and re-reading the letter on the train home yesterday afternoon was that Mary Galbraith had died in a manner that was somehow similar to the way in which Alison Dickson had died. There also seemed to have been some kind of scandal attached to his mother's death.

Mum had told Michael that Aunty Mary died of cirrhosis of the liver, as a result of her long-term drinking. But I don't remember Mum telling me anything at all about how Mary had died. Perhaps I was considered too young when it happened to have really understood or taken it in. Also, Mum hardly ever mentioned anything about Dad's family after he died. In fact, I could probably count the number of times that she did on the fingers of one hand.

It takes me a little while to get used to how the online archive works but within a few minutes I have logged on and set up my subscription. I place a notebook and pencil next to the keyboard.

The sun is now blazing through the tiny side window of the study. I wrench it open to its full extent to let some cooler air in. I feel absolutely no remorse for sitting in front of a screen in this little room on such a glorious day. I simply won't be able to focus on anything else until I've checked out this information.

The archive proves to be very user friendly, but I still need to scroll through a huge amount of data, just like you would have done a few years back, with the old microfiche machines. I am checking the main Glasgow papers for articles from 1973 and early '74 which contain the names 'Mary', 'Galbraith' and 'Nichols'. When I don't get any results for this, I remove the 'Nichols' from the search. From this new combination of terms I am informed there are three results that match these criteria.

A list of three publications appears on the screen. For some reason, I choose 'The Garansay Recorder' first, probably because I am keen to know if there is a possible Garansay connection. The article pops up, looking as if it has been scanned from an original copy. There is an option to print so I tap my foot impatiently whilst Hugh's printer churns out the forty year old article.

The piece is dated Monday 23rd July 1973. It is written by John Campbell and there seem to be no accompanying photographs. I scan through the columns, eager to get the gist of the events being described.

The article tells me that the body of a woman, found in the mountains of Garansay on the morning of Sunday 15th July, has now been identified as that of Mrs Mary Anne Galbraith of 54, Carmichael Buildings, Motherwell, North Lanarkshire. She was formally identified by her husband, who claimed to have no idea why Mary might have been on Garansay at the time of her death. It says that Mr Edward Galbraith claimed his wife was often absent from the family home and this is why he had not reported her missing or become concerned until she had not returned for over a week. It finishes by stating that the cause of Mrs Galbraith's death still remains undetermined and that she has sadly left behind two young sons.

As I read through this article it becomes clear I am going to have to find a piece from earlier in that week in order to get the actual details of Mary's death. I click back to my original list. I can't see any dates given so simply use trial and error in order to find what I am looking for. Finally, I print off an article that was written on Monday 16th July 1973 in the Glasgow Herald.

The piece is penned by the Herald's chief news reporter, Jenny O'Keefe, and is written in a very matter-of-fact and un-sensational style. According to O'Keefe, the body of a white female was discovered on Sunday morning by a group of walkers on the holiday island of Garansay. The hikers were apparently setting out to climb the 'twin peaks' of Ben Mvor and Ben Keir by crossing over the 'saddle' of rocks that lies in between.

Their walk was cut short when one of them spotted the body of a woman, in a state of undress, floating face down in the small loch that lies at the foot of the hills. The walkers immediately proceeded back down the hillside for help. The emergency services arrived within thirty minutes.

Sadly, they were unable to revive the woman, who was pronounced dead by the ambulance crew at the scene. O'Keefe states that the body remains unidentified and she repeats the local police's appeal for anyone who might know the identity of the woman, who they estimate to be aged in her late thirties to early forties, to come forward immediately. There is a Garansay number given at the end of the article which you could call with any relevant information.

I spend a bit of time looking through all of the other articles that mention the case, just to see if they add any additional information, but they do not. It's evident that if I want to find out Mary's final cause of death, I will have to see the police report or the Procurator Fiscal's report.

I collect up the print-outs and take them into the garden with me. After concentrating hard on the faint, dark text for so long, walking out into the glare of the sun hurts my eyes. So I sit under the shade of the parasol and balance the bundle of papers on my lap. The information is pretty much what I was expecting, but I am still struggling to make sense of it. I was only three years old when Aunty Mary's body was found and have no memory of it. Michael didn't seem to have any knowledge of the incident either - but I will need to double check that with him.

Why is there no reference in these reports to the fact that Mary had a brother who lived on Garansay and this provided the connection between her and the Island? Eddie Galbraith didn't seem to have mentioned it to the police at the time and that seems very odd to me.

The most unsettling element of the tragedy is how it so closely mirrors the way in which Alison Dickson committed suicide, nearly forty years later. Had Alison known about the circumstances of Mary Galbraith's death and somehow wanted to recreate it? I just can't imagine what purpose it could possibly serve. But the facts speak for themselves. Both women were found dead at the foot of 'Aoife's Chariot', both partially undressed, both drowned and both lying face down in the shallow, peaty water. That couldn't possibly be a coincidence, could it? No wonder Andy Galbraith was so upset when he read about the details of Alison's case.

I look about me at the beautiful order that Gerry has brought to our garden. The grass has been neatly mowed into straight parallel lines and the borders have been turned and carefully weeded. Gerry will happily return next Tuesday to restore the uniformity that the progress of Nature in the intervening week will have sought to overturn. I wonder if it is simply human nature to strive to bring order to chaos. Do we have a fundamental need to feel it is possible for us to exert some kind of control over the unruliness of the world around us?

Wincing, I picture the conversation that I will have to have with Hugh this evening. Firstly, we need to resolve this dispute with Ian over the party, but then I will have to tell Hugh about the decision that I've just at this moment made, and he isn't going to like it one little bit.

## Chapter 15

Hugh and I very rarely have a full blown argument. This doesn't mean we never have disagreements or lose our tempers with each other, but we are usually quite good at discussing our problems and coming up with a workable compromise. Our relationship is not perfect by any means but at times of stress in our marriage we are in greater danger of drifting away from each other than of coming into direct conflict.

We are both people who have our own private worlds. Hugh has his research and his work and I have the children and my books. If we are going through a difficult patch, such as we did when the children were small and Hugh was working around the clock to gain his professorship, the house will tend to be silent and unhappy. We do not have the explosive and bitter rows that I know some couples do. But last night we did have one of our rare arguments, although it ended with an unexpected and not altogether unwelcome resolution.

The issue of Ian's party was fairly easily dealt with. I called up the mother of the boy who had issued the invite. She informed me it is the couple themselves who are throwing the party and the whole family are welcome to come along. I contacted the mothers of some of Ian's closest friends and we have resolved to attend together. It turned out we were all keen to keep tabs on the boys.

After dinner, when the kids had disappeared off to their rooms and the dish washer rumbled into action, I made a couple of milky coffees and encouraged Hugh to come and sit with me on the armchairs by the window in the living room. It had been a beautiful day and the sun was bowing out in a blaze of deep orange over the channel to the west. I sombrely told Hugh about the death of Mary Anne Galbraith back in the summer of 1973.

'Do we need to tell the police,' he had immediately asked, 'about the similarities between the two cases?'

'I hadn't even considered that. Do you think that we should?'

'Well, I very much doubt they are connected in any way, but I still think the police would want to know. The incident with your Aunt Mary, did they think she was killed by someone or was it just an accident?' Hugh enquired.

'I couldn't find out the cause of death from the newspaper cuttings so I don't know. There are no more articles relating to the case which were printed after July 1973. No reports of an arrest, or a trial or anything so I assume they must have decided that it was an accident or suicide. Just like Alison Dickson.'

'Well, it certainly is a puzzle.' Hugh gazed out at the dying embers of the evening light.

'Yes, it is.' I slipped off my chair and perched on the corner of Hugh's, taking his hands in mine.

'You know what I'm going to say, don't you.'

'Yes,' Hugh replied, holding my hands tight but gazing out towards the calm stillness of the shimmering water.

'I need to go back to Scotland, to find out exactly what all of this means. I need to speak to my cousins in Glasgow and do some digging into the way in which Alison died. Something about this is very, very wrong.'

Hugh turned around to face me. I could see then that he was angry. 'But that is a job for the police. We pass on the information and let them do their job. I certainly don't want to get all Victorian husband about this, but there are people who are qualified to do that sort of thing. Besides, you've got your own children to consider.' Hugh immediately looked embarrassed about his choice of words.

'I'm only talking about a few days. I have given you and the kids eighteen years of my life and now I am asking for some time to find out what the hell is going on with my family. I'll be back in plenty of time for the 'Barge Match' next Saturday.'

Hugh went quiet then, as if he were considering all the possible options. 'Only yesterday you practically flaked out just going up to London. You were as white as a sheet when you got back. If you start digging into all of this stuff again I have a feeling you're going to find out some things you'll jolly well wish you hadn't.'

'You are probably right, but the bottom line is that I need to know. At the moment I feel as if everything I believed was true about my Mum and Dad is a lie. It is as if the ground has suddenly shifted underneath my feet. You of all people should understand my need to find out the truth.'

'Okay,' Hugh said. 'But if you are going to go and do this then it will have to be on one condition.'

'Fine, what is it?'

'That I will come with you.'

## Part 3

## Chapter 16

I did take some persuading this would be a good idea. Hugh assured me that most of his students have finished their end of year exams and if he arranges to work for a couple of weeks over the summer holidays the Principal won't have a problem with him taking a few days off.

Hugh suggested his parents take the kids up to their caravan in West Mersea for the weekend as the weather has been so lovely. He said that if it takes us a little longer than a couple of days to do what we need to do then Kath and Gerry will take them back to their house in Maldon, where they are within walking distance of the school.

So here we are, in a large suite of a modest hotel in central Glasgow. The hotel is on West George Street. We are in a fantastic location for a variety of shops and galleries. I have to keep persuading Hugh, and myself, that this is not a holiday, but an investigation of sorts, and to this end I am sitting on the edge of the bed in my sensible cotton nightdress, carefully examining a map of the city centre.

Hugh steps out of the bathroom, which is tiled from top to bottom in alternating squares of cream and beige. The taps are made of sparkling gold plate and automatically dispense water as soon as they sense your hands approaching the faucet. In fact, the entire hotel appears to be decorated in every conceivable shade of brown, from dark chocolate, to a creamy off-white. The visual effect is not at all unpleasant.

Hugh comes and sits down next to me on the king-sized double divan. He slips his arms around me and slowly levers me backwards onto the bed.

'This is exactly what I was worried might happen,' I say with a grin. 'It isn't a dirty weekend.'

'Yes, I know, more's the pity,' Hugh sighs and leans in for a quick kiss. 'We haven't had one of those since we left a screaming baby Ewan with my parents while we had a night away in Paris sixteen and a half years ago. I seem to remember you were calling home every fifteen minutes, which did kill the romance somewhat.'

'Once I have found out everything that I need to know, we can have a trip away somewhere, just the two of us,' I say, temporarily discarding the map and pulling him back towards me.

He gently rolls his body on top of mine and kisses me more deeply than before. Then he shifts onto his side, rests his head of thickly dark hair in his hand and says playfully, 'so, Mrs. Croft, tell me the plan.'

\*

Hugh and I are meeting Michael at his flat, which is in a modernised Victorian building in the West End of the city. Michael bought the place a couple of years after Miriam died, when he felt that he could no longer stay in the family home. At the time, I worried that Michael was making a mistake by moving to the centre of such a busy and cosmopolitan city. But I was wrong to be concerned.

Sarah visits him most weekends from Edinburgh, occasionally bringing her friends or her boyfriend, Ross, with her. The rest of the time, Michael is just a short walk from his office. He can meet up with his pals in the city and indulge in the theatres, galleries, numerous coffee houses and restaurants on his doorstep whenever he chooses. This means he has less opportunity to brood.

I still hold out a vain hope that Michael might one day meet someone he can share his life with. He is not yet an old man and has certainly had his fair share of admirers from amongst the widows and divorcees within his circle of friends. But he has never shown the slightest bit of interest in them. I suspect he will remain on his own, just like Mum did for all of those years after Dad died.

Michael has arranged for us to meet up with Andy Galbraith at his house in Motherwell. It is Saturday, but Andy told Michael that his wife, Sally, will take their girls out for the afternoon. He said that Sally knows all of the depressing details about his mother, but his daughters do not and they both want it to stay that way. Andy had made this statement sound very much like a warning.

Michael has booked a taxi to take us there. This makes me wonder if he does not feel comfortable about parking his new sports car on a council estate in the centre of Motherwell. Perhaps I am being unfair and he simply does not wish to flaunt this symbol of the vastly different paths our two families have taken. I would like to think it is the latter.

Hugh and I are running late, so when we arrive at the flat, the taxi that Michael booked has already pulled up. As the driver makes a second toot on the horn, Michael steps out of his grand front door. We exchange a brief greeting before jumping into the cab.

Michael and Hugh chat away to each other during the journey but I just sit quietly and gaze out of the window. The traffic is very heavy as we make our way out of the city centre. The taxi progresses at no more than a crawl along Duke Street. When we finally get onto the M74 it doesn't take us long to reach the turning for Motherwell.

Finally, we pull up outside the correct address. It has started raining and the sky is grey with cloud but the Galbraiths' semi-detached ex-council property still looks welcoming. The frontage is covered by the light grey pebble dashing that seems to be the standard for Scottish social housing. The front garden is large and very well maintained. A line of rose bushes, currently in full bloom, marks out a path that leads to what looks like a newly fitted front door.

Andy Galbraith answers this door almost immediately after Michael has pressed on the bell. I wonder if he is keen to get this over and done with before his wife and daughters get back. If that is the case, he shows no sign of it in the manner in which he greets us and invites us in.

'Well, hello there Michael,' he says with genuine warmth.

'Andy, this is my sister, Imogen, and her husband, Hugh.'

The man reaches out to shake our hands.

What I had worried might be an awkward and difficult meeting does not turn out to be that way at all. Andy seems like a friendly and hospitable type of chap. Glancing into the kitchen I see that his wife has left some freshly baked cakes and what looks like their best tea set laid out for us. Clearly unused to entertaining on his own, Andy suddenly remembers to offer refreshments. After he has furnished us with a cup of tea and a fruit scone each we discuss our jobs and children and various other necessary pleasantries.

I'm not sure what I was expecting, but I am surprised by Andy's physical appearance. The Nichols' look is certainly evident in his facial features but that is where the similarity between us ends. His hair is thinning, but was obviously at one time quite fair in colour and although he is by no means short, he is not as tall as Michael or Allan. His build is what I would describe as stocky. It makes me wonder what his father must have looked like.

Whilst I am surreptitiously studying Andy for signs of a family resemblance, our host introduces the topic that we are all here to discuss.

'Michael, I want to apologise for sending you the letter. I got myself into a bit of a state after reading about that lady's suicide. Sally suggested that if I was so worried about it then I should get in contact with you. I feel silly about it now,' he says.

'Not at all,' Michael responds in his most reassuring voice. 'We are very glad that you did. The truth is that we didn't know anything about what happened to your mother until you wrote me that letter. It came as a complete surprise to us. It seemed from what you had written that you assumed we did.'

Andy is silent for a few seconds before he eventually says, almost incredulously, 'you mean that no one ever told you about it?'

'That's right,' I join in. 'We knew your mother had passed away and Michael remembers our father going to the funeral. But we had absolutely no idea she had died on Garansay or,' I cough tactfully, 'the circumstances in which she had died.'

'There was an awful lot of press attention about it,' Andy says. 'Alec and I were only very little, so we weren't told the exact details at the time. All Dad told us back then was that our Mum had gone to heaven and wouldn't be coming back.'

'The newspaper report said your Mum and Dad were separated when she died and Mary hadn't been living at home. Was that the case?' I ask tentatively.

'Yes, pretty much,' Andy replies. 'I was only six years old and my memory of Mum is very vague. I think that she came and went from our lives from quite soon after Alec was born. From what Dad had told us it was him and my granny who brought us up. Gran was certainly with us most of the time after Mum died, but my recollection of anything before that is hazy I'm afraid.'

'When did you find out what had really happened to your mum?' Hugh asks.

'Dad told us. He waited until he thought we could properly understand it. I think that Alec was about sixteen years old and I was fourteen. He sat us down at the kitchen table and brought out all these cuttings from the newspapers. He didn't actually let us read them, but sort of explained what was written there in his own words. He was worried, you see, that someone else would tell us about it. This was a pretty rough area back then and he didn't want someone really nasty breaking the news to us about our drunken, good-for-nothing mother. Dad wanted the chance to do it himself.'

'It sounds like he was a very good father,' I say quietly.

'Aye, he certainly was. He told us the police decided our mother had taken her own life, drowned herself in that loch, whilst she was 'under the influence' of alcohol. The doctor had said she was probably depressed and that was why she'd done herself in. He even went as far as saying she'd been suffering from 'post natal depression' ever since Alec was born. But Dad wouldn't have that at all.'

'What do you mean?' Michael asks.

'Dad declared that none of those experts had known Mum. She was not depressed and never had been. She simply enjoyed the booze and didn't like the responsibilities of having little kiddies. He said there was no way she'd have taken her own life. He believed she must have had an accident on that hillside. Dad always claimed Mum had fallen into the water and because she was blind drunk she couldn't get out.'

I don't ask Andy how she came to be undressed if that was the case but instead say, 'do you remember much about our parents, Isabel and Angus?'

'I'm afraid not. The first time I ever recall meeting your mother was at Dad's funeral a couple of years ago.'

'And have you got any idea why your mother was on Garansay when she died?' asks Hugh.

'None at all. That was the greatest mystery for Dad. He was used to Mum being away for weeks at a time on her drinking binges, but he always had a basic idea of where she was. There were a number of local pubs where she could usually be found and a group of drinking cronies who would put her up on their sofas. Dad had no knowledge of her ever having gone over to Garansay. He said that your father couldn't cast any light on that issue either. Dad just couldn't understand it because the boat and train fare would have eaten into her boozing money. That's why at first he didn't think the woman who had been found on Garansay could have been Mum. Only when she'd been away for over a week did Dad start to get concerned. When he couldn't locate her in any of her usual haunts he contacted the Garansay police. They asked him to come and identify the body.'

There is a short break in the conversation as we sip our tea. I take the opportunity to run through what Andy has told us in my head. Then I turn towards Michael and add, 'Andy said there was a lot of press interest in the discovery of Aunty Mary's body. Are you absolutely sure you don't remember it?'

'I have been thinking about that myself,' Michael replies, 'and the only way I can explain it is that around that time I had gone on a trip with the Marshes, do you recall? They had a holiday cottage up on Glen Nevis. Jenny had been badgering her mother to allow me to come with them for the summer holidays. I wasn't keen, because I didn't like her father very much. But I did go in the end. For a couple of weeks in July I think it was.'

'And was that during the period when Mary's body was discovered and then identified?' I enquire.

'I can't be sure, but it certainly could have been. It would explain why I didn't hear anything about it at the time. When I got back home, I was concentrating on my studies.' Michael goes on, 'I was also starting to feel that my relationship with Jenny was coming to an end and was a bit preoccupied with that to be honest.'

'But your parents must have decided to deliberately keep the information from you,' says Andy, articulating what we have all been thinking.

'Yes,' I say without enthusiasm, 'that's the only conclusion I can come to. Allan and I were too young to have known the difference but Mum and Dad must have made a decision to give Michael a false story about how his Aunt had died. I suppose because the lady identified on Garansay had a different surname, they hoped that nobody would find out she'd been Dad's sister.'

'They must have wanted to protect their reputation on the island,' Hugh adds and then turns towards Andy. 'You said that Angus told your father Mary hadn't been visiting him at the time she had her accident. He couldn't explain why she was on Garansay, is that correct?'

'Aye, that's right. Dad really pushed for a reason why Mum had been on the island. If I'm honest, Dad probably thought she had a fancy man there, so he kept pressing your father about it. Angus insisted she hadn't been visiting them. Your father said that like him, they had no idea the body found on the hillside was Mary's. So Dad never did find out what she was doing there.' Andy says this with a note of finality.

This is not the only issue we have come here to discuss, so I take a deep breath and say, 'I was at the loch on the day Alison Dickson's body was found last October. When reading the details of Mary's death I was struck by the similarities between the cases. Hugh thinks we should inform the police.'

Andy shifts about in his seat. For the first time during our conversation he looks uncomfortable. 'I don't want the details of Mum's case raked up all over again. My girls know nothing about what happened. Sally would never forgive me if we got involved in some kind of scandal.'

'It seems very unlikely there can be a concrete connection between two suicides that occurred forty years apart. But I do believe we have a duty to inform the police of the striking similarities between the cases. It may shed some light on Alison's motives or state of mind at the time of her death. The police might just ignore it, but we really must tell them,' Hugh states.

Andy looks decidedly unhappy with this suggestion. He noisily tidies away the cups and plates. Michael follows him out into the small kitchen. I can hear his soothing and gentle tones as they share a private conversation. When the two men return to the living room, Andy seems visibly less anxious. He reluctantly agrees that Michael may contact the police and tell them about the possible connection between the two deaths.

Andy suddenly announces that his family will soon be returning and he doesn't want to be rude but he would like us to be gone by the time they get back. I tell him that on the contrary, he has been extremely hospitable and we all agree to stay in touch in the future. Andy gives us directions to Motherwell Railway Station, as we have decided to take the train back to Glasgow rather than attempt to battle our way through the Saturday afternoon traffic in a taxi.

As we are saying our goodbyes in the narrow hallway, a thought suddenly occurs to me. 'Andy,' I ask, 'do you have a photo I could have a look at - of your mother I mean? Only, I've just realised that we have no idea at all of what she looked like.'

'I'm afraid I'll have to disappoint you there. I've never seen a photograph of Mary, not even my Dad possessed one. I've got hundreds of photos of me and Sally and the girls. There are albums and pictures all over the house.' he gestures towards the happy family shots which line the walls on either side of us. 'But I haven't got a single one of my mother. What you need to understand, Imogen, is that Mum and Dad and Alec and me - we just weren't that kind of family.'

I tell Andy not to worry and the three of us make our way down the well-kept pathway, past the pretty pink blooms of the Floribunda rosebushes guiding our way out. Before we even reach the little wooden gate that protects the Galbraiths' home from the outside world, we hear the front door being firmly closed behind us.

## Chapter 17

Michael's Victorian tenement conversion is immaculately presented. The living room has tall 'sash and case' windows that look out over Kelvingrove Park. Despite Michael's passion for modern architecture, his own home is surprisingly traditional. He has spent much of his free time lovingly restoring the original nineteenth and early twentieth century features of this flat.

The results of his labours have taken exquisite form in the refurbished decorative plaster cornices that adorn the ceilings of every room and the art-deco glass panels that provide a stunning contrast to the solid ash doors. Tenements such as this, located in such a salubrious part of the city, have always been occupied by the wealthier class of Glasgow resident.

The rain has cleared away to reveal a beautiful sunset over the park, which hints at the possibility of a better day tomorrow. Michael has cooked us a simple meal in his small but functional kitchen. We are now setting out to have a drink in a small 'unfussy' pub that Michael knows.

We walk past the university and along the Byres Road where the young Saturday night drinkers are spilling out into the street with their loud chatter and high-pitched laughter. It makes me think of Ewan in Manchester who is most likely doing the same. I take Hugh's hand and give it a squeeze, hoping that he too is thinking about our eldest son.

Michael leads us down a side street running parallel to the Western Infirmary. He pushes through the door of a small and inconspicuous pub which stands on the corner of a quiet junction. We order our drinks and find a table in a snug that sits between two glass partitions.

Hugh and I are feeling tired after our journey yesterday and our meeting with Andy this afternoon. We plan to get back to the hotel soon. But I want to make sure we have properly discussed the information Andy has given us first. I am keen to get Michael's take on things.

Sipping from my glass of Merlot, which is surprisingly drinkable I ask, 'what do you make of it all? What's your view on what Andy told us?'

Michael picks up his glass of stout and absentmindedly swirls around the liquid so that some of the creamy white top penetrates into the darkness that lies below. 'Well,' he says, 'I think Dad's sister was someone he was ashamed of. You know what he was like - more than averagely judgemental and intolerant. So when Mary turned up dead on Garansay, semi-clothed and drunk as a skunk, he and Mum did their best to hush the whole thing up. As to why Mary was on Garansay in the first place, that I couldn't tell you. I think Eddie Galbraith probably had it about right when he said she had a fancy man, someone who could give her money to cover the fare to get over there.'

Hugh looks up. 'Might I offer an opinion - as your resident psychologist?' Michael and I nod enthusiastically. 'Whilst I can totally understand that the two of you are mainly concerned with the role played by your parents in all of this. My interest lies in the connection between the deaths of these two women. What really strikes me is the similarity in their profiles. We don't know a great deal about Mary Galbraith and anyone who did know her is now dead themselves. However, she was probably an alcoholic, had a chaotic lifestyle, she was most likely seeing other men and had, at least partially, abandoned her young children.'

'She was so different from Dad,' I can't help but point out.

'Indeed,' says Hugh. 'Now, Alison Dickson, please correct me if I am wrong, also had a drinking problem, which in the months before her death had been getting worse. She had no children that we are aware of, but we do know she could be sexually promiscuous.' Hugh does not expand on this point as he knows Michael isn't aware of Alison's relationship with Allan all those years ago. 'There is some suspicion surrounding both women that they had lovers whose identities are as yet unknown.'

'Alison was found to have a significant income stream the police couldn't account for. This money may have been provided by a man she was involved with,' I suggest.

Hugh nods. 'The question is do we believe the two women committed suicide, as was concluded, or do we think there is another party, let's call him 'X', who had a role in their deaths?' Hugh leaves this question hanging as he takes a hearty swig of beer.

'I hadn't really considered that possibility,' I say. 'Are you suggesting this could be the same person- this X- in both cases? Because I just don't see how that could be possible. If he had been in his thirties or forties in the early 1970s then he would have to be at least seventy or eighty now. It doesn't make any sense.'

'Unless he was a much younger man back in the 1970s,' suggests Michael.

'It's possible,' says Hugh. 'However, my gut feeling is that there is no mystery individual responsible for the two deaths. What I do suspect is that Alison Dickson knew about the manner of Mary Galbraith's demise. Somehow, consciously or unconsciously, that knowledge contributed to the method and location she chose for her own suicide.'

'That theory makes more sense,' agrees Michael. 'I can't imagine some deranged killer striking in the same way after four decades with not a dicky bird in between.'

'So have we decided,' I say, feeling suddenly exhausted and impatient, 'what we are going to tell the police?'

'I promised Andy I would contact the police,' says Michael, 'and all I will tell them are the absolute bare facts as we know them.'

'Good,' says Hugh, taking my arm firmly. 'Then let's drink up and get back to the hotel. I don't know about you but I am just about ready for that super cushioned king-sized bed.'

*

Hugh and I treat ourselves to a lie in the next morning. As a result, we miss the hotel breakfast. It is worth the sacrifice, as we get a chance to laze in each other's arms under the thick duvet, with absolutely no one to disturb us with questions or demands. As I nuzzle my face into his neck, Hugh says, 'I thought this wasn't allowed.'

I giggle and raise my head up so that my face rests on the pillow next to his. 'Well, it is Sunday. I don't think we'll be able to do very much sleuthing today.'

Hugh lets his hands slide down my back. I shift so that my body slots comfortably into his, as if I have placed together two pieces of a favourite jigsaw puzzle. He murmurs into my ear, 'let's just stay here a little while longer then.'

***

When we are finally showered and dressed we head out of the hotel, stopping for brunch in a vegetarian café on Buchanan Street before heading to the Gallery of Modern Art in Royal Exchange Square. I take a photograph on my phone of Hugh standing between two of the impressive classical pillars that line the entrance. As we wander around the exhibits which are alternately vibrant and challenging, I feel the strains of the previous week start to recede.

Strolling along arm-in-arm like newly-weds, I feel ridiculously pleased that Hugh offered to come with me. I am finding his insights invaluable and remembering what a great team we made at university.

The sunshine has returned today. Hugh and I are wearing our cool cotton shirts and linen trousers. When we have had enough of the modern art we amble out of the gallery and Hugh suggests we take one of the unoccupied tables fanning out from a little Italian café on the square. The seat I have chosen is positioned directly in the glare of the sun. My shades are required in order to look at the drinks menu.

After we have ordered our coffees we sit in companionable silence. Hugh lounges in his seat reading the city guide whilst I languidly observe the comings and goings of the bustling, sunlit square.

A couple, who are walking slowly and carefully down the stone steps of the GoMA, catches my eye. The man is about my age, well dressed and quite good looking. He is supporting a very old lady by the arm. She is wearing a straw hat with a pretty purple ribbon tied around it, like a little girl's.

As they move closer to where we are sitting, I suddenly realise that the well-dressed man is Colin Walmsley. The lady he is escorting around the sights of Glasgow on this sunny day must be his mother, Kitty. They don't seem to have spotted me. Then I remember that I am wearing my sunglasses and have an opportunity to observe them for a while without being noticed myself.

They eventually take a table at another café across the square from us. I am slightly surprised by the solicitous way in which Colin is taking care of his mother. Firstly, he makes sure that she is comfortable in her chair. Then he starts fussing with the parasol, getting it at the correct angle, so Kitty does not have to contend with the direct glare of the weak Scottish sun.

Totally engrossed in what the Walmsleys are up to, I nearly jump out of my skin when the waiter comes up behind us with the coffees.

'Feeling a little on edge darling?' Hugh jokes, pouring cream into his Americano, 'guilty conscience perhaps?'

'As a matter of fact, yes.' I point as subtly as possible towards the Walmsleys' table at the café opposite. 'I've been watching those people over there. Do you see the man?'

Hugh looks across and nods.

'That's Colin Walmsley, the one who we're selling the farm to and the old lady next to him is his mother, Kitty. She was great friends with Mum. They were our neighbours for years and years.'

'We should go over and say hello.'

'Yes, we will. But let's finish our coffees first.'

Hugh picks up his guide book again.

'What do you think of the way they are behaving with each other?'

Hugh indulges me by looking over at their table for a few minutes. In that time, Colin carefully lays a napkin across his mother's lap and cuts up what looks like a piece of sponge cake.

'I'm not an expert in body language. But, I would say he is a very devoted and loving son. Perhaps he fears she hasn't got very long left. There is probably another sibling - a sister maybe. I'd suggest she is married and has a family of her own. He is left with the responsibility of looking after his mother. By the way that he is behaving, I very much doubt he is married himself.'

'Why do you say that?'

'I just would,' Hugh replies without glancing up. 'Why, is he married?'

'No, not that I'm aware of.'

Taking off my sunglasses, Hugh and I stroll towards the couple. Colin looks over and I spot the flash of recognition. Colin's eyes move fleetingly across to Hugh and then back to me again, but he quickly adopts a broad smile. 'Imogen! How great to see you, please come and join us.'

I introduce Hugh to Colin and Kitty then take the chair next to my mother's old friend, holding her frail hands in mine and asking if she remembers me. I tell her I am Isabel and Angus' daughter.

Kitty seems a little confused about who I am but she returns my smile and holds my hands tightly for the rest of our conversation. Colin informs us he will be returning his mother to her nursing home later this afternoon. He asks whether or not we will be visiting Garansay whilst in Scotland.

'Yes,' I say, 'but we'll have another day or so on the mainland first. The sale seems to be proceeding well.'

'Aye,' he replies, 'we're still waiting on some of the land surveys, but there's no rush to complete. If you let me know when the two of you are coming over to Lower Kilduggan I'll make sure the lawns are mowed and everything is looking neat and tidy.'

'That's very kind of you, but there's really no need,' I say.

'It's no problem at all. It's best to keep the place in decent nick, otherwise I'll end up with one hell of a job when I take over,' he explains.

As we are discussing the maintenance and condition of the farm I sense Kitty shifting about uncomfortably in the chair next to me. Colin jumps up to assist her. She is looking flushed and I help Colin to remove her cardigan.

'I should probably be thinking about getting her back,' he says fretfully, 'she's okay for a few hours and likes to get out and about, but it's not a good idea for her to get over tired.'

'Of course, we will leave you to it,' I say, leaning down to give Kitty a kiss on the cheek. We each shake Colin by the hand before heading in the direction of our hotel. When we have gone far enough to be out of earshot I turn to Hugh. 'So, what did you think of them?'

'I thought it was awkward,' Hugh says cryptically.

'What do you mean?'

'Well, the old lady seemed distressed by our presence and I got the distinct impression that

Colin was a bit put out to see you up here with your husband in tow.'

I sense a response is not required, so we continue walking towards our hotel in the pleasant afternoon sun without either of us uttering another word.

Chapter 18

Hugh took a bus to Pollok Country Park first thing this morning. He wants to visit the Burrell Collection whilst we are here. I have decided to do some research into Dad's family instead.

Hearing from Andy Galbraith about the short and chaotic existence of his mother has made me want to know more about what it must have been like for poor families living in the City in the years before the Second World War, at the time when Dad and his sister were children. I feel that Mary must have experienced a very difficult early life in order to abandon her own children in the way that she did. Perhaps I am just making excuses for her.

Firstly, I head along Argyle Street towards the Kelvingrove Art Gallery and Museum where I know they hold some of Avril Paton's well known paintings of the iconic tenement buildings of Glasgow. To me, this Scottish painter's work has always best captured the architecture and atmosphere of the city. Upon arriving at the gallery, I head straight for the room which houses the painting, 'Windows in the West.' This is probably the best known of Paton's pictures depicting 'ordinary' Glasgow life.

The gallery is almost empty at this early hour of the morning. I take advantage of the peace and quiet to linger beneath the imposing picture. Paton has reproduced a typical four storey tenement building. What really captures my imagination about this piece of artwork is how it draws you into the warm and inviting interiors of each of the flats. The orangey glow that lies beyond the sash windows contrasts sharply with the cold white of the snow outside. The sky even has that purplish colour that you only get when there has been a snowstorm and when another is on its way. If you look closely, you can see the everyday situations that are being played out behind the glass.

A painting is a perfect medium for evoking the experience of ordinary folk but I want some solid information about the life my father lived as a child. I am not completely uninformed and do know that living conditions south of the Clyde during those years were amongst the very worst in Europe. I direct myself towards the section of the museum which might tell me more.

Whilst engrossed in an exhibit about the construction of the first tenement buildings, one of the museum employees moves across the room to hover beside me. She asks tentatively if I am looking for anything in particular.

'Actually, yes,' I reply gratefully. 'I'm looking for information about the area of central Glasgow south of the Clyde, particularly during the era of the 1920s and 30s.'

'The Gorbals, do you mean?' the assistant asks.

'Well, I'm not sure really. My father's family lived in a tenement somewhere to the south of the river. After the slum clearances of the early 1960s, they moved into more modern social housing in the Motherwell area,' I clarify.

'I can certainly provide you with plenty of information about living conditions in the Gorbals around that time because it was really quite notorious. It sounds as if your family would have lived somewhere within that vicinity.'

The lady, who introduces herself as Stella, shuffles off into another room. After some considerable time she brings back an armful of documents and files. She guides me over to a small leather sofa that rests against the far wall. 'Now, I'm sure you already know about the terrible overcrowding in the tenement buildings of Glasgow at the end of the Victorian era. When we hear the word *tenement* we conjure up visions of communal middens full of human waste and of whole families living and sleeping together in just one or two rooms.'

I nod encouragingly.

'The reality was often even worse. The Gorbals area of south Glasgow had become a treacherous slum by as early as the 1860s, when terrible overcrowding in the area led to high levels of disease, drunkenness and crime. For the period that you are interested in and particularly during the 1930s, when the effects of the Depression were at their worst, the Gorbals was often known as the 'most dangerous place in Britain'. Street gangs and casual violence were simply a fact of life.'

'For an ordinary family like my father's, what might their day-to-day existence have been like?' I enquire.

'No doubt your grandfather would have been an industrial labourer of some sort, perhaps in and out of work, depending on the economic climate of the time. The family would have lived in two or maybe three rooms, if they were lucky. The children often had to share a bed, which in a typical tenement would have been a 'cavity bed', so-called because they were literally built into tiny holes in the walls. One writer describes them as being like 'little tombs'. Toilets would have been shared by all of the inhabitants of a block. Human waste was often described as 'flowing' down the stairwells, so you can imagine the effect this had on the health of the residents. These families would have had very little money. As soon as was possible, the children would stop their schooling in order to go out to work and bring in a wage. Of course, the Education Act of 1870 meant children had to have some basic schooling, but your father would have left education by the time he was fourteen I would expect.'

'That's right,' I add, 'my father had very little formal education. He joined the Navy, as soon as he was able to.'

'Yes, that was one way to have escaped the poverty, certainly. Look, Imogen, was it? I can tell you these facts all day long, but really, the best way for you to get a picture of what things were like back then is to hear the voices of those who actually lived through it.' Stella shuffles off again and comes back, more quickly this time, with two worn and very battered looking paperback books.

'These are my own copies and I've had them for years but you are very welcome to borrow them.'

I have a brief look at the two books. They are both memoirs of childhoods spent living in the Gorbals. One of them is quite well-known and I recall reading it many years ago but have long since forgotten the details. The other is a more recent account that I don't recognise and haven't read. 'Are you sure? This is very kind of you,' I say sincerely.

'Of course, I haven't touched those books in years. I would like to know that someone is getting good use out of them,' she explains.

'I am going to be in the area for a few more days and will drop the books back to you before I return home,' I promise.

'There's no rush,' says Stella brightly. 'You can always post them to me if you need a bit more time.'

'Thank you,' I say and without planning to lean over and give the surprised library assistant a hug and a peck on the cheek.

'Och, you are very welcome,' she says, chuckling, thankfully taking my over enthusiasm with good humour.

I place the new reading material into my satchel and head out of the museum, proceeding purposefully back towards the centre of the bustling city so I can find myself somewhere quiet to have lunch and take a good look at Stella's old books.

## Chapter 19

The next morning, in the deep comfort of our hotel bed, Hugh is fast asleep. I am propped up against the eiderdown pillows next to him, sobbing quietly as I finish reading the last few pages of the second of Stella's books.

I had started with the older and more battered of the two paperbacks yesterday lunchtime and continued dipping into it for the rest of the day. Later on, after Hugh had come back from seeing the Burrell Collection, I stayed up late into the night, eagerly turning the pages. Hugh kept me company for a while, skipping through the channels offered by the hotel's extensive TV package, until, finding nothing worth watching, he finally went to bed.

Maybe because of the sunlight that is streaming in through the gaps in the curtains, or simply as a result of my early morning movements, Hugh suddenly wakes. Seeing my red and blotchy face, he sits bolt upright.

'Is everything okay? Are the kids alright?'

'They're absolutely fine. I've just received a text from Bridie. Right at this moment Kath is making them all breakfast.'

Hugh glances at the dog-eared paperback lying discarded on the duvet in front of me. He falls back onto his pillow with a sigh. 'I see. You haven't pulled an all-nighter on those books have you?'

'No, not quite, but I have finished them. And I'm not upset, just feeling a bit emotional. This second book is so beautifully written. The main character, the one who grew up in the Gorbals at a similar time to my father, manages to get himself out of the slums, totally against all of the odds, by educating himself and spending hours and hours in the library. He finally gets to Oxford University. It's an incredible story,' I gush.

Hugh sits up again and puts on his reading glasses. 'This one was made into a film about twenty years ago, we saw it in Edinburgh - don't you remember?'

'Oh yes, I think I do. It was a real tear-jerker and came out around the time there were all those books and films being released about people's traumatic childhoods. There was another one set in Ireland, when all the children kept dying from various diseases. You wanted to go and see it but it was just after Ewan had been born and I refused.'

'Yes, I remember that,' Hugh says, cuddling up to me as we slip comfortably into this long forgotten memory.

'The other book of Stella's is much more positive about life in the Gorbals. It is set a little bit later than this one, in the fifties and sixties. It makes more of the community spirit and work ethic there was in that part of Glasgow. The author claims it was one of the most exciting places in the world to live during that time. He laments the clearing of the older tenement housing in the early sixties as he says that it meant the people were cleared out too, along with their common customs and identity.'

'That sounds a little too romanticised,' suggests Hugh. 'There is nothing desirable about living in poverty.'

'No, but I don't think he is suggesting that. What is interesting about the first book is the author's idea there was a kind of 'Gorbals mentality', which dictated that you had to work hard in order to survive. Those who remained idle were the ones who succumbed to the drink and the criminal culture. When I read that, it really struck a chord with me because that was Dad's philosophy exactly. He could be a tough task master and he never showed us much love or affection, but he had such a strong work ethic. I think he pushed Michael so hard because of that.'

'You're probably right. Especially when you look at how his sister had turned out. What were the rest of the family like? You mentioned that your father had a younger brother?'

'Yes, Michael has been in contact with him. His name is John and he moved out to Canada with his wife in the 1980s. He was just a toddler when Dad left home to join the Navy, John kept in touch with the family but he hardly knew Dad at all. He was from a younger generation really,' I pause to take a sip of water from the glass on the bedside table. 'Mum said at one time there was an older brother too, Frank, he was called, but he must be long dead now and I've never heard him mentioned by anyone else in the family.'

Hugh thinks about this. 'So there were four children that we know of, all of whom were living in a 'single end' in one of the roughest parts of Glasgow before the war. It must have been very tough.'

'But Mary and John were younger than Frank and Angus, so they wouldn't all have been children at the same time. The older boys must have gone out to work by the time they were fourteen years old. There would only have been the two wee ones at home after that.'

'What about your grandparents, do you know much about them?'

'Almost nothing at all. I don't think Mum ever met them when she and Dad were first together. They had both died by the time I was born. I had a look at Dad's birth certificate and his father was called William. He was recorded as being a 'shipyard labourer'. His mother was called Netta and her maiden name was O'Donnell, so she may have been of Irish descent.' I shift myself out of Hugh's embrace and stiffly swing my legs around to the side of the bed.

Hugh spreads himself out into the space I have vacated and muses, 'the area where the Nichols lived would have been totally cleared in the early sixties and superseded by the concrete high rise estates that replaced them. There is no physical evidence left of their existence.'

'No, and that seems very sad, but in a way I'm not sorry. I have a feeling Dad wouldn't have minded at all. He hardly ever went back there, even when we were only just over the water. I don't think he can have had any good memories of the place.'

Hugh makes us tea whilst I have the first turn in the shower. The bathroom is so impressively well-appointed that I take this rare opportunity to luxuriate under the powerful jet of water. By the time I finally emerge, with my wet hair wound up into a fluffy white towel, Hugh is sitting on the edge of the bed with a concerned expression on his face. He is holding my mobile phone tightly in his hands.

'That was the police.' Seeing my face contort with horror, he quickly clarifies, 'the kids are fine. It was the Glasgow police. They have re-opened the case into Alison Dickson's death. In the light of new evidence received, is what the man said. And they want you to come down to the station, today, in order to be re-interviewed.'

\*

We'd brought hardly any formal clothes with us for this trip, so Hugh and I are looking very casual and a little out of place when we arrive at Strathclyde Police Headquarters, which turns out to be just a short walk down West George Street from our hotel.

We both look very much like tourists. Like a couple who has lost their travellers cheques or had a handbag or wallet snatched. We certainly have the appropriate confused and disorientated expressions on our faces when we approach the uniformed officer at the reception desk.

We are informed that the Detective Inspector who is in charge of the case is expecting us. We are buzzed in through a heavy door and led into a waiting area. Hugh and I sit side by side on uncomfortable plastic chairs. I whisper to him that it feels as if we are waiting to receive a good telling off by the Headmaster.

'Do you think the new evidence they have has come from Michael, telling them about Mary Galbraith, I mean?' Hugh whispers back.

'It must be, unless there's something else. If it is, then they've taken it more seriously than I thought they would.'

A large balding man in a dark suit comes down the corridor towards us. Hugh and I spring to our feet.

'Good morning, Mr. and Mrs. Croft. My name is Detective Inspector O'Neil. I have been put in charge of reviewing Alison Dickson's case. I am very grateful to you both for coming down here at such short notice and believe that we are lucky to have caught you whilst you were here on your holidays.'

'Yes,' I say nervously, trying desperately to relax.

'One of my Detective Sergeants is going to take you into that room over there and ask you some questions about the day you found Miss Dickson, okay?' Inspector O'Neil asks this in a kindly way, clearly noting my anxiety, 'Mr. Croft, if I could ask you to wait outside and one of my officers will fetch you a tea or a coffee.'

The burly Inspector turns and disappears into an office area divided from us by a glass partition. Hugh gives my hand a quick, reassuring squeeze as another, younger man, emerges from an interview room opposite.

'Mrs. Croft? My name is Detective Sergeant Bruce, if you could just follow me in here please.'

The interview room is very small and a little claustrophobic. I sit in yet another plastic chair which has been placed in front of what looks like a school desk. I have been interviewed before, in the days after Colin and I found Alison's body. The Garansay police station was not as daunting as this one.

Detective Sergeant Bruce has a copy of my previous statement in front of him. He runs through all of the main points with me again. I confirm the reason why Colin and I had been at Alba Cottage that afternoon and describe once again exactly what we saw when we got into view of the overflowing loch on that wet October day.

This time, Detective Sergeant Bruce appears to be concentrating on the behaviour and actions of Colin. He asks me whether it was my decision that he should accompany me to the cottage. I confirm that Colin was there entirely at my request.

Bruce then asks, in detail, about Colin's reactions upon the discovery of Alison's body. I do my very best to convey to the detective how shocked and horrified Colin was and how he fought valiantly to save her life.

D.S Bruce seems satisfied to conclude this line of questioning. He moves on to discuss Strathclyde

Police's reasons for the re-opening of Alison's case.

'As you may know, Mrs. Croft, your brother, Mr Michael Nichols, contacted us a few days ago to inform us of a historic case which he felt may have a bearing upon the circumstances of Miss Dickson's death.' Bruce shuffles the papers that sit on the table in front of him until he finds the document he is looking for. 'The death of Mrs Mary Anne Galbraith, née Nichols, whose body was discovered in the early hours of Sunday 15th July 1973, but who had died as a result of drowning at some time between the hours of 10pm and 2am on Saturday 14th - Sunday 15th July 1973. This lady was your paternal aunt, is that correct?'

'Yes,' I say clearly, suddenly conscious of the tape recorder sitting on the shelf next to us.

'I can certainly say we were rather struck by the similarities between the deaths of these two people. Although, having said that, their causes of death are not quite as identical as they may at first appear. We have had a team looking into the file relating to Mrs Galbraith's case. They have turned up some interesting and relevant information.

There had been quite an extensive police investigation into your aunt's death conducted by the Glasgow and Bute Constabularies. I am not sure if you are aware but the reason for this was that although Mrs Galbraith had died of asphyxiation due to drowning, she was also found to have suffered a head injury, as the result of a blunt trauma impact, sometime before her death.' Bruce sits back for a moment to allow me to absorb this piece of information. 'This meant that her death was initially treated as suspicious. Her movements in the hours leading up to the Saturday night of her death were very closely investigated. In the course of that investigation, a number of individuals were interviewed by detectives, including your father, Angus Nichols.'

I must have looked surprised by this, because D.S Bruce then asks, 'did you know that your father had been interviewed about the case, Mrs. Croft?'

'No, I did not. But I was a very young child at the time and probably wouldn't have been aware of it.'

'Okay. It says here that your father had denied having seen his sister in the days and weeks leading up to her death on the 14th July. No evidence emerged to contradict his statement.'

Bruce asks if I would like to stop for a break but I politely refuse his offer.

'The investigating officers at the time of Mrs Galbraith's death did a good job of tracing her movements on the Friday and Saturday of the 13th and 14th July. She was seen by witnesses in a pub in Govan Road, Glasgow on the Friday night. She was then observed by several fellow passengers taking the ferry from Gourock to Garansay at lunchtime on Saturday the 14th. Mary was quite conspicuous it seems, as she attempted to drink from a bottle of wine she had brought with her and got herself into an altercation with the Steward. Unfortunately, Mary's whereabouts for that Saturday afternoon remain unknown, as no more witnesses reported having seen her until about

9pm that evening when she was spotted in the Chariot Bar of the Gilstone Hotel.

Now, according to those statements, Mrs Galbraith spent the rest of the evening drinking in the Chariot Bar, but she was not alone. There were a group of local men in the bar as well. Mary spent a large part of the evening with one man in particular. This individual was then questioned by detectives on several occasions, becoming a suspect of sorts for a short period of time. Until it was decided there was not enough evidence to support a conclusion of foul play in Mary's death. Would it surprise you, Mrs Croft, to hear that the man who was seen with your aunt just a few hours before her demise and who was repeatedly questioned by police in connection with it, was one Malcolm Ronald Walmsley?' Bruce enquires.

'Yes,' I say shakily, 'it certainly would.'

## Chapter 20

'Bloody Hell,' says Hugh, as the barman places down a couple of neat single malts. We are perched up high on metallic stools that service an extensive, shiny chrome bar in a very trendy establishment on Douglas Street. Upon reflection, Hugh and I would perhaps not have chosen such a glossy and expensive place to stop for a drink. But after leaving the police station just fifteen minutes ago, I had demanded a stiff drink from the nearest available hostelry.

'Indeed,' I reply, taking the tiniest sip possible from my single malt.

'Just go easy on that,' Hugh advises sagely. 'Remember what happened the last time you tried to get drunk in the middle of the day.'

This makes me laugh and I'm grateful to Hugh for relieving the tension.

'I'm not planning on getting drunk. This,' I say, pointing firmly at the chunky glass of golden liquid, 'is for medicinal purposes only, after having received the shock of my life back there in that interview room.'

'It looks very much as if Mary Galbraith's mystery man - her 'Mr X' if you like - was actually Colin's father,' Hugh concludes.

'Yes, it would appear that way but I just can't believe it. D.S Bruce told me the witness statements from the Chariot Bar suggested that Mary and Malcolm were both drunk and they were 'all over each other' for most of the evening.' I pause to take another sip of my whisky, 'poor old Kitty. It must have been awful for her.'

'He was cleared of any wrong-doing. They never charged him with Mary's murder.'

'No, but from what D.S Bruce was saying that was only because they didn't have enough evidence. No one saw Malcolm go up the hillside with Mary and there was no physical evidence that could link him in any way to her death. Because she had died of drowning and was found to be pumped full of alcohol, the Procurator Fiscal decided the death was accidental and most likely suicide.'

'You knew Malcolm when he was alive. What do you think - was he capable of killing her?'

'Malcolm Walmsley was a kind and gentle man. He loved his farm and seemed devoted to his family. He and Kitty were so supportive of Mum when Dad died. I honestly don't think we could have stayed on at Lower Kilduggan without their help in those early years. So I would say definitely not. But then I would never have thought he'd have an affair either. That shows you how good my judgement is.'

'We don't actually know that Malcolm and Mary were having a full blown affair, do we? They may have only met that evening in the Chariot Bar. Mary was drunk and Colin's Dad was drunk too and they just hooked up, had a flirtation, a kiss and a cuddle maybe. We've no actual evidence to suggest they knew each other before that night.'

'Yes, but our whole rationale for why Mary was on Garansay in the first place and not just in one of her usual Glasgow haunts, was that she was intending to visit her fancy man. If she wasn't travelling to Garansay to see Malcolm, then who *was* she coming to see?' I cannot mask the exasperation in my voice.

Hugh takes a swig of whisky to give him a bit of Dutch courage before venturing, 'I'm afraid I haven't been able to shake this thought from my mind. If Mary Galbraith was on Garansay, then the most logical reason for her being there would be to meet with your father. *He* was her connection to the island. I think Eddie Galbraith knew that too and this was why he kept asking your father if he'd seen her. To Eddie, it was simply the most obvious reason for his wife to be there. I think Malcolm Walmsley may be a red-herring in all of this. Mary's link to Garansay was through your Dad and whatever she was doing there must surely have had something to do with him.'

\*

I'm cross with Hugh for a short period of time. But I have to admit the thought had occurred to me too. If it turns out Mary and Malcolm had never seen each other before that night in the Chariot Bar then I will have to accept this is actually the most likely scenario.

Hugh and I finish our drinks in silence. Then, as we walk in the direction of the river in order to have the pleasant stroll down to the Millennium Bridge that we had planned earlier in the day, I slip my arm through his and say, 'so, if Aunty Mary had visited Mum and Dad at some point during that Saturday afternoon, why did they lie about it, not only to the police, but also to us?'

'Well, that I can understand. Your father was most likely ashamed of his sister and didn't want his own respectable family dragged into her murky affairs. He probably hoped he'd left that chaotic life of drunkenness and violence behind him. It must have been very unsettling to feel as if it had followed him over the water to his safe and peaceful haven in Garansay.'

'If that was the case, and we assume Mary met up with Dad, then maybe she asked him for money. Perhaps she took whatever Dad gave her and went straight into the hotel bar in Gilstone to spend it. Okay, I can see that happening. But the next day, when Dad and Mum find out a body has been discovered and they hear the description, they're bound to know it's Mary. So why did they never go and identify her? It took another week for Eddie Galbraith to start getting worried about where she was. If Mum and Dad left her lying unidentified on that slab, then I think it's pretty unforgivable to be honest.' I stare blankly at the river.

Hugh slips his arm around my shoulders and stands firmly by my side. 'Really?' he asks, 'because I can understand that too. Your father would only have given Mary money if she had promised she was leaving the island. I can even imagine your father buying her the ferry ticket himself. So, your Dad goes back to Lower Kilduggan, thinking that his sister has headed straight back to her drinking cronies in Motherwell. He had no idea she was going to stay on in a quiet, conservative backwater like Garansay. So when the body was found it perhaps never occurred to him that it might be his sister. He expected her to be propping up the bar in her grubby local by then, three sheets to the wind on his hard earned cash. By the time his brother-in-law had identified her body a week later, when it had become obvious there were no witnesses who had seen your father with Mary on that Saturday afternoon, he realised he didn't need to admit to anything. He decided to 'let sleeping dogs lie' and denied he had ever seen her at all.'

'It still doesn't show Dad in a particularly good light,' I say, quietly looking out at a group of rusty container ships moored up on the opposite bank. This part of the Clyde has not been cleared and modernised in the way that it has a mile or so up stream.

Just below the stone barrier marking the division between the footpath and the steep bank that shelves down to the river, there is a small muddy beach. It is scattered with pieces of rotten driftwood. Just at this moment, a large passenger boat goes past us on its engines and sends a surge of wash in the direction of the bank. As I watch the wave approach it breaks unexpectedly on the mud flat down below and the strength of it makes me jump.

'Hugh!' I exclaim.

'What is it darling?' he says, with a tender concern that makes me want to cry.

'The wave, it made me think of something. There was a clear image in my mind. Hugh, I think I might remember it - the day that Dad met Mary, back on Garansay all of those years ago. I can't believe I didn't consider it before, because I had a sort of flashback, whilst staying at the farm back in the autumn.

It was a really hot summer's day. Michael, Allan and I had gone to the Kilduggan shore with the dog to play. Dad had taken us down there for the day. We had a picnic in a basket and the football with us. Then Dad just disappeared. I probably wouldn't have remembered it at all but for the fact I got caught by a big wave. Mum had to run into the water to pull me out. I don't think she was meant to be there. Mum happened to come along the path at that moment, most likely to check up on us. I was really lucky she did because Dad was supposed to be looking after us - but he wasn't, do you see?'

'This isn't making a lot of sense,' Hugh says patiently.

'I know, but look, I would have been about three years old when this happened. It was a really hot sunny day, an absolute scorcher, so it must have been July or August. What I have just recalled is that when we got back to the farmhouse after Mum had brought us back up from the beach, there were all these bags in the hallway. They were there because someone was going away the next morning.

I think it was Michael who was going away with the Marshes, to their little cottage in Glen Nevis, just like he said they were when the police discovered Mary's body. That was why he didn't know anything about it.

The events of that afternoon have been floating around in my head like little snapshots for all these years. Only now are they coming together to form a picture. What if that hot summer's day, when I nearly drowned in the sea at the Kilduggan shore, was the Saturday that we've been talking about, the 14th July 1973? And the reason why Dad disappeared off the beach was because he'd gone to meet her - Mary, I mean? Of course, I can't be certain of it because I was so very young when it happened. I'm going to have to speak to Michael and see if he remembers it too.'

Suddenly, the need to perform this action feels so urgent and the implications of these returning memories so terrible that it is almost impossible for me to bear. I cling on tightly to Hugh until the worst of the sensation has passed. He says nothing but holds me firmly and reassuringly for as long as necessary.

Hugh is silent during this time but I know that he is thinking. His mind is running through the disjointed information I have just given him. I also know, very well, that Hugh always reaches what he believes to be the most logical deductions based on all the evidence. I have an uneasy suspicion I am not going to like the conclusion that his shrewd and rational mind has just drawn.

## Chapter 21

Hugh managed to persuade me not to be too hasty to confront Michael with my suspicions. He suggested we take a little time to get our ideas in order first. I gave Michael a call at work and without any prompting he informed me that my niece, Sarah, is coming over to his flat for a meal this evening. He invited us to have a post dinner drink with them. This gives me a few hours to consider exactly what I am going to say to him.

Knowing I will be seeing Sarah later on gives me the perfect excuse to spend the rest of the day in Buchanan Street, looking for an engagement present for her and Ross. This distraction will allow me, temporarily at least, to take my mind off my worries. Hugh bows out of the shopping trip and stays behind at the hotel to catch up with some work. We agree to meet later on in the hotel bar for dinner.

After a few hours of window shopping, I finally decide upon a set of crystal wine glasses. Whilst queuing up to pay, I start to wonder if it would be a good idea for Hugh to leave me up here for a few days so he can return home to help Gerry and Kath with the children.

When Hugh and I are having dinner in the hotel, he tells me how much he is looking forward to seeing Garansay again after all these years.

'Do you think the two of us spending all of this time away is such a good idea? Perhaps you should head back home and give your parents a break. I can tie up the sale of the farm and try to unearth whatever I can about Mum and Dad's relationship with Mary Galbraith. I'll be back by Saturday.'

'I'm not going to let you go over to that island on your own. I don't want to jump to any conclusions here, but it's a pretty strange coincidence that Colin Walmsley was the one who happened to discover the body of Alison Dickson when his father was the chief suspect in an almost identical death forty years ago. Until that little issue has been resolved by the police, I wouldn't be happy for you to be on Garansay without me. Besides, Mum and Dad are fine. Stop feeling guilty.'

'As long as Kath and Gerry can cope, we will go back to Garansay together. But as to your concern about Colin, I just cannot believe he had anything to do with Alison's death. I would swear that when we spotted her body Colin was absolutely shocked. He was as appalled as me to see her floating there, completely lifeless. The way he gave her mouth-to-mouth when it was perfectly evident she had been dead for some time just shows how devastated he was.'

'It may have been guilt. If Alison was killed in the heat of an argument, with Colin storming off and leaving her body in that way, coming back to the scene again a few hours later would have triggered terrible feelings of remorse and regret. This could easily be mistaken for shock.'

'If that was the case, and Colin knew what we were going to find when we went to Alba Cottage, I don't think he would have agreed to accompany me there that afternoon.'

'Fine. I trust your judgement. Just promise me you will keep an open mind about this. Simply because you like the man and he has helped you out at the farm doesn't mean he is innocent. It could be that he is trying to keep you sweet, darling. Quite successfully so, it seems.'

I decide to let this comment go as I know Hugh is only trying to encourage me to be more objective. I can't help but wish he would have a bit more faith in my instincts, though. In this instance, I believe them to be fairly sound. But I simply take a deep breath and finish off my mushroom risotto in silence before suggesting we make our way over to Michael's flat.

It is a mild and pleasant evening. We stop to buy a bottle of French red on the way to the underground Station. Hugh and I maintain a comfortable silence until I suddenly say, 'do you think my father could have killed Mary Galbraith?'

Hugh stops dead in his tracks, turns me around to face him and replies, 'I can honestly say that the thought had not even entered my head. Why on earth do you ask?'

'Because if I have remembered rightly and Dad did actually meet Mary on the Saturday afternoon of the day she died, he lied about it to the police and possibly to Mum as well. I thought the most logical conclusion of all this would be that he must have murdered her. You said yourself that Malcolm Walmsley was just a red-herring.'

Hugh cups both of his hands around my face and looks me straight in the eye. 'Imogen, I promise that I do not think your Dad murdered anyone. I may not have known him, but I have known you and your mother and your brothers for a long time. A husband and father of those fantastic people could not have killed anyone. So it doesn't bloody matter what the logical conclusion is.'

'Thank you.' I kiss him tenderly. This was exactly the kind of reassurance I needed. It gives me the confidence to pursue my inquiries to the bitter end.

By the time we reach the flat and are buzzed in it is nearly nine o'clock. As we push open the inner door to his apartment we hear Michael busily clearing away dishes in his small kitchenette. He calls out to us that we should take a seat in the sitting room and he will be out to join us in a minute. We make ourselves comfortable on the long and well-worn leather sofa. Sarah emerges from one of the spare bedrooms and sweeps majestically into the room.

My niece is in her late twenties and is a self-confident and highly intelligent young woman. Unlike the rest of her cousins she has almost none of the physical traits that are common to the Nichols family. She is tall, certainly, but her hair is a light auburn colour and her eyes a deep emerald green. Sarah is an almost exact replica of her beautiful late mother. I have often wondered whether this is a source of comfort to her father or a constant reminder of his terrible loss.

Michael enters his grand living room with a tray of coffees and petit fours. After Hugh and I have properly greeted our niece we sit down, appreciatively taking a cup. The conversation is dominated by talk of Sarah and Ross's upcoming wedding. We indulge in a lively discussion about the best and worst potential venues in Scotland.

Ross's family hail from Perthshire and the couple have not yet decided upon the best location for their nuptuals, partly because they do not wish to offend either side of the family. Sarah would like her mother's relatives to be able to attend. Most of them live in Aberdeen and the surrounding area. They need a venue which will suit everyone.

When we have finished our coffees, Michael offers us something a little stronger. He heads towards the kitchen to fetch some brandies, I follow him out. Helping him to rinse the tiny espresso cups and place them onto the dishwasher tray I say, 'Michael. I didn't want to talk about this in front of Sarah, but I need to ask to you about something.'

My brother stops what he is doing and turns around to face me. We can hear Hugh and Sarah talking happily in the other room so Michael pulls out a couple of stools from underneath the breakfast bar and gestures for me to take a seat.

'It's just that after I had my interview with the police today it got me thinking,' I begin. 'Now, you knew Malcolm Walmsley as well as I did - better probably. I just cannot picture him being Mary

Galbraith's fancy man. If he was drunk yes, perhaps, but when Hugh and I talked about the possibility that Mary came over to Garansay specifically to meet up with the shy, unassuming and middle-aged Malcolm, I just couldn't see it.'

'What are you suggesting?' Michael asks warily.

'I can't help but conclude that the most obvious reason why Mary came to Garansay would be to visit Dad - probably to ask him for money. Only, because he denied it so many times - to the police and to Eddie Galbraith - I had just dismissed the possibility. But what if Dad *did* meet Mary on that Saturday?' I lean in closer, 'I think that I might remember it, the day Dad went to meet her. It was lovely and sunny and we had gone down to the shore. Dad set out with us in the morning but at some point he left the beach. I think now it was to go and meet Mary. I need to know if you can remember it too.'

To my disappointment, I can't identify any signs of recognition so press on, 'the only reason I recalled it at all is because I had an accident whilst playing down by the shore. I got too close to the water and was suddenly pulled under by a wave. Luckily, Mum had just come down to check on us and she dragged me out.'

At this point in my account Hugh comes into the kitchen. Sensing he has interrupted something, he silently pours out a couple of brandies, leaving the drinks on the breakfast bar. He takes the bottle and the remaining two glasses and re-joins Sarah in the living room.

Michael takes a swig of brandy and says, 'Miriam and I took Sarah on holiday to Florida once. She was only four or five years old and we had rented a lovely little villa. We took her to Disneyland and visited all of the usual sights while we were there. The villa had a small pool on its terrace. One day, Miriam said she was going to the local shop for some groceries. She told me to keep an eye on Sarah, who was playing with her dolls outside in the sun.

A few minutes after Miriam had gone, whilst I was clearing away the breakfast plates in the kitchenette, I suddenly felt as if the place was just too quiet. I stopped what I was doing and rushed out onto the terrace. There was Sarah, lying face down and motionless in the swimming pool, with her bright red hair splayed out all around her.'

'Oh my God.'

'I jumped straight in and turned her over, quickly hauling her out. She started coughing and spluttering as soon as her face was out of the water. I was terrified. I dried Sarah off and massaged her back until her breathing seemed back to normal. When Miriam returned a few minutes later, that's how she found us, huddled on the sofa in soaking wet clothes. Both of us were shaking and shivering uncontrollably even though it must have been at least thirty five degrees outside.' Michael pauses and has another sip of brandy.

'What did Miriam do?' I ask, knowing full well what I would have done in the same circumstances.

'She was very business-like at first. She got Sarah into dry clothes. All the time she was checking her breathing and trying to soothe her. But she wouldn't even look at me and I certainly didn't try to explain myself. I don't think she spoke a single word to me for the rest of the holiday, not beyond asking me to set the table, or collect the beach towels.' Michael falls silent and I can see his eyes are glistening.

'I'm so sorry. I should never have brought up such an upsetting memory for you.'

'Not at all. I like to think of Miriam and what a great mother she was. The point I am trying to make is that those types of incident we never forget. They stay with us forever. When we recall them, even twenty five years later, they are as painful to us as they were at the time. Even the suffering of a bereavement eases with time, and I should know, but a near miss with a child haunts you always.'

'What are you saying?'

'I'm saying that of course I remember the day you nearly drowned down on the Kilduggan shore. Allan and I were playing football. I was trying to keep an eye on you but we got so engrossed in the game that when I next looked over, you had completely disappeared. I didn't even know you were in the water.

Then Mum, who must have seen you get swept under, came running past us from the direction of the path that led up to the house. She ran straight into the waves and dragged you out, thumping you on the back a few times until you coughed up all the sea water you'd breathed in. Then you were okay.'

'What else do you remember?' I ask eagerly and by this time both Hugh and Sarah are standing in the kitchen doorway, listening.

'Well, I know Mum had the exact same look on her face Miriam did that day in the villa, as if she had been totally betrayed and let down. But she wasn't angry with me. In fact, she was really kind to us all for the rest of the day, do you recall? We sat playing board games and eating cakes until Dad came home later on.'

'You can remember Dad being there?'

'Only when we set out in the morning and when he helped me to bring my bags down into the hall, because I was getting the first bus to Kilross the next day. But I'm not sure why he wasn't there with us on the beach.' Michael thinks for a few minutes, obviously trying to resurrect the events of that long forgotten summer's day from somewhere in his subconscious.

'Take your time,' says Hugh, 'and try to remember the day in stages, starting from when you first brought the bags down into the hallway.'

'We had a rushed breakfast because we were excited about spending the day at the beach. Mum was dressed nicely. I think she was going to visit Kitty that morning. She had made us a packed lunch and Artie was going crazy - trying to eat up all the scraps that were falling from the sandwiches and cake that mum was cutting up.'

'Yes,' I add. 'He kept running in and out of our legs as we set off down the path and Allan nearly tripped up. I remember Dad really shouting at him - Artie, I mean, not Allan.'

'We waved goodbye to Mum as she stood at the kitchen window. Dad was in front of us, holding your hand, Imogen. Did you have on a white dress? I have an image of you with your jet black hair falling in thick curls down your back and of a white cotton dress floating around in the breeze.'

'Yes, I did,' I reply softy.

'Then we got to the beach and set down our blankets and our picnic basket. Artie started chasing the waves. We sat on the sand for a while and then Dad played football with us. He was gently dribbling the ball to you and it was irritating Allan and me because we wanted to have a proper game, so we started having races up and down the beach instead. Then we had our lunch. You kept nagging Dad that you wanted to paddle in the sea. Dad said you could but only once you had eaten your sandwiches.'

'It sounds like I was a really annoying child,' I add without thinking. Hugh looks daggers at me for breaking Michael's flow, but my brother carries on, undeterred.

'He didn't end up taking you for a paddle. Allan and I started having our football game after we finished our lunch and you began to toddle down to the water's edge, but I don't remember what Dad was doing after that point. I don't recall him telling me to keep an eye on you, because he was just going off to do so and so, which is what you would have expected him to say. But then I don't recall

Dad being present at all at any point after lunch, not until he arrived home later that evening.'

'Why would he just leave us there like that?' I ask, puzzled.

'Maybe because he had arranged to meet someone, like Aunty Mary, and had rushed off to keep the appointment,' Michael suggests.

'But then surely he wouldn't have agreed to take you all to the beach in the first place,' Sarah chips in. 'If he knew he had a prior arrangement, I mean. He would have just told your Mum that he was too busy. All she was doing was visiting a friend. She could have done that at any time.'

'Unless it wasn't pre-arranged,' Hugh interjects. 'If Mary had simply turned up on Garansay and your father saw her. Perhaps she was coming down the path towards you all on the beach. She might have arrived at the farmhouse and found no one at home, so she came down to the shore to look for you. Angus could have turned around and spotted her. Remember, she'd had quite a lot to drink by then already and would probably have looked a bit of a state. He may have wanted to head her off, so the rest of you wouldn't know she was there. Perhaps it all happened on the spur of the moment and wasn't planned at all.'

'So Dad hustled Mary off somewhere, to give her money to get rid of her maybe. Or he even took her right back to Kilross to get her a return ticket for the ferry - just to make sure she was really going,' I suggest.

'But there were no witnesses who saw your father with Mary at any time during that Saturday afternoon. I don't think they can have gone into any of the villages. More likely they were somewhere quiet and secluded where Angus could remonstrate with her and there was no chance of any of his friends or neighbours seeing them. He was ashamed of her, remember,' Hugh conjectures.

'Why was he so worried about us kids seeing Mary?' Michael asks, 'he was concerned enough to leave us on our own on the beach rather than let us come into contact with her.'

'Maybe he thought she would be some kind of terrible influence on us,' I suggest weakly.

Michael has now finished his brandy. My brother gently rubs his forehead with his fingertips, prompting Sarah to step towards him and place a protective arm around his shoulders.

'Come on Imogen, it's getting late. We've imposed on these people's hospitality for long enough. Not everyone is on holiday you know,' Hugh says, suddenly taking my arm and leading me out into the hall.

We exchange heartfelt goodbyes and Sarah thanks us profusely for our gift. I give Michael a long hug and thank him for being so patient in entertaining my wild imaginings. He assures me that he is always happy to help.

Hugh and I decide to call a taxi to take us back to the hotel. We wait outside the flat in the pale moonlight until it arrives. I hardly feel weary at all when we return to our suite but I try my best to get some sleep, as tomorrow is when Hugh and I will return to Garansay, where I am determined to solve this conundrum, once and for all.

## Chapter 22

As soon as dawn breaks the next morning an idea comes to me. I slip quietly out of bed so as not to wake up Hugh, pick up my satchel and take it with me into the en-suite bathroom. Rummaging through the contents, I find a piece of paper with the number for Strathclyde C.I.D scrawled on it. Checking the time on my watch I sit down on the edge of the bath and use my mobile phone to make the call.

I ask to be put through to Detective Inspector O'Neil, or, failing that, to Detective Sergeant Bruce. After a few minutes of silence the administrative officer informs me that both men are currently on the Isle of Garansay, in the middle of an on-going investigation. So I relay a message for the Detective Inspector.

I carefully explain that Mrs Imogen Croft would like to know if his officers had found any letters or papers belonging to a Mrs Isabel Nichols when they went through Alison Dickson's personal effects after her death, clarifying that I may have reason to believe she had in her possession some important documents which were the property of my late mother. I give the officer my mobile number and the landline of the farmhouse at Lower Kilduggan as contact details.

It is a long shot but I feel it must be worth a try. I put aside my phone and begin the process of packing up the bags, ready for our trip to Garansay. If D.I O'Neil is still on the Island, I can always make my request face-to-face.

Hugh is a little slow to get started this morning, most likely because of our late night brandies with Michael and Sarah. Once I have made him have a cup of strong instant coffee from the hot drinks tray, he begins to liven up a bit. Our bags are packed in plenty of time for us to take advantage of the hotel breakfast.

There is a real sense of urgency to this trip. We need to get over to the Island and tie up all of the loose ends quickly. Both Hugh and I have to get back to Cooper's End by Saturday morning or we seriously run the risk of letting down our kids.

They have been looking forward to the barge race on the River Blackwater for months. As soon as we have breakfasted, we take ourselves and our bags straight down West George Street on the five minute walk to Central Station. We say a wistful farewell to Glasgow City and catch the train to Gourock from where, on this calm and beautifully clear day, we will sail to the Island of Garansay.

\*

I can tell that Hugh is trying hard to stifle his excitement as we cross the small bridge which takes us into the Kilross Harbour building. From here we have a perfect view of Ben Ardroch, rising majestically over Kilross Bay, where the water today is as still as a mill pond and the hills are so clear that you feel as if you are viewing them through a magnifying glass.

I am a little uncomfortable, to think that Hugh feels he cannot enjoy himself during this visit. I slip my hand into his and say, 'It's still a wonderful view isn't it?'

'It certainly is,' he replies, 'and it's not often we get to see it on such a perfect summer's day as this.'

Our appreciation of the spectacular scenery is curtailed by the sound of a muffled bleep coming from the depths of my bag. The mobile signal in this part of the world is so patchy that there is no guarantee as to how long it might take for a message to reach you.

Listening to my voicemail, I am surprised to hear the voice of DI O'Neil. In calm and surprisingly quiet tones he suggests that if we are back on Garansay any time over the next couple of days we should drop into the Police Station to speak with him. He has some information for me that I might find of interest.

The Garansay Police Headquarters is at the opposite end of Kilross village from the Harbour. Hugh and I leave our bags in the left luggage office and take a stroll along the sea front to find out what O'Neil has to tell us.

Kilross is a very different place on this sunny June day than it was when I was here back in the autumn. The promenade is full of holiday makers and day-trippers. The jetty is thronging with people in wet suits and bright orange life jackets who are taking part in the various recreational water sports that are on offer here during the summer months.

On the grassy area down by the golf course there is a huge inflatable slide and a small collection of fairground rides have been set up for the visitors to enjoy. Placed amongst the many attractions are two huge speakers which are currently pumping out loud and rhythmical music.

'Things have certainly changed around here,' Hugh observes with a wry smile. 'Ian would love it.'

'The Island had to move with the times,' I say, a little defensively. As much as I want to see Garansay full of happy visitors, I am also deeply nostalgic for the time when this little harbour possessed no more sophisticated a diversion than to explore the rock pools or the tiny creeks and waterways which trailed off from the beach. Where the boys and I would take our wooden rowing boat out in summer and end up stranded somewhere, having run aground in the gravelly shallows.

When we reach the old Police Station, opposite the Kilross Primary School, Hugh leads the way into the dark, wood panelled reception area. We introduce ourselves and are taken through a thick connecting door into a corridor, that in all my years growing up on Garansay, I have never before seen. We wait here for a few minutes before the bulky form of DI O'Neil emerges from one of the nondescript grey doors.

'Good afternoon, Mr and Mrs Croft, do come in.' O'Neil uses a voice that cannot be anything else but intimidating.

The office itself is quite pleasant and its generously sized window looks out over the tennis courts that back onto the gently rolling landscape of the Kilross Golf Course. DI O'Neil squeezes behind the desk, gesturing for us to take a seat.

'As my assistant may have told you, Mrs Croft, my team are very kindly being allowed to commandeer the Kilross Station for a couple of days whilst we pursue our enquiries into the Alison Dickson case. For the time being, this has involved the extensive interviewing and re-interviewing of witnesses. I received your phone message, Mrs Croft and was a little intrigued, I must admit.'

'I appreciate you taking it seriously.'

'My team did not discover anything in Ms Dickson's effects which related to your mother. But another piece of information has emerged in the course of our enquiries. It is something you may find of interest.' The detective searches for a document amongst a vast and haphazard pile on his desk. When he selects what he is looking for, he smooths the paper out carefully with the palms of both hands. 'Since re-opening the case, we have looked over Ms Dickson's financial affairs in greater detail. We examined her bank transactions covering the last five years. We were aware the lady had a considerable sum of money in her savings account and were keen to know how she had accumulated it. We discovered a large, single deposit made to Ms Dickson's current account, about eleven months ago. The deposit was for the sum of twenty thousand pounds and was transferred from the account of a Mrs Isabel

Nichols of Lower Kilduggan Farm, North Garansay, on the 31$^{st}$ July 2012.'

After delivering this piece of information, O'Neil sits back in his chair and makes a steeple out of his hands.

'There must be a mistake,' I blurt out, perfectly aware of what a hackneyed cliché this must sound. 'Why on earth would my mum give Alison Dickson twenty thousand pounds?'

DI O'Neil lets this question hang in the air between us for a few seconds before he replies. 'There *is* some kind of explanation attached. The Scotiabank queries all credits and deposits to and from their accounts which are over ten thousand pounds, for prevention of fraud purposes. So they asked Ms Dickson on,' he glances at the sheet of paper in front of him, 'August 2$^{nd}$ of last year, to explain the reason for such a large transfer of funds. It appears that both parties confirmed the money was for the purchase by Mrs Nichols of a piece of artwork by Ms Dickson.'

I almost snort with laughter. My mother had very little interest in works of art and in Alison's paintings she had even less. I take a deep breath and say, 'Detective Inspector O'Neil, I don't know what my mother told the Scotiabank at the time, but there is no way she would have paid twenty thousand pounds for one of Alison's paintings.' I pause for a moment. 'Where is this incredible picture supposed to be? Because I certainly haven't seen it hanging anywhere in Mum's house.'

'A handwritten receipt of sorts was photocopied and added to the bank's files. This suggests the painting was entitled, 'The Queen of the Night'. No more detail is given about it than that I'm afraid.'

I look at Hugh, who is sitting beside me and staying very quiet. If I didn't know any better I would say he was trying to avoid my gaze.

DI O'Neil shuffles the papers on his desk before he looks towards me and says, 'now, imagine the scenario if you will. I had just discovered that your mother, less than a year ago, paid a very hefty sum of money for one of Alison Dickson's paintings - well over the market value if I understand you correctly. Then, on the same day, I receive a phone message from you, Mrs Croft, asking me to have a look to see if Ms Dickson had in her possession some important documents you believed had rightfully belonged to your mother. You can perhaps see now why I was so intrigued by your request.' O'Neil pauses again and then his commanding tone of voice returns, 'perhaps you had better tell me the *whole* story this time. If you wouldn't mind, Mrs Croft.'

\*

## Chapter 23

Hugh and I sit in the stuffy office for another couple of hours. We tell O'Neil the whole story, about Mum's lost bag and the contents which still remain a mystery to us. I inform the Inspector about Alison's relationship with Allan - the latter being information O'Neil already knew, because of my letter to the Procurator Fiscal. I also tell him about Andy Galbraith's note to Michael and of the Nichols cousins we had not previously known we had. I even tell O'Neil that I may remember the day when Mary Galbraith had come to Garansay, back in 1973, and how Dad had been unaccounted for in the afternoon for at least a couple of hours, but that he had been back at home again by the evening. When I have finished my account, having tried very hard not to leave out any details, DI O'Neil asks me a question which I had not at all been expecting.

'So, if we are to presume that Alison Dickson never did dispose of the contents of your mother's satchel, do you believe it's possible that whatever was inside could have been worth paying twenty thousand pounds to get back?'

And suddenly the penny drops. This was why Hugh had been avoiding eye contact for the last few hours. He had already put two and two together and realised my mum must have given Alison that huge sum of money because she was being blackmailed. Which means Mum must have done something so awful she was prepared to pay a small fortune in order to cover it up.

Hugh must sense I've finally grasped the full implications because he suddenly takes hold of my hand and says, 'my wife has had a bit of a shock here. I'd like to take her somewhere for a cold drink. I promise we will consider what you have told us and come back to talk again tomorrow, if you'd like.'

O'Neil says nothing, simply nodding his head, presumably feeling he has successfully made his point. With some effort, he gets out of his seat and stands awkwardly within the cramped space between his adopted desk and the window, signalling to us that we have been dismissed.

Hugh has to guide me out of the room and along the dark corridor. He proceeds to bang rudely on the connecting door in order for us to be released. Once back outside, in the still bright sunshine of the late afternoon, Hugh takes hold of me and says kindly, 'I'm going to find you a comfortable chair in the 'Glenrannoch', darling. Then I'll go and fetch our bags. When I get back we can have something to eat before we get a cab over to the farmhouse, alright?'

I nod feebly and with some relief, let Hugh take temporary control of the situation.

The Glenrannoch Hotel is surprisingly quiet this afternoon, but then it is too early for dinner and I assume most of the residents are still out and about on the Island, enjoying this preciously rare sunny day. Hugh leaves me curled up in an armchair, hidden from public view and with a wonderful outlook onto the Bay, having ordered me an ice-cold water with a brandy chaser on the side.

It must be the effects of the brandy, but whilst Hugh is gone I doze off for a little while in the armchair. Coming round, I see Hugh sitting on the stool next to me, with our bags laid out around his feet and wonder how on earth he managed to carry them all by himself.

'Hugh,' I ask, 'what did DI O'Neil say the painting was called? The one that Mum was supposed to have bought from Alison?'

'Something about a queen wasn't it?' he replies, whilst dabbing at the beads of sweat on his forehead with a handkerchief.

'That's it - 'The Queen of the Night'- it's familiar to me for some reason but I can't for the life of me remember why.'

'Well, don't even try for the moment. Let's order food and get back to the farmhouse before it gets dark.'

Hugh and I have a lovely meal, looking out across the Kilross Bay whilst the sun goes down in a shimmer of gold behind Ben Ardroch. The bay is full of sailing boats this evening, who will have navigated their way from the ports and marinas of Ayrshire and Kintyre to take advantage of the glorious conditions the weather has created for them.

When we have finished our dinner, we ask the hotel receptionist to call a local taxi firm. Contrary to our plans, by the time the cab drops us off at the bottom of the stony driveway, the evening light has faded to dusk.

When Hugh and I reach the square courtyard of Lower Kilduggan Farm we are unexpectedly bathed in a beam of bright, artificial light. Our movements have triggered the security system that Colin had fitted for us last year. It proves to be very useful as I am easily able to locate my key and slot it carefully into the stiff and ancient lock of the under used front door.

We dump our bags in the hallway. As I automatically throw the nearest switch it activates a single, bare light bulb, which harshly reveals the stark emptiness of the place. I note how uninviting the house looks, now that it has been almost entirely cleared of its previous contents.

I did have the presence of mind to leave the beds made up in two of the guestrooms and spare sheets and towels in the airing cupboard. I also left some cutlery and utensils in the kitchen, just in case we needed to return for any reason before the sale was finalised. Colin had also requested that we leave a few of the oldest pieces of furniture, for the use of any potential future tenants.

I tell Hugh that I am going to get myself a glass of water from the kitchen and ask if he would like one too. Hugh declines the offer and takes himself off in the direction of the front sitting room, where I suspect he is going to see if there is any of Mum's single malt left in the cabinet.

Standing at the butler sink, running the tap, I look out across the courtyard towards the outbuildings and sheds. Despite the lovely clear weather we enjoyed today, the clouds have rapidly moved in. Without any moonlight it is almost pitch black outside. I can barely perceive the outlines of the buildings at the far end of the yard and certainly can't see anything in the little passages which run in between them. For some reason, this makes me feel suddenly nervous.

I take off my shoes and leave them by the kitchen door, with its newly fitted, thick panes of glass that were expertly installed by Colin's handyman all those months ago. Although standing by the kitchen door has reminded me of it, I try not to think about the break-in. It's spooky enough simply being back here at the farmhouse again. It seems crazy to have imagined I could have come back again on my own.

Padding across the stone floor of the kitchen to find out what Hugh is up to in the sitting room, I stop dead in my tracks. A loud and heavy thud has just reverberated from the ceiling above me. I hold my breath and daren't move a muscle, waiting for any further sound to emanate from up there.

When there is nothing but silence I tell myself it must be have been Hugh, deciding to use the upstairs toilet or something. With a monumental effort of will-power, I carry on walking out into the hallway, peering up the twisting stairwell, into the complete blackness beyond. There is no sign of light or movement coming from upstairs so I turn around and tip-toe back towards the sitting room, finding Hugh lounging in the threadbare armchair by the bay window, with a large glass of scotch in his hand.

'Did you hear that noise?' I ask in a whisper.

'I thought it was you,' Hugh replies calmly, sitting forward in his seat.

'No, it wasn't. It came from upstairs, from the room directly above the kitchen.'

Hugh carefully puts his glass of scotch down on the side table and stands up. 'You stay here. I'll go and have a look.'

Before he gets the chance, a clearly audible creak comes from the floorboard directly above our heads. There then follows the sound of a series of heavy footfalls which are advancing rapidly towards the top of the stairs.

'Stay in here,' Hugh orders. He glances frantically around the room, obviously looking for something to use as a weapon. The sitting room has very few items left in it, so Hugh simply picks up the nearby bottle of whisky, taking it out with him into the hall.

By this time, the heavy footsteps are making their way purposefully down the poorly lit stairwell. Hugh quickly positions himself at the bottom of the last flight, crouching behind the wooden bannister with the whisky bottle held firmly in both of his hands, which it disturbs me to see are shaking uncontrollably.

I gasp in apprehension as a tall figure turns the final bend in the staircase, moving out of the shadows and descending swiftly towards the final few steps. Hugh has just about managed to maintain his composure and at this moment, he lifts the bottle up above his head and turns, ready to confront the intruder.

In the light of the hallway, I get a chance to have a proper look at the person who is running down the stairs. I immediately call out, 'No - Hugh, Stop!'

And for a fraction of a second, all three of us are absolutely still and silent. Finally, I step out of the doorway of the sitting room. Standing squarely in the centre of the hallway I declare, 'Allan - what on God's earth are *you* doing here?'

\*

## Chapter 24

I have just about resisted the urge to batter my brother senseless, largely because Hugh was able to see the funny side of the whole thing. When Allan turned and saw his brother-in-law wielding a half-full bottle of whisky, like a claymore above his head, both men collapsed in a fit of hysterical laughter. This, for Hugh at least, was the release of an incredible build-up of nervous tension.

I did not manage to find the situation quite so amusing. Even as we sit in the bay window of the living room, on the only remaining furniture in the house, rapidly polishing off the ill-used bottle of whisky, I remain annoyed.

'I still don't understand what you're doing here,' I say sulkily.

'Well, I was summoned by the imposing DI O'Neil to come in for questioning. In order to "help them with their enquiries" were the exact words he used. I expect they're regarding me as their 'prime suspect',' Allan declares proudly.

'I'll have to disappoint you there. I think that role has been assigned to poor old Colin Walmsley,' I quickly retort.

'How long have you been here on the Island?' Hugh asks.

'Only since this afternoon. I'm afraid I overdid the 'in-flight hospitality' somewhat. I was sleeping it off upstairs when I heard someone knocking about in the kitchen. I decided to leap out of my pit and come down to defend my property,' Allan says with relish.

'I didn't even know you had a key to the farmhouse,' I say.

'I don't. But I knew that old Heathcliff next door was looking after the place for us. When my cab pulled up I saw him, measuring up the outbuildings for their addition to his farming empire. He very kindly let me in and left me with the spare key.'

'Well, you could have told me that you were coming,' I say huffily.

'And I could say the exact same to you, darling. I've had a bit of a shock myself, you know. You do realise this is *term time* don't you? And you've got offspring that you should be ferrying around rural Essex and *feeding* every so often?' Allan says this with a wicked grin on his face.

This time I do take a swipe at my brother, more gently than I would actually like to. 'Let's just try not to have any more secrets shall we?'

\*

The next morning, Allan has to go into Kilross for his interview with DI O'Neil's team. After we've had our breakfast, Hugh gives him a lift over there in Mum's car.

Whilst they are gone, I take advantage of the peace and quiet to pad around the farmhouse, trying to get my head around the odd relationship Mum seemed to have had with Alison Dickson.

The first thing I would like to do is check whether or not Allan and I could somehow have missed the painting Mum claimed to have bought from Alison, when we cleared out the house a few months ago. This seems impossible, as we had emptied out every room, but I decide to have another look, just in case. Even going as far as to climb up the ladder into the attic space and then down the stone steps, leading off the hallway, into the damp and disused cellar. But, as I had expected, find nothing.

I have a thought. Perhaps Mum had put it in one of the outbuildings. It wouldn't be a very good place to store a painting as none of the buildings is properly sealed off from the elements, but we've searched everywhere else. I put on my canvas pumps and light cotton cardigan and leave the farmhouse through the kitchen door, crunching through the gravel courtyard towards the first of the old animal sheds. Most of these outbuildings have fallen into disrepair. The first one I enter is empty except for the two ride-on mowers we use for the front and back lawns of the farmhouse.

Sliding across the large corrugated iron door of the next of the old sheds, I hear a vehicle pulling up the long, steep driveway. I know it is too soon for Hugh to be returning from Kilross. Turning around, I see Colin Walmsley's 4x4. He drives the vehicle right up into the centre of the courtyard before climbing down from the driver's seat.

I give my neighbour a warm smile, striding over to greet him. 'Hi Colin, how are you?' I ask this perfectly sincerely, knowing the re-opening of Alison Dickson's case cannot have been easy for him.

'I'm fine, thank you, Imogen. You arrived here safely, I see,' he replies, just as politely. 'I was coming over to check on your brother, in case he needed me to do anything for him. I was planning to send Charlie over to mow the lawns and tidy up a bit.'

I notice that Colin looks tired and immediately wonder how many times he has been questioned by Detective O'Neil and his team. Then, a notion hits me. I consider the possibility that Colin had not previously known about his father's involvement in the Mary Galbraith case. If he did not, it must have come as a terrible shock when the police told him.

'Would you like to come into the farmhouse for a coffee?' I ask, hoping that someone had the foresight to buy some milk.

'I'd love to, thanks.'

We walk quietly together, back towards the side entrance to the kitchen. I am very relieved to discover that Allan must have brought a fresh pint of milk with him when he arrived yesterday afternoon. I note to myself that my brother is not quite as undomesticated as he likes to make out. I place the old kettle on top of the stove and while we wait for the water to boil ask Colin how his mother is keeping.

'She is very well, thank you. Physically, Mum is good for her age. She's becoming increasingly confused about what is going on around her though. Perhaps at the moment this might not be such a bad thing.'

'The police haven't been interviewing her too have they?' I ask, horrified at the thought.

'No, thank goodness. But they've questioned me plenty of times, particularly about my father and the death of your aunt all of those years ago. They keep going on and on at me about that,' Colin says this quietly, without displaying any obvious emotion.

The kettle starts to whistle and while busying myself making a couple of instant coffees I ask, 'Colin, did you know anything about the death of my father's sister and the fact your Dad had been seen with her that evening, *before* we found Alison, up on Aoife's Chariot?'

'You sound like the police,' Colin says and then breaks into a smile. 'But as it's you I might be persuaded to answer the question one more time. Yes, I did. My mother told Sandra and I about it a few years ago. She also told us the police case had been dropped and Dad hadn't had anything to do with that lady's death.'

I place the mugs down on the table top and sit opposite my guest. 'I don't think for a second your father had anything to do with it either. But the way that Alison died, it was so similar to the death of Mary Galbraith, I just don't know how to explain it.'

'I can explain it,' Colin says and for the first time his voice is filled with emotion. 'She did it deliberately. Somehow she knew all the details of Mary Galbraith's death and she killed herself in exactly the same way as a kind of sick joke. Whether it was designed to upset you or me or another poor sod I just don't know.'

'But why would she do that?'

'You didn't know her, Imogen. She was capable of terrible things.' Colin looks away then, deliberately avoiding my gaze as he slowly sips his steaming coffee.

I get up and give myself some thinking time by rummaging around in the cupboards to see if anyone has bought any biscuits. Whilst I carry out this fruitless search Colin changes the subject and says, 'I read that book you know.'

This makes me stop suddenly and turn around to face him. 'Which book?'

'The Return of the Native,' he reminds me. 'Did you know she drowns at the end? Eustacia Vye, I mean. There is a terrible storm. Damon and Eustacia fall into the weir and are never seen again. It made me think that, actually, *Alison* was more like Eustacia Vye than you are. I know that in looks she was uncannily like you, with her jet black hair and her full, perfect lips: 'formed less to speak than to quiver, less to quiver than to kiss,' Colin recites this romantically whilst staring down at the table top.

'Hang on a minute,' I say. Colin immediately looks up. 'That description of Eustacia Vye - I haven't read the book for years, but I heard something just recently that brought those words back to me. Colin, how did Hardy describe Eustacia in that early chapter of the book? He explains how she loathes the heath and is desperate to escape from the isolated and lonely life that she leads there. Hardy also compares her to it. She is described as roaming the dark hillsides, at one with the barren countryside around her.'

'The Queen of the Night,' says Colin, like an obedient sixth-former.

My face lights up in recognition. 'That's it! I knew I'd heard it before.'

Colin looks a little confused. He finishes his coffee and says, 'thank you so much for the drink, but I'd best head off for now. I'll send Charlie over to sort out the grass for you. I don't want to upset your husband by being here when he gets back.'

'Oh, Hugh wouldn't mind at all,' I say unconvincingly. But Colin has already stood up. With a firm shake of my hand, he walks back to his jeep. Manoeuvring it expertly out of the courtyard, he disappears in a cloud of grey dust down the steep drive.

## Chapter 25

When Hugh arrives back from Kilross, he brings much needed supplies along with him. Allan told Hugh not to bother waiting for him to finish at the Police Station. He said he'd spend the remainder of the day in the village and get a taxi back here later on.

'I hope he's not going to while away the rest of the afternoon in the pub,' I say to this, chopping up the salad vegetables for lunch as Hugh puts out a couple of ill-matching, chipped plates on the table.

'I think he was actually planning to do a bit of sight-seeing, oh ye of little faith,' Hugh chuckles. 'I hope he was okay in his interview. The guy was pretty nervous on the way in.'

'In spite of the act he puts on, Allan is actually really upset about his part in Alison's suicide. He blames himself for having confronted her so brutally and for revealing he was about to tell the world about their teenage shenanigans,' I explain.

'I really don't think he should blame himself,' Hugh says with his mouth full of the cherry tomato he has just plucked out of the salad bowl. 'I think Alison Dickson had been up to far worse things in her lifetime than rolling around on hillsides with a border-line under-age boy.'

'That's what Colin said. This morning, when he came around to offer to mow the lawns for us, he suggested that Alison was capable of 'terrible things' but I didn't want to press him on what he meant by it.'

Hugh stalks round the kitchen table. Catching me around the waist, he says, 'entertaining handsome farmers whilst I've been out have you?'

I laugh and give Hugh a reassuringly long kiss before saying, 'poor Colin has been put through the ringer a fair bit by the police. I'm feeling quite sorry for him. Oh, and he has solved a little mystery for me.'

Hugh raises his eyebrows curiously at this.

'The title Alison had given to the painting, the one that was apparently written on the receipt: 'The Queen of the Night'. I said that I thought it was familiar. Well, it turns out it was a reference from the Thomas Hardy novel, 'The Return of the Native'. The character the phrase refers to is Eustacia Vye. The day Alison blew up at me at the diary farmer's show, she said I used to "moon about the hillsides like some kind of Eustacia Vye". I am the same physical type as her, so that's what I thought she meant at the time.'

'Then what is the significance of giving the painting that name? The picture was supposedly for your mother, not for you.'

'I don't think there was ever any such painting. I have searched through the house and it's definitely not here. I mean, if you had felt that a picture was worth twenty thousand quid you'd have it on show somewhere, wouldn't you?'

'So the money was for something else. To stop Alison from revealing the information she had discovered. Or to buy back an item Alison had taken from your mother,' Hugh summarises.

'I think Alison was having a joke with the name she chose for the painting. It was something Colin said that got me thinking. He suggested that Alison's whole suicide was staged to mirror the death of Mary Galbraith as some sort of 'sick joke'. He seemed to believe that Alison would be trying to get at him or possibly me through doing it.'

'Why does Colin think Alison had a grudge against him? They didn't have any connection to each other, did they?' Hugh suddenly says.

I hadn't considered this point and fall silent for a little while.

Once we have finished eating our lunch I ask, 'will you help me to finish the job of searching the outhouses? I had an idea that the painting, if it exists, may be out there.'

Hugh and I tidy up the kitchen before venturing outside. By the time we do the sky has clouded over. The atmosphere has become very warm and humid. There is a kind of oppressive feel to the air which indicates we could be in for an impromptu summer storm later on.

We take a tour around the outhouses, looking carefully behind the straw bales and the carcasses of ancient farming machinery that lie abandoned in these long defunct buildings. The only structure which has seen any recent use is Mum's pottery shed. This was converted by the Monroes just a couple of years ago. I discover that we need to go back into the kitchen in order to find the little key that opens the padlock securing the entrance.

As we push the heavy doors open I silently chide myself for being so stupid as to not clear out this shed last year. As we gaze around us we are confronted by dozens of shelves, all filled with beautifully decorated plates, vases and paper weights. There are several wooden trestle tables jam-packed with hand-made ornaments, some of which still have the price tags attached to them bearing Mum's eccentrically looped and sloping handwriting.

I have to gulp down a sob, as seeing the contents of this room invokes Mum's spirit to me, more than anything in the farmhouse ever did. The wheel and kiln are located in the far right hand corner. There is a new wash basin positioned next to a set of fitted wooden desks. Mum had used these when the children came to throw and decorate their own pots.

I nearly jump out of my skin as I glimpse, out of the corner of my eye, an almost life-sized pottery owl, wisely marking the entrance to the place with the inscription: 'We Are Open,' carefully written into the clay border running around its sturdy base.

It takes us a little longer to search this shed but it is already evident there is no room in here for any kind of picture to be stored. Once we have searched all of the outbuildings to no avail we walk back out into the courtyard again. I am immediately struck by the warm and sticky thickness of the air outside, certainly compared to the damp chilliness of the atmosphere in the barns.

'Gosh, it's permanent winter inside those places,' I say, shivering slightly at the thought.

'What is Colin Walmsley going to do with the outhouses?' Hugh asks. 'They'll need a lot of work if he wants to bring them back into operation.'

'I'm not sure. I suppose it depends on whether Colin wants to rent the whole farm as it is, in which case he will probably need to reinstate the barns and outhouses. If he is just going to annex Lower Kilduggan onto his existing business then I suspect they will have to go.'

'How do you feel about the place being sold? You may never be able to come back here again,' Hugh asks, as we stand together in what was once the centre of the old farm.

'If you'd asked me that question a year ago I would have said that I would be devastated. But now I really don't know. I'm actually starting to find the place sinister, even after spending so many happy times here. As we stand in the courtyard now, and look back up towards the house, all I can picture, in my mind's eye, is Alison, leading Allan out of that kitchen door and down towards the cow shed. She has a triumphant look on her face and has just stolen and hidden Mum's bag. The next thing I can see, through the kitchen window, is Mum, slumped at the table and weeping bitterly for its loss.'

Hugh takes hold of me in an embrace. We stand together, locked in each other's arms for some time, whilst the clouds accumulate into tall billowing towers above us and the breeze abruptly picks up, disturbing the dust on the gravelly farmyard floor. It lifts aloft the minute particles into perfect tiny spirals, suddenly causing the open doors of the pottery shed to slam shut, with a loud, cracking noise which echoes sharply up the glen.

## Chapter 26

As the swollen droplets finally begin to fall, we rush back inside the farmhouse to shelter from the coming storm. Not long after we have got ourselves dried off, filled up the old kettle and lit the stove, the phone in the hallway starts to ring.

I hurry out in search of the plastic handset, eventually finding it sitting on an ancient Garansay phonebook, on the hall floor by the cellar door. It is wrapped up tightly in its own flex. I have to frantically unwind it before I am able to lift up the receiver and connect to the call.

It is DI O'Neil, who politely informs me that he will not be requiring us to come back in for any further interviews. He tells me it is a courtesy call to let me know that his team have completed their investigation into the death of Alison Dickson and have uncovered no conclusive evidence that would overturn the original findings of the Procurator Fiscal. I ask him about the mysterious money in Alison Dickson's account. O'Neil replies that they cannot prove Alison had accumulated her money in a way that was illegal, but if I should find any evidence to the contrary, to contact him straight away.

'But what about the death of Mary Galbraith?' I ask quickly, sensing the Detective Inspector is about to ring off.

'The connection between the two cases remains an enigma, Mrs Croft. After so many years we would not hope to be able to draw any solid conclusions about what happened to your aunt. The evidence you gave us which suggested your father might have met up with Mrs Galbraith on the afternoon of her death is certainly very interesting. But Angus Nichols is sadly no longer here to be interviewed about it. Your testimony, the disjointed memories of a three year old girl, would not be admissible in any court in the land. In addition to this, your father was back at home, with several witnesses during the hours that Mary met her fate, so we never had him in the frame.'

He goes on to say that if any new evidence comes to light he will inform me immediately.

Just as he is about to end the call, I quickly add, 'what is the weather like over there in Kilross DI O'Neil?'

'It's rather hot and sunny at the moment,' the man answers, momentarily disconcerted.

'Well, I'd batten down the hatches if I were you,' I reply cheerfully, 'because there's a storm coming.' Without another word, I gently place the receiver back into its cradle and go through to the kitchen to tell Hugh the news.

As we sit, drinking tea at the kitchen table, it looks as dark as night outside. The rain is falling in thunderous sheets which almost completely obscure the view out of the window. Where the rain encounters the smooth, concreted areas of the driveway, the water is bouncing back up again to form little geysers that rush towards lower ground like a fast flowing stream.

I remark to Hugh how fortunate it was we had the drainage system installed at the farm last year. Thankfully, most of this water will be contained within the pipes and gutters that Danny Monroe had skilfully created for us. Then I remember, that without Danny's ground works last October we would never have unearthed Mum's satchel, or not for a good few years anyway and possibly never. Maybe I wouldn't have started digging around into what Allan and Alison had done back then and perhaps if I hadn't, she would not be dead.

I try not to dwell on this thought, saying instead, 'Are we agreed that if Mum did not have this so-called, 'Queen of the Night' painting in her possession, then the money she gave to Alison must have been for something else.'

'Yes,' says Hugh who is reclining in the kitchen chair with his legs stretched out to their full extent. 'But, if Isabel paid that money to get something back from Alison and, for argument's sake, say it was whatever had been in the lost satchel. Then she *must* have got those items returned to her. If so, where are they now?'

'That's right. We've been searching for the painting, when in fact we should have been looking for whatever it was that Mum was prepared to pay Alison Dickson twenty thousand pounds for.'

'My other thought,' says Hugh, 'is why now? Alison had whatever was in your Mum's bag for thirty years, so why did it take her so long to extort the money for it?'

I think this through for a little while before suggesting, 'what if it was some kind of final payment? Alison had nearly thirty thousand pounds in her bank account. Maybe Mum had been paying her, in smaller amounts, for a long period of time but she said enough is enough and gave her a lump sum to end it, once and for all.'

'And then your Mum died, which dried up the supply anyway,' Hugh says. 'So we can't know if there would have been any further payments after that.'

'Somehow I feel that was the end of it. Mum didn't have the kind of money where she could dole out tens of thousands of pounds at the drop of a hat. If she paid Alison twenty thousand then that would be it. Mum wouldn't have expected to give her more.'

'After your Mum had paid her off, and especially after she died, Alison had suddenly lost her 'cash cow', if you will excuse my expression. Wasn't that when she started to behave strangely, drinking more heavily and becoming uncontrollable?'

'That's correct. The thought that Alison might have been living off my mother for all of those years makes my blood boil.'

There seems to be absolutely no relief from the driving intensity of the rainfall outside. I begin to get concerned about Allan. The road between here and Kilross has a low lying section that tends to flood when there are high volumes of rain. I become worried that Allan won't be able to get a taxi to bring him back over here tonight. Fetching my mobile, I decide to give him a call.

Allan's phone rings and rings but there is no answer. My mind starts to run away with itself, thinking about Allan's drinking and the effect that today's interview with the police will have had on his mood. I start to consider what Colin had said to me this morning, about Alison trying to rub our noses in something, having a joke at our expense. It abruptly occurs to me that if Alison had an undisclosed ally in any of this, as she had wanted me to believe, it certainly wasn't Colin.

'Hugh, I'm starting to get really worried about him. I've been so wrapped up in the mystery of the money that I haven't given a minute's thought to Allan.' I start to pace slowly around the kitchen, with my mobile phone clutched tightly in my hand.

'He's a grown man. He's always been a big drinker. We all were, for heaven's sake, back in the day.' Hugh comes over and places an arm around my shoulders, but I am so tense that I shake it off.

'Yes, back in the day - when we were students, or on holiday, or at a special occasion, but not all day, every day,' I say, starting to get agitated. 'Something's not right about this, I know it's not. Don't even try to fob me off.'

Hugh walks out of the room and I worry that he might be really upset. But he comes back in a couple of minutes later carrying the old and battered telephone book. The one which has been serving as an impromptu table for the hall phone since the sideboard was shipped out last year.

He places the book down on the kitchen table, gets his mobile phone out, and sits it on top. 'Right, let's make a list of all the pubs and hotels that Allan might have gone to between here and Kilross. We can take half each.'

I give Hugh a quick kiss on the cheek, grab a pen and a piece of paper from my bag and start searching for numbers. After half an hour of ringing around, Hugh has managed to ascertain that Allan was in the Glenrannoch Hotel for most of the afternoon. He is not there now. We haven't been able to find out which drinking establishments he might have visited since.

'Did Allan give you any idea of what his plans were today, when you talked to him this morning?'

'He just said not to bother waiting. He would stay in Kilross for a while and might do some sight-seeing, maybe the Castle or the craft-shops. He was moaning about having to buy a gift for Abigail.'

'Well, that's the eastern side of the Island then. I'd be very surprised if he made it as far as the Castle but we could try Skilling Bay and Gilstone. There are only a couple of hotels in each village and only one pub that I know of.'

I take the hotel and guest house in Skilling Bay and Hugh takes Gilstone. But I only get as far as dialling the number for my second hostelry when Hugh walks back into the kitchen, with the phone held up to his ear and his other hand raised in the air, a signal he has found something out. Hugh expresses his gratitude to the person on the other end of the line and hangs up.

'That was the bar manager at the Gilstone Hotel. He said that Allan has been the life and soul of the party in the Chariot Bar for the last couple of hours. He left about twenty minutes ago and the manager has no idea where he was heading to next.'

I drum my fingers impatiently on the table. After a couple of minutes of contemplation, I jump up from my seat and cry, 'that bloody fool! I know where he has gone.'

Rushing out into the hallway, I find my shoes, which are made of a flimsy canvas material that won't be very practical in the rain that is falling remorselessly down from the leaden sky outside.

'Haven't you got any other shoes with you?' Hugh asks impatiently.

Just as I am plucking up the courage to inform him that the only other footwear in my luggage are sandals with a four inch heel, he suddenly says, 'hang on, wasn't there a pair of your mum's wellies in the pottery shed? I saw them underneath the sink. She must have worn them when handling the wet clay. Wait here, I'll go and get them.'

We hadn't had time to lock the doors to the pottery shed earlier on, after the rain had started falling, so Hugh simply pulls on his mac and runs across the courtyard, through the torrential downpour, to fetch Mum's old boots. The clay stained wellingtons are a bit tight but I don't have the heart to tell Hugh. I just pull on my travel mac, zip it up to the neck and with my satchel hanging across my shoulders, we both make a dash for the car.

As soon as we get inside the vehicle and close the doors I have a terrible, sinking feeling. The rain is coming down so hard that it is drumming off the car roof. The sound is deafening. When Hugh starts up the ever reliable engine and flicks on the wipers they barely make a dent in the wall of water obscuring the windscreen. Hugh puts on the lights full beam, but the visibility is still awful. Regardless of this, he valiantly manoeuvres the little car to the top of the steep slope which leads to the main road, lying about three hundred yards below.

We can't see it from inside the vehicle, but after the sheer volume of rain that has fallen, the water is now gushing down the driveway in torrents. As soon as Hugh has edged us, very slowly, to the point where we are just over the brow of the hill, he starts to lose control.

We are sliding fast towards a thick line of bushes at the left hand side of the track. Luckily, the driveway bends sharply at this point and before we can gain any more momentum we hit the undergrowth head on. Hugh and I are thrown forwards in our seats but the car has come to an absolute standstill. If we had carried on down to the main road, with no control and at the speed the car was travelling, we would have been in real trouble. Neither of us has uttered a single word throughout this whole terrifying experience but now I shout, 'Hugh! Are you alright?'

At first, there is no reply. I undo my seat belt and lean over to check his breathing. Hugh must have hit his head hard on the steering wheel because a big red lump is forming on the side of his forehead. I put my ear to his mouth and just about hear his even breathing over the thunderous noise of the rain. I realise then that in the rush he can't have put his belt on. I move him gently backwards into a more comfortable position and during this procedure, he begins to come round.

'Hugh,' I say in a loud but calm voice. 'Can you hear me?'

He is mumbling a little, but as he starts to regain consciousness properly I look closely at his eyes and see they are focussing well.

'How are you feeling?' I persist.

'Okay,' he croaks, 'but I'm pretty sore.'

My side of the car is jammed up against the thick foliage so I climb into the backseat and get out through the rear door on the driver's side. I am immediately pelted by rain and nearly lose my footing because of the sheer velocity of the water sweeping down the driveway towards us.

Thankfully, Hugh is a bit more with it by the time I open up the driver's door. All I need to do is support his weight a little whilst he gets himself out of the seat. We are sheltered from the worst of the flow here but once Hugh is out of the car I shout, 'just to warn you, as we walk out of the shelter of the car, we are going to get hit by a strong current of water. It's not deep, but it's fast. Keep holding onto my hand. If we lean into the slope we should be able to make it back up.'

Hugh nods his head.

After we have navigated ourselves past the car, we try to keep to the edge of the track, where the flow is not quite as strong and we can grab onto any protruding undergrowth we find to keep us on our feet. By the time we get back up to the farmhouse we are both completely exhausted.

I lead Hugh in through the kitchen door, sit him down at the table and throw my arms around him.

'I'm so sorry darling. That was totally my fault. How are you feeling now? Do we need to get you to a doctor?'

Hugh takes hold of my arms and pushes me away from him so that he can see my face. 'Imogen, I'm absolutely fine. Just a bump on the head, that's all.'

He looks better. There is colour in his cheeks and his eyes are still focussing well. He promises that his head is feeling okay and he is not nauseous. There is some ice in the freezer section of the fridge so I chip off a few pieces and wrap them in Hugh's handkerchief before giving it to him to hold to the lump on his forehead.

After removing Hugh's wet clothes and getting him comfortable and warm in the tatty old armchair in the sitting room, I squat down on my haunches in front of him and look him squarely in the eye. 'You're not going to like what I am about to say, but I need you to hear me out, alright?'

Hugh nods cautiously.

'I've been thinking, about all the messages Alison has left for me. She called that fictitious painting, 'The Queen of the Night', which is the way that Hardy describes Eustacia Vye in the early chapters of 'The Return of the Native'. Alison must have known I would understand the reference. She was trying to rub my nose in something, but I hadn't been able to work out what. Then, when Colin said it was *Alison* who was like Eustacia Vye and not me, it all started to come together. There were always the two of them in the book, you see. Eustacia and Damon were childhood sweethearts who both ended up married to other people. But Damon still loved her, throughout all of it, and in the end they both die because of that love.

I think Alison was trying to tell me there were always two of them, that it was her *and* Allan all the time. She was letting me know that things had never ended between them.'

Hugh looks unsure of where this story is leading.

'Allan has made some really stupid mistakes. I'm afraid he is about to make an even worse one now. I've got to try and stop him. You do understand, don't you? He's gone up to Aoife's Chariot, but there's absolutely no way the car will get over there in this storm.' I pause, putting my hands up to Hugh's face. 'I know how to get there on foot. It's straight up the hillside to Loch Crannox and then over the 'saddle' between Ben Keir and Ben Mhor. There are no high peaks it's just a straightforward scramble. I've done it a hundred times before.'

'But not in this weather,' Hugh whispers almost inaudibly.

'I've got to do this. I can't prove my theory, so there's no point in calling the police or anything. I'll have to go it alone. I'll take the flashlight and your proper rain jacket. I need you to stay here and take care of yourself, man the phones and I'll be back before you even notice that I've gone.'

Hugh nods his head but says nothing. As I take hold of both his hands to say goodbye he looks away. standing up to go I see that he can no longer hold onto the tears, which are running, gently and uncontrollably, down his face.

## Chapter 27

I am absolutely terrified at the thought of what lies ahead. Taking several deep breaths, I keep myself occupied, rushing around the farmhouse, gathering together equipment and supplies.

I tip out the contents of one of our rucksacks, filling it instead with two spare jumpers, the flashlight, my mobile phone and a packet of chocolate biscuits that Hugh bought in Kilross this morning. I fill an empty plastic bottle with water and place it in the string pocket at the side of the bag. Putting on Hugh's waterproof Macintosh and Mum's wellie boots I try to forget about how badly they pinch my feet and concentrate on the fact they are probably the best form of footwear to be sporting out on the hillside today.

As ready as I will ever be I step out through the kitchen door, closing it gently but firmly behind me. The rain is still lashing down into the glen, but looking ahead of me along the footpath, I feel it is not quite as heavy as it was before. Setting off at a fast pace I resolve to make good time where the going is reasonable, as there will be sections of this walk where the terrain will become slow and difficult. As I look to the side of me, along the meadow bank, I become aware of what a great job Danny Monroe did for us. The rainfall today has been amongst the worst the valley has ever been subjected to but the path along this section is almost unaffected.

The water has flowed into Danny's extensive system of ditches and pipes, leaving the farmhouse and its surrounding area little touched by the flood. I quickly reach the first stile and from here have a good view up the mountainside. I figure there may be roughly two to three hours of daylight left. The plan is to reach the basin of Aoife's Chariot by then. Every ten minutes or so I try Allan's mobile phone but there is no reply.

I ascend the steep and rocky section which runs along at approximately two hundred feet above the farmhouse. The ground here seems little disturbed by the massive volume of water that has fallen over the past couple of hours. As I climb further up, beyond the second stile, the path follows the course of the burn and as this higher section comes into view I gasp. What is usually a gentle stream of peaty brown water is now a torrent of white spray, bubbling in deep plunge pools and cascading down the steepest sections like a dozen impressive waterfalls.

I pull my hood up tighter and carrying on walking, trying to keep focussed on where to place my feet and not on what the conditions will be like when I reach what will be the worst section of the trek, the huge expanse of boggy marshland at the foot of Ben Keir. I make good progress along this section and wherever the path has been encroached upon by the swollen burn I make a zig-zag motion across the slope, moving towards drier terrain where I can hold on to the limpit-like heather and gorse to help me stay on my feet. I am careful never to lose sight of the path, which remains my greatest fear in this poor visibility.

When I reach the first summit and Loch Crannox finally comes into view, it becomes clear just how much I have been sheltered from the elements by the hillside up to this point. The wind in this scooped out, glaciated valley suddenly drives the rain directly into my face. For a few moments I wonder if it will be possible for me to carry on. But keeping my head right down and edging my way around the side of the loch, seems to work, as the softer hills which enclose this natural pool provide me with some protection. Loch Crannox itself appears to have doubled in size. The water is lapping at the base of the hills and the pebble beach is completely submerged.

I find a decent bit of shelter behind a large rock halfway up the side of the hill and wedge myself in to take a sip of water and eat some chocolate biscuits. I take out my phone to call Hugh but there is no signal. Hills surround me on three of four sides and they must be blocking any reception. It probably won't be of any use to me until I've got beyond the mountains so the mobile goes back into my pocket.

I keep leaning into the hillside, sidestepping gingerly around the ridge until I've reached the main path again. As I look back in the direction from which I have come, it appears as if there may be a break in the iron grey clouds that hang over the Kilbrannan Sound. But straight ahead lies the worst of the storm, which seems to be following a steady course from west to east.

The brow of the hill is situated about two hundred feet above Loch Crannox. From here, the sight that I have been dreading comes into view. Between this point and the foot of 'the saddle' is a huge area of boggy and waterlogged marshland. Today, from this elevated position, it simply looks like a vast, dark green sea. I stand in the pouring rain, looking out at this totally unfamiliar landscape. For a little while at least, I truly believe it will be necessary to turn back. But then I see a recognisable landmark, lying to the south-east of the marsh.

There is a set of ancient standing stones here which are sited in a long and precise line across this section of the marsh. They lead right up to the foot of 'the saddle'. I have visited these ancient monuments many times with my brothers, when as kids we would climb up onto them, laying ourselves out flat on the smoothest ones, like lizards in the desert sun.

Today, they are almost unrecognisable as that natural playground of my childhood, but they do offer me just the faintest glimmer of hope. I scramble down the slope and keep bearing to the right, continuing for as far as possible until I have got to a point where the water is so deep it reaches a quarter of the way up the hillside. All of the features I would usually recognise are gone, submerged underneath these unprecedented levels of rainwater.

Then I see the first of the large and sturdy stones, narrowly protruding out of the deep water. It is probably about five feet away from me. I am going to have to jump for it. Making sure my rucksack is secured tightly to my back I take a short run-up and leap towards the smooth edifice.

I get my arms and upper body comfortably clear of the water but my legs and feet go in, causing me to draw a sharp intake of breath as the ice cold sludge starts to fill up my boots. I wriggle onto the top of the sandstone rock, pulling my lower half out of the water. I note with relief that the other stones are not positioned quite so far apart. All that should be necessary from here is to take a small running jump between each of the rocks. However, I can't prevent myself from pausing to look out at the unearthly scene and it immediately makes me want to roll up into a ball and panic.

I make a concerted effort simply to focus on the rocks themselves. I examine the contours of their reddish brown surfaces, each one being totally unique after having withstood thousands of years of natural erosion. I notice that the weather is most definitely lifting. The east coast of Garansay is probably being pounded right at this moment but at least I am getting some relief and the rain has diminished now to a steady drizzle.

The visibility is improving. When I get into my stride I am able to reach the last of the stones in good time. The very final standing stone is not as tall as the others. As a result, it is totally submerged beneath the surface of this artificial loch. The gap between me and dry land is probably about the width of a standard swimming pool. With time running out and little choice left I decide to make a swim for it.

Taking off my rucksack and using all of my strength, I toss it as far as possible. It lands in a gorse bush on the opposite bank. I take a deep breath and lower myself into the freezing, muddy water. I know the greatest danger is the risk of hypothermia so I try to keep moving, kicking my arms and legs frantically in a vain attempt to propel myself forward.

I had no idea what effect this terrible, enveloping cold would have on my already exhausted body. My feet and hands are growing numb and only about half the way across it feels as if I've completely lost control of my limbs. I resolve just to float here for a while until I can regain some energy. Suddenly it seems a little warmer and the thought occurs to me that if I can stay like this for a little while longer, I will be able to find the strength to continue to the other side.

Then I see her, standing on the opposite bank, holding out her hand to me. She is calling my name and encouraging me to swim towards her. She's telling me to lift my feet up off the ground and kick myself back to the shore. It's lovely and sunny and the water feels so beautifully warm, almost like a deeply filled bath. I call back to Mum that I'm coming, that I can do it, look at me, Mum! I can do it!

Happily drifting away into this beautiful dream I experience a stabbing pain in my side. Suddenly, I don't feel the lovely warmth any longer and instead the overriding sensation is one of being appallingly cold. The jabbing in my side comes again and this time it is accompanied by a painful scratching against my skin. It feels as if I'm being brutally dragged through the glacial water. During this onslaught I battle to open my weary eyes and when I do, see that I'm now lying on the bank. It's impossible to make out much else because of the thick covering of grasses and gorse which surround me.

Being aware of the need to make myself wake up, I keep fighting to move every one of my leaden limbs, in order to get the blood flowing back into them. I become aware that somebody else is doing the same thing. A large figure is leaning over me, rubbing vigorously at my arms and legs. After a few minutes of this, I feel myself being hoisted up into a sitting position.

A disembodied voice says, 'I need to get these wet clothes off okay? And then I'm going to put you into my dry ones alright?' The voice mutters to itself, 'you bloody well know how to sober a man up, Mrs Croft, and that's no mistake.'

I close my eyes again and smile, letting Allan pull off my sopping wet trousers and shirt and wrapping me up in his own jacket which smells of fags and whisky and pubs in general, but at this moment in time, I find it the most reassuring and wonderful smell in the world.

## Chapter 28

Once I have regained some movement in my limbs and can sit up unaided, I tell Allan there are two of Hugh's jumpers in the bottom of my ruck-sack. After he has gone over to fetch them we each put one on. Allan empties the water out of my wellington boots and pushes them back onto my bare feet.

'Are you going to be able to walk back up the hillside with me?' he asks warily.

'I'll give it a try,' I reply.

Allan helps to lift me up onto my feet. With my arm around his shoulders, he leads me slowly to the top of the muddy bank. After that, it is a fairly short scramble down to the small loch at the foot of Aoife's Chariot. The ground here is not quite as waterlogged as it was on the other side of 'the saddle'. Allan informs me that the storm has not been as bad on this side of the Island as it must have been in the west. He says the weather seemed to just blow itself out. I find that walking is a little easier now and the final descent, the one that leads down to Alison's little row of cottages, I can manage without Allan's assistance.

When we reach the bottom I am amazed to see my brother walk confidently through the back gate of 'Alba Cottage'. He goes straight into the house through Alison's weatherworn French doors, calmly entering the tiny kitchen beyond. 'It's okay,' he calls out to me when I hold back, unsure of whether to follow him, 'you can come in, Imogen.'

I shuffle into the cottage and Allan escorts me into the sitting room, which is empty except for a sofa, coffee table and sideboard that runs the entire length of one of the white washed walls. He sits me down on the sofa and goes back into the little kitchen where I hear him carefully filling up a kettle and flicking on the switch. I wait quietly until Allan comes back into the sitting room with two mugs of steaming tea. He places them on the small wooden table whilst lowering himself into the empty space next to me.

'I owe you an explanation,' he says softly.

I do not reply, simply allowing him to continue.

'Davy told me the landlord just couldn't get anyone to rent this place - not after what had happened here. I still had a key, so I came over this afternoon and spent a bit of time here, before going to the pub.'

'Why do you have a key to Alison's cottage?'

'I'm coming to that, I promise. Just let me start with today okay?'

I nod patiently.

'I had planned to come here, get totally plastered and then head up to the loch with a bottle of whisky. Just to drown my sorrows you understand, not necessarily myself. Well, I wasn't quite sure what I was going to do, if I'm honest. Then the rain came on and it seemed to be particularly bad just over the hill, so I climbed up to have a look, get to higher ground and all that. From there I saw, in the distance, some damned fool trying to cross the flooded moor. I couldn't quite believe my eyes but it looked like it was you. I shouted and shouted but you didn't seem to hear me. Then you just disappeared into the mire. I ran down the slope, well, slid most of the way, and found a big stick and dragged you onto the bank. The rest is history, as they say.'

'I do appreciate it, thank you,' I say quite sincerely.

'But I expect you were only doing it because you were out looking for your idiot brother. It kind of cancels out the good deed, doesn't it?' Allan stares into his mug of tea.

'Just tell me what you've done. We will deal with it, whatever it is, I promise.' I lay my hand on his damp knee.

Allan lets out a sigh. 'Everything I told you about Mum's satchel is completely true. I still have no idea what was inside it. She never told me. But when I said I'd not had any contact with Alison since we all lived at home here, that was a lie. We did break up after the incident with Mum's bag and I had nothing to do with her for years afterwards. I swear that nothing happened whilst I was married to Suz. For all of that time, I thought Suz was the one for me and would never have cheated on her. But when she had that affair, down in London, everything changed. It was so devastating and I just couldn't get it out of my head. I couldn't look at her in the same way. After Suz moved back to Scotland and we'd got our divorce, I happened to be up in Glasgow on business. That's when I bumped into her again - after all those years.'

'Alison.'

'She was taking part in some kind of arts festival and was in town getting materials and stuff. We went for a drink. Hell, you know what she was like. She was charming and funny. I just forgot about what happened when we were kids because it felt like it hadn't been real, you know?'

'You started seeing one another,' I prompt.

'On and off. If I was in Scotland on business we would meet up, with me coming here for a weekend sometimes. She gave me a key a couple of years back. It was nothing regular, I swear.'

'What about Abigail?' I can't stop myself from asking.

'It never meant I didn't love Abigail, I still do. But nothing was the same after Suz. It just felt like that part of my life - the family and the marriage and all that stuff was over and done with. So it didn't really matter what I did.'

'Oh Allan.'

'Alison and I weren't still together when you found the bag last October and we had that confrontation. I'd broken it off with her three months before then. That part was all true.' Allan appears almost proud of himself.

'Did you know Alison was blackmailing Mum?' I ask sternly.

Allan looks genuinely shocked. He clasps hold of my hands and says, 'I had no idea she was doing that. You've got to believe me. I've been a bloody fool but I wouldn't do that to Mum, or to you and Michael. I love you,' he pleads.

I sit quietly for a little while, trying to get my head around what Allan is saying to me. I desperately want to believe him but just don't know if I can. 'Okay, if I say that I believe you didn't know about the blackmail, can you tell me if you ever spoke about me with her. Did the two of you laugh about me behind my back?'

Allan lets go of my hands and his eyes drop down to his lap. This gives me my answer before he even utters a word. 'It wasn't like that. But we did speak about you, yes. It was mostly Alison. She just had this thing about you being a real 'goody two shoes', with your perfect family. You know what I'm like, I enjoy teasing you. I don't bloody well mean it.'

I take a sip of tea and find there is a huge lump in my throat. I swallow it down as best as I can, desperate not to let Allan see how upset this has made me.

'The simple explanation is that she was jealous. I certainly know *I* was. You and Hugh were still together after all this time and there was me having lost my marriage and ballsed everything up, *of course* I was jealous. But it wasn't your marriage and your kids that Alison had a thing about. It was you and Michael.'

'Me and *Michael*?' I repeat, genuinely puzzled.

'Fundamentally, she was stuck in the past. Alison wasn't interested in real, adult relationships. She had that obsession with Michael when we were teenagers. I always knew I was the poor substitute for the real thing. She used to think you had 'bewitched' him. That was the exact word she used, because when we were all together he always put you first. In her mind, I truly think she believed that if it wasn't for you, she and Michael would have been together.'

'But that's crazy - I was only a baby. Michael was looking after me, especially after Dad died. He was my big brother for heaven's sake.'

Allan shrugs his shoulders.

'Look, there are some things I need to think through here. I'm going to give Hugh a call first.'

Allan nods and says he's going to go and make himself presentable. He gives me a peck on the cheek as he stands up. I sit, rigid in my seat and don't respond. I'm not quite ready to forgive him just yet.

I go into the kitchen and dial Hugh's mobile number. He picks up almost immediately. I tell him I'm safe and Allan is fine too. Hugh informs me that Colin Walmsley came over not long after I had gone. He had brought his 4x4, but even that couldn't get up the flooded driveway. Colin walked up the track to see if we were all okay, getting a bit panicky when he saw the crashed car. Since then, Colin has been keeping Hugh company at the farm. I tell him to stay put and make sure he has something to eat because I'm stuck here for the time being and can always get a room at the Gilstone Hotel if necessary.

I feel stronger for having spoken to Hugh. Allan has come back downstairs and is moving about in the living room. I go along the dark, narrow corridor, stand in the doorway to the dingy room and say, 'why did you break it off with her, three months before we came back to Garansay? If it wasn't serious then why break up? That makes it sound like a proper relationship.'

'I can assure you it wasn't - not on my part anyway. I had to end it because I found out something about her that I didn't like. Something which reminded me of the person she used to be.' Allan turns to look out of the bay window.

'What was that?' I ask, venturing further into the room.

'You should ask your mate Heathcliff, because he knows more about it than I do.'

'Colin? But Hugh's with him now. Do I need to warn him?' I start to become alarmed.

'Oh, he's not dangerous at all, just a fool, like me.'

I storm across the room, take hold of Allan by the arm, spin him around to face me and say, 'you'd better tell me exactly what you know Allan Nichols and tell me right now, because I've lost all patience with your cryptic bloody jokes alright?'

Allan looks penitent and replies, 'look, I'm sorry. I'll tell you absolutely everything Imogen, I promise.'

## Chapter 29

Allan was starting to get twitchy about staying in the cottage, in case one of the neighbours heard us and mentioned something to the landlord. So we tidied away all traces of having been there and headed down the long garden path to the sea-front, finding ourselves a bench facing out towards the more gentle gradients of the Ayrshire hills.

You would never know now there had ever been a storm at all. The dark clouds have completely dispersed and although it isn't warm, there is just the faintest hint of a sunset still lingering over the Clyde. Within a few minutes of us being there, the dim orange light is finally extinguished along the water's dark horizon.

I have on Hugh's jumper and a pair of leggings we found upstairs in the cottage which must have somehow got left behind. I do not feel at all queasy about wearing a piece of Alison's clothing. Instead it pleases me, because I consider that she owes me a favour.

Allan is starting to look tired. I think to myself that he has been living a life no self-respecting man approaching his fifties should be living. He should be playing golf on a Sunday, growing plump on his wife's home-cooking and looking forward to retirement. Not going on pub-crawls and hanging about with an old flame from his childhood who was nothing better than a blackmailer and a thief. He has really made a mess of things.

As if Allan can tell what I have been thinking he has the good grace to look ashamed as he carries on with his sorry tale. 'I turned up here one Saturday. Abigail was on a hen-weekend and I decided to get an early morning flight up to Glasgow and surprise Alison. I got off the mid-morning boat and jumped straight into a cab. That's what I always did, just to make sure no one I knew in Kilross spotted me. The taxi dropped me off at about 11ish.

There was a great big 4x4 parked up on the grass verge at the end of Alison's front garden but I thought nothing of it. As I was walking up the path towards the cottage, Colin Walmsley came storming out with a face like thunder. My immediate thought was that Alison had another bloke on the go. I couldn't exactly have blamed her. I thought he was about to thump me. But Colin just carried on past and shouted back that he didn't know what on earth I was doing with someone like her. He just got into the car after that and drove off.'

'Did you ask Alison about it?'

'Well, she was overjoyed to see me at first, or she pretended to be.' He clears his throat awkwardly. 'Later on, I challenged her. She said that Colin was a fool because he'd paid her to keep quiet about a piece of evidence she no longer had. Alison said the expression on his face when she told him this fact was priceless.'

'She'd been blackmailing Colin?' I blurt out, 'as well as Mum?'

'She didn't actually spell it out, but that was how I interpreted it. I never had the slightest idea she'd done the same thing to Mum. When she told me she'd been getting money from Colin I did not like it one little bit and Alison had that look, the one she'd had when she produced Mum's bag from behind the hay bale all those years ago. Seeing it again made me feel physically sick.'

'So you finished it then. When was that exactly?' I enquire.

'It must have been at the end of July or early August last year.'

I think about this for a while, considering whether to take Allan into my confidence after everything he has done. In the end, I decide there isn't much choice, turn to face him and say, 'at the end of July, Mum paid Alison twenty thousand pounds. They both claimed it was for a painting, but the painting doesn't seem to exist and there is no way Mum would have paid that kind of money for Alison's artwork,' I pause whilst trying to gauge Allan's reaction to this news. He simply looks confused. 'Hugh and I decided this money must have been some type of pay-off. Mum gave Alison a lump sum in order to stop the blackmail or, more likely, to return whatever it was that Alison had in her possession which rightfully belonged to Mum.'

Allan is utterly aghast. 'You don't think it was whatever was in Mum's bag do you? What if Alison never got rid of it and she'd been blackmailing Mum for all those years? I don't believe I could bear it if that were true.' He rests his head in his hands.

'I'm very sorry, Allan. That's exactly what I think.' I lay my hand on his back. 'You are the only person who ever got a glimpse at the contents of the bag. Can you remember anything about it at all? What on earth could have been in that satchel? Why would Mum have allowed herself to be at the mercy of Alison Dickson for all that time and not tell us about it, when we might have been able to help her?'

Allan is concentrating hard. It is getting quite dark now, but the bench we are sitting on is illuminated by the yellowish glow of the street light outside the Gilstone Hotel. Allan is sitting so that the artificial beam is behind him. His face is in complete shadow. I cannot read his expression at all.

'I've tried to recall what Alison took out of that satchel a hundred times, but I just can't picture it. All I can tell you is that it contained papers of some kind and maybe an envelope, like a letter. It didn't appear to hold any jewellery or larger objects, yet I couldn't absolutely swear to it, because she stuffed it all in her bag so quickly. I'm sorry Imogen.'

I've been concentrating hard myself during this time. 'You said it was the end of July or early August when you saw Colin storm out of Alison's cottage. Alison had just told him she no longer possessed whatever it was she had been blackmailing him with.'

Allan nods.

'And this was a few days after Mum had paid twenty thousand pounds to get back whatever material Alison had on *her*. So, what if it was one and the same thing? That whatever Alison was blackmailing Mum with, was the *same thing* she was blackmailing Colin with? I have no idea what it could possibly be but I just have a feeling that whatever damning evidence Alison had on Mum, was directly connected to what she had on Colin.'

\*

I give Hugh another call on the mobile to see if Colin Walmsley is still at Lower Kilduggan Farm. It turns out he is. Hugh says that once the water levels had sufficiently dropped, Colin went to tow our car out of the hedge with his 4X4. It wasn't an easy job so Colin stayed for a drink. Hugh was just about to offer him dinner. I tell my husband to keep Colin there for as long as possible. Allan and I will join them as soon as we can.

It is nearly nine o'clock. I can't imagine how on earth we are going to get ourselves back over to Lower Kilduggan from a sleepy backwater like Gilstone at this hour. I say as much to Allan, who immediately declares, 'well, I do know a chap. He's a fisherman and lives in one of the little cottages opposite the harbour. He's not licensed or anything, but he drives people about the Island. He takes the tourists back to their holiday homes when they've had a drink in the pub and that sort of thing. I've used him quite often myself, he's very discreet, if you know what I mean. We could give him a try if you'd like?'

I never cease to be amazed at the ways in which Garansay can be a law unto itself, but say absolutely nothing, simply allowing Allan to take the lead. We pass the Gilstone Hotel, round the sharp corner at the tip of the headland and proceed towards the pretty little harbour on the other side of the village. The fisherman-cum-taxi-driver is exactly where Allan said he would be and is extremely grateful to get a job in before the holiday drinkers start spilling out of the hotel in a couple of hours from now, looking for a cheap lift home.

Our driver turns out to be called Dougie and seems to know Allan very well. The two men chat contentedly for the whole journey. We drive back along the coastal route to Kilross and then over the Glenrannoch road, cutting straight through the mountains and the low lying moorland which delineate the western side of the island. Finally, we reach Lower Kilduggan Farm just as the daylight has been completely usurped by the bluish radiance of a huge circular moon.

There is still plenty of evidence left of the earlier storm. The single-track road that runs through the low lying heathland and then meanders up to the farm is quite flooded in places, but not enough to give the car any real trouble. I tell Dougie he can drop us off at the end of the drive. When Allan has paid him with a couple of crisp Scottish notes and bid him a fond farewell we both walk purposefully up the steep pathway.

Approaching the front of the farmhouse, we see a cheery triangle of light projected onto the gravel of the courtyard. It seems to have been created by the warm glow emanating from the kitchen window. Suddenly, I am reminded of Avril Paton's painting of the Glasgow tenement building and of the cosy interiors of those refurbished flats, contrasting sharply with the cold white of the snow outside.

When Allan and I open the kitchen door we find Hugh and Colin sitting at the kitchen table. I can immediately tell the atmosphere is jovial and friendly. Hugh jumps up to embrace me, his face a picture of relief.

'Thank goodness you're back,' he declares, 'although Colin has done an excellent job of keeping me buoyed up. He kept reminding me how you knew those hills like the back of your hand.'

I look at Colin and smile in gratitude. Somehow he realised that staying with Hugh would be more useful to me than him tearing up the hillside in hot pursuit. Hugh asks if we have eaten yet, when he finds out we have not he busies himself, making sandwiches and pouring out glasses of beer and wine.

When we are all supplied with food and drinks, I take a deep breath and say, 'Colin, I know this is absolutely none of my business, but Allan told me he saw you once, in the summer of last year. It was just after you'd had an argument with Alison Dickson at her cottage. Allan said he got the impression Alison had some kind of hold over you. The reason I am asking you about this is because we believe Alison had a hold over our Mum too. We are desperate to find out what it might have been. I sense you can help us to discover what it was, is that true?'

The query hangs in the air between us for a few seconds. Hugh looks at me and furrows his brow in puzzlement.

Colin gazes around the table. 'I knew you would be asking me this question at some point, Imogen. Before answering, I want to let you know that I always wanted to tell you and your brothers what was going on. There was a very good reason why I didn't. Your mother swore me to secrecy. She did not want her children to know, so you need to think very carefully about whether you would like me to tell you. Once I have, there is no going back.'

I glance at Allan. His face is tired and drawn, suddenly giving me a clear image of what keeping secrets has already done to our family. I say, without any hesitation, 'we have to know. Whatever the consequences, we will deal with them.'

'I'm very relieved to hear you say that, because I have found the burden very difficult to carry.' Colin adds, 'so has my mum.'

'Kitty?' I exclaim.

'Yes, it was Mum's secret to carry really, not mine. She was the one who swore to Isabel that she would never utter a word and she never has, but there has been a cost to that pledge. I want Mum to be able to get it all off her chest before she goes.' Colin's eyes glisten in the subtle glow of the oil lamp flickering on the kitchen sideboard.

I have a strange sensation which is a mixture of both excitement and dread as Colin continues.

'I will tell you my side of the story first. If you can bear to wait another night, I would like to take you to see Mum in the morning and she can tell you her side of things. She may be a bit confused and hazy about the here and now but Mum remembers the past perfectly clearly. That is why this business has upset her so much.'

I nod my head, feeling it would be best to follow Colin's lead otherwise we may never find out the truth. We make ourselves comfortable in our seats, cupping our hands around our drinks and remaining perfectly silent whilst Colin begins his story.

'Alison Dickson had managed to get her hands on a bag of your mother's. This bag contained some important and personal documents that Isabel had not wanted anyone else to see. There were some family papers in amongst them and it was in one of these that Alison first saw the name, Mary Anne Galbraith. Alison had gone through your mother's bag with a fine-toothed comb. Even at this young age she had a kind of special instinct for useful information. A blackmailer's eye you might call it. When she saw the name Mary Galbraith, it rang a bell with her. Alison said she had heard it before somewhere, perhaps in her childhood. So she decided to look into it further. It happened that Alison had a young man friend who was a police constable down in Kilross. He had made sure a blind eye was turned to her drinking in the pubs when she was underage and that sort of thing. Alison asked him about the name she was so sure she had heard mentioned on Garansay. He dutifully did some checks for her, having a good look through the police records.

This was how Alison Dickson found out all the details of Mary Galbraith's death and the police investigation which followed. What she also discovered from her policeman friend, information that had not been released publically at the time, was how my father had been the chief suspect in that investigation. The constable told her the police back then had been utterly convinced Dad killed Mary. They just didn't have enough evidence to prove it.

Alison knew she could use this information to her advantage. She waited and planned. Then, one day when she saw Mum in the General Store, Alison asked if she could come up to the farm some time to do her sketching. She mentioned the lovely views from Glen Crannox and the smugglers cove. Of course, Mum said yes. Alison came over quite regularly during one particular summer holiday, during the day time, when Sandra and I were at home in the farmhouse with Mum and Dad would be outside working.

One day, Alison was up the glen with her sketch pad while Dad was tending the sheep in the next field. Alison went to chat to him over the fence. She asked politely about his flock and the sheepdog, seeming very interested and quite sweet. Then, without warning, Alison abruptly took off down the hill to the farmhouse, running as fast as her legs could carry her.

Sandra and I were in the kitchen with Mum. I remember it as if it were yesterday. Alison came rushing in, looking terrified and with her dress all creased. She was covered in grass stains and straw. She cried out that Dad had attacked her, "tried it on", she claimed, and then got heavy when Alison had refused his advances.

Mum appeared completely shell-shocked. She quickly ushered me and Sandra out of the room, but we hovered in the hallway and listened. Alison was very clever. She must have known that Mum had probably lost a bit of faith in Dad after the Mary Galbraith case, and there might be that tiny part of her which could believe her husband capable of such a thing.

Perhaps Mum did believe her story, for those first few minutes, but then it started to become crystal clear what Alison Dickson was really after. When Mum was pouring her a glass of water and Alison was sat down at the kitchen table, the young woman's tears seemed to suddenly dry up.

She looked at Mum and said to her, in a very matter-of-fact way, 'I know what your husband did - back in 1973 - to that woman who was found dead in the loch. I know it was him that killed her. I'm going to tell everyone on this Island. Then I'm going to tell them what he tried to do to me, too.' After she said it, she folded her arms, sitting back in the chair with an expression on her face which must have persuaded Mum this was no idle threat.

Mum asked her what she wanted. She knew what Garansay was like. Mum was aware that if they got caught up in that kind of scandal they would have to flee their farm. Sandra and I would be forced to leave school. They loved it up there in the glen, it was their life.

Alison was clever with the blackmail too. She didn't ask Mum for very much at first, just some money here and there for her art equipment. Occasionally, she would ask for the fare to Glasgow so she could attend an interview at one of the art colleges there.

Sometimes months would go by and it seemed she had forgotten about us. Then, Alison would be back, wanting something else. But it was never too much. I think she knew that if she asked for more than we could afford to spare we would call her bluff. As it was, the whole thing dragged on for years. After Dad died I took over the payments, which I could quite easily manage as the farm got larger and more profitable.

There was another reason why I kept paying up too. I am very fond of Davy and his parents. I didn't like the idea of them finding out exactly what kind of a sister and daughter they really had.' Colin turns towards Allan. 'That morning, when you saw me coming out of Alison's cottage, we had argued. The day before, I had gone to visit Isabel. As I pulled up to the farmhouse, Alison was leaving. She had that triumphant smirk on her face - the one she had when she confronted Mum in the kitchen all those years ago. Alison quickly got into her little car and drove away. I went around to the open kitchen door and called out to Isabel, but there was no reply. When I entered the house, I found her sitting, slumped in the armchair in the living room. I couldn't recall ever having seen your mother sitting down before, she was usually always on the go.

I knew instinctively why Alison had been at Lower Kilduggan that day. I asked your mother if she would tell me all about it and she did. That's when I discovered how Alison had been tipped off about Mary Galbraith from the material she'd taken from your mother's bag. Isabel explained that she'd finally persuaded Alison to let her buy back the documents which had been so cruelly taken from her thirty years before. When she finished her tale Isabel sobbed with relief.

It turned out Alison had got herself into arrears with the rent and heating bills. She also told your Mum she needed to buy a plane ticket, she was going away somewhere. So, for the first time in all of those years, she was finally prepared to let your poor mother off the hook. Finding out Alison had been blackmailing Isabel for all that time made me furious. I left Lower Kilduggan and marched straight over to Alison's cottage where we had a blazing row. In the heat of the exchange I suddenly didn't care about Davy, Susie or Jimmy anymore - I just wanted her out of my life.

I told her that if she no longer possessed the evidence then she wouldn't be getting another penny out of me and stormed out. I figured that with Dad having passed away there wasn't much she could do to us anymore. Then I bumped into you, Allan.'

Allan nods but he has a hangdog expression on his face which indicates to me it has finally sunk in what a truly wicked person he was involved with for all that time.

'Now, this last part of the story is the one I am least proud of. I sincerely hope you can find it in your hearts to forgive me for my actions, once you have heard me out. After the end of July of last year, Alison's behaviour started to become increasingly erratic. She was drinking heavily and causing trouble in a number of local pubs. Then, at the start of October, just after your mother had passed away, Davy was called out to pick Alison up from a pub in Kilross where she was making a nuisance of herself. He asked me to come with him.

As I helped to steer Alison's drunken body up the path to her cottage, Davy said he had to go back to the car for the spare key. For a moment, Alison and I were alone. She whispered something in my ear during that moment which made my blood run cold. She told me she knew exactly where Isabel had put the documents after she'd sold them back to her. Alison said that now Isabel was dead she was going to break into Lower Kilduggan Farm and get them back. She said it as if they were *her* property - like she had some kind of right to have them in her possession once more.

I knew then, as she uttered those words, that it was going to start all over again. She would use the evidence to blackmail someone else in your family. I just couldn't let that happen.'

I start to feel very uneasy about what Colin might be about to confess to us but remain silent.

'What Alison had said to me on that evening kept preying on my mind for the next few weeks. Then, when you arrived on Garansay during that time, I became even more concerned. I was worried you see, that as you and Allan were clearing out the farmhouse, one of you would find your Mum's documents. You would then discover the secret that your mother had, at all costs, tried to protect you from.

So, against all of my instincts, I went back to 'Alba Cottage'. I knew you had gone over to the mainland because one of my pals had seen you get on the boat. I confronted Alison and told her she needed to show me where Isabel had put those documents. My plan was to let Alison lead me to the papers and then I would burn them, so that you would never find out your mother's secret and Alison couldn't use them to blackmail anybody else. We argued for some time. I became quite rough with her, finally bundling her into the jeep, taking her over to Lower Kilduggan with me in the vain hope she would tell me where to look.

I frog marched Alison up to the kitchen door. Mum had told me where Isabel kept the key, but when I looked under the rock there was nothing there. I am deeply sorry for this. I took the rock and threw it through the top pane of glass. I didn't want to cause any more damage so we cleared away the remaining shards from the frame and I forced Alison to climb through.

She was as skinny as a child so she slipped in very easily. Then I made her go round and open the front door. I am not proud of this, but we both wore gloves, which came out of the back of my 4x4. We searched for hours but couldn't find a thing. The place where Alison thought the papers would be - under a loose floorboard in one of the back bedrooms - contained some old porn mags but nothing else.

When there was nowhere left to investigate we went outside. I suddenly felt exhausted, humiliated and disgusted with myself. So I left Alison there. I didn't even look at her. I climbed into my car and drove off home without giving her a second thought.'

I think about this for a few minutes. 'Alison must have trekked back home over the hills, just like I did today.'

'Yes,' Colin says, 'and I promise she was still alive when I left her. She would have had a lot of time to think on that long walk home. She thought about what she had lost. She no longer had any power over me or your mother. She was very angry, that much I do know.'

'She no longer had her relationship with me either,' Allan mutters, so faintly we almost can't make out his words.

Colin states with feeling, 'I'd known Alison Dickson for most of my life and like to think I've a good idea of what made her tick. She wasn't really interested in the money she received from the blackmail. What Alison enjoyed was having power over people. To be able to play around with folk and manipulate them is what drove her on. What I believe happened on that day, as she was walking back from Lower Kilduggan Farm, over the hills and the glens to the foot of Aoife's Chariot, was that she was plotting her revenge. One more act designed to cause terrible problems for those she'd left behind.

When she finally reached home she got herself steaming drunk, took a few pills and then calmly walked up the steep footpath to the flooded loch. She removed her clothes down to her underwear, maybe even burying them somewhere to add to the effect and then she drowned herself in the water.

Alison wanted her own death to be a mirror image of the way in which Mary Galbraith had died forty years ago. I believe she hoped the details would encourage the police to make a link with the old case. Then all the sordid details about my father's involvement with Mary Galbraith would be made public.

She couldn't have predicted how perfectly her plan would work. As it turned out, it was me who found her body, which had meant it was an absolute certainty the police would start making connections. Alison Dickson managed to cause problems for me and my family right up to the last.'

I want so much for Colin to carry on and tell me what it was that Alison had discovered about my mother and my family that I did not know, but I don't. I realise this will have to be Kitty's story. If I am patient for just a little while longer, I will be given the final piece of the puzzle. I decide to empty my mind of everything tonight, because after tomorrow, things will never be the same for us ever again.

# Chapter 30

Although determined not to brood on what Colin had told us, I spent last night drifting in and out of sleep. Various images and phrases kept floating into my fractured consciousness. Over an early breakfast, I put vocal form to some of my ideas.

'I've been thinking about where Mum might have put the documents she bought back from Alison.'

Allan looks up from the buttered toast he has been pushing around his plate but not eating.

Now I have his attention, I continue, 'Colin and Alison looked everywhere in this house for them but to no avail, right? So, if we are assuming that she didn't just shred or burn them which, somehow, I don't think she did then perhaps we have been looking in the wrong places.'

Hugh appears interested now, his curiosity having been pricked enough to divert him from his plate of bacon and scrambled eggs. 'Of course,' he adds, 'who said that she put the papers in the house at all? There are loads of places around the farm they could be. She might even have given them to a trusted friend to look after.'

'Exactly. But I don't think she would have had time to do that. I still believe they are around the farm somewhere,' I suggest.

'We have to try and think like Mum,' Allan says. 'She would have wanted them to be close to her. She'd lost the stuff once and would put them in a hiding place she could keep an eye on nearly every day - just to reassure herself they were safe.'

'Yes, I agree,' I say excitedly, impressed by Allan's unusual flash of insight.

'Well. There's only one place that Isabel went to every day in the months leading up to her death,' Hugh says. 'It was the summer season and Isabel spent all of her days in the pottery shed, either making pots or manning the shop.'

I give my husband a pat on the back then begin rummaging in the cutlery drawer, bringing out a rolling pin and two heavy, stainless steel kitchen utensils; a ladle and a pasta drainer. Both of which get handed to a bemused Allan and Hugh.

'Follow me.'

I lead the two men out of the kitchen and across the courtyard to the pottery shed. It is a little alarming to discover that no one remembered to lock up the doors last night, in all the excitement of the flood. But when I peer inside, everything appears to be just as it was yesterday afternoon.

'Right. If you needed to hide something really precious in here, then I know exactly where you'd put it.' I stand with my hands on my hips in the middle of the barn. Hugh and Allan look nonplussed. '*Inside* one of the pots.'

'Can you do that?' Allan asks as he picks up a vase and examines it carefully.

'Of course, you could put an item into the base of a pot quite easily. Who is ever going to think to look there?'

'You obviously,' says Hugh with a cheeky grin, adding with relish, 'I think I'm going to enjoy this next bit.'

I inform Hugh and Allan that we are going to smash all of the pots, vases, cups and plates in the entire barn until we find what we are searching for. Allan still looks highly sceptical but he joins in any way. For the next twenty minutes, the shed is filled with the tremendous cacophony of crockery being smashed to pieces. A thick cloud of clay dust envelopes us as we work our way through all of the pots. If any one were to happen to come along at this particular point in time and see what we are doing, they would think we had completely lost our minds.

Stopping to cough away some of the dust in my lungs, I take a moment to look around me at the mess we have created. For an instant, I wonder if I have got it completely wrong, panicking that we might have destroyed Mum's precious work for no good reason at all. But then, my eyes settle on a large, portly owl - the one that gave me such a fright the last time we were in here because it was so life-like. It is perched high up on a shelf, just behind the door, a little out of direct sight. Mum had obviously used it to sit outside the building as a notice to visitors. I remember how it announces, around its thick and sturdy base, that the pottery shed is open for business.

'That's it!' I exclaim, realising this was an article Mum had never intended to sell. The wise old owl was meant to stay permanently in the pottery shed with her, year after year, performing an important and irreplaceable function.

Much to Hugh and Allan's surprise I leap across the room and lift the heavy object down from its shelf. I carry it out into the courtyard and lay it down on its side. With the three of us standing over the poor defenceless creature, I strike heavily at the base with my rolling pin. The pottery cracks into several large pieces. There on the ground, lying amongst the jagged fragments of clay is a rolled up bundle of papers, tied around the middle with a quite ordinary looking piece of string.

*

It takes all of our collective willpower, but we leave the documents tightly secured within their strong binding. We take them with us, unread, to our meeting with Kitty Walmsley. Colin has arranged for us to meet outside Kitty's nursing home in Gilstone at ten this morning. Even though we arrive early in our taxi cab, Colin is already standing outside waiting for us.

The home is in a large and attractive sandstone villa which looks straight out over the Firth of Clyde. There are a number of sturdy wooden benches and seats dotted around the large front garden, so the residents can gain the full benefit of the tremendous views.

Yesterday's storm has cleared the air and there is barely a cloud visible in the blue sky. Colin asks one of the nurses to bring Kitty out into the front garden so we can take our morning coffee out here. While we are waiting, Colin glances down at the bundle of documents I am holding in the crook of my arm, but makes no comment on it.

As Kitty is guided down the three stone steps leading out into the garden I am struck by her almost childlike appearance. She is wearing a cream cotton summer dress that is secured around her middle by a pink shiny belt. I am immediately reminded of an outfit Bridie had worn to every single party she attended in the year that she turned five.

Colin takes over from Kitty's nurse. He sits her carefully down on one of the sturdy seats and slowly introduces us all to her. Colin takes his mother's hand and speaks in a kind and gentle voice when he says, 'they've come here to talk about Isabel, Mum. These are Isabel's children.' Colin gestures to us all and absolutely no one contradicts his attempt to simplify things. 'They've come to hear about that terrible winter on the Island. Isabel has said it's time for them to know the full story. She wants *you* to be the one to tell them.'

I expect Kitty to look distressed by this news but she does not. For the first time since meeting her, I think that I see her smile.

'Does she really Colin? Can I tell them at last? I would very much like to.' Kitty's voice is unexpectedly strident.

Colin nods reassuringly.

After a nurse has brought over a tray of coffees and cakes he goes on to add, 'I'll let you tell the story Mum, but if you need any help to explain anything then I will chip in, alright?'

It is Kitty who nods this time. She completely ignores the dainty china coffee cup that has been set down in front of her. Instead, she places her bright, cornflower blue eyes directly upon us and begins her story.

'It was a terribly cold winter. It had started in the December of the previous year and just went on and on, through Christmas and continuing well into the months that followed. There were snow drifts reaching the roofs of the barns during that January and February. It was a very difficult period for all of us farmers. I was not married to Colin's father yet and my parents were still running Loch Crannox Farm. But Isabel and Angus were up at Lower Kilduggan all by themselves. Isabel's father, Donald, had passed away a few years earlier and Elizabeth had retired to a little cottage in Kilross. It was very tough for them, being all alone up there. I would often trek over, across the deep snow covered fields, to give them a hand when the weather was really bad. Sometimes I would help Angus to guide the sheep and cows down into the barns, so the poor things could keep warm.

On one of these occasions, all three of us had just come down from the hillside. Isabel and I were in the kitchen. Your mother, I recall, had the stove door wide open so we could gain some heat from it to warm our freezing cold hands. Whilst we were preparing the kettle and lighting the fire, Angus came in holding a letter.

He was angry about something, but he didn't want to talk about it in front of me. Isabel told him I was a good friend and we had no secrets from each other. Angus nodded and started to tell us what the letter said. I had never before heard Angus utter a single word about his family, so I was amazed to hear that the letter he was holding in his hand had come from his mother. She had written to tell him how she was at her wits end and needed his advice. The letter said that his younger sister had got herself pregnant and the baby had been born a few weeks earlier. His mother had added that no one knew who the father of the bairn might be, so there was no point in his even asking.

It sounded to me as if this sister of his was no better than she ought to be. She had left the baby with her mother whilst she was out until all hours of the night doing goodness knows what. But that wasn't the worst of it. Your grandmother was writing the letter because she was desperate. Their tenement flat was damp and cold. They'd not enough money to heat it and the terrible chill of that long, cold winter was taking its toll. The wee bairn was coughing all of the time and she wrote of her fear that the poor thing might not make it through another freezing night. Your grandmother explained how the baby had never taken to Mary's milk and the wee mite was getting weaker each day. When Angus read out this part, Isabel gasped and looked really distressed.

I remember then, that Angus put the letter down in disgust and said they'd be wanting more money from him he supposed and when would it ever end and other words to that effect. But Isabel was just sitting there at the kitchen table, as white as a sheet, and that's when she started to recount a story of her own.

She told us about how she once had a cousin, who was a little older than her; a beautiful and fair-haired girl, she said. But this cousin, I forget her name, had fallen ill with consumption. Isabel had never forgotten the girl's pale and anguished face and her constant rasping cough which was followed by a terrible battle to catch her breath.'

'Aileen,' I mutter quietly, almost to myself.

Kitty doesn't hear me but simply carries on with her tale. 'Isabel insisted that the clean Garansay air had kept that young girl alive. Once she went off to the Sanatorium on the mainland she just got worse, but when she had been on the Island she'd lived perfectly comfortably for quite some time.

Then, and I remember this part as if it was yesterday, Isabel took hold of Angus by his arms, and he wasn't someone you did that to lightly. She said to him, quite forcefully - the baby must come here.

Isabel was suggesting they could look after the bairn until the bronchitis had cleared up and the weather had got a little warmer. She said she was sure this was what his mother must be hinting at in her letter. Angus took an awful lot of persuading that it would be a good idea, but eventually he seemed to agree.'

Kitty takes a break here and sips at her coffee which must by now be stone cold. I am unsure of where this story is taking us, but sit patiently and obediently, waiting for Kitty to be ready to continue.

'I heard no more about it until Isabel came knocking on our door one evening, a few weeks later, to say that the baby was poorly. I put on my coat and boots and rushed back across the fields with her to help. When we arrived at the farmhouse, Angus was cradling a baby in his arms.

The poor wee thing was red in the face and bawling away at the top of its lungs. I had a quick look and decided the bairn probably had a fever so we sent Angus out for the doctor in one of the vans. Luckily, the weather had improved by this time so we were no longer cut off from the other villages as we had been for the previous few months.

When Angus returned with the doctor, the baby was looking a little better. We'd given the wean plenty of milk and loosened its clothes a little and the fever seemed to have come down. The doctor examined the baby. He told us that it was just a virus and all should be fine within a few days and how it was perfectly normal in an infant of this age.

Isabel looked very relieved to hear this, but then the doctor started to ask her questions about the baby's age and what the birth had been like. He even suggested that he should examine Isabel whilst he was there. Your mother drew the line at this, but at no stage did she explain to the doctor that the bairn wasn't hers, she just quietly and measuredly answered his queries.

Then, as he was leaving, the doctor turned back towards us for a second. He said that it was funny, because he too had been a 'snow baby'. His mother had been cut off by bad weather at their farm when she was due to give birth. No one outside of his family had set eyes on him for at least a month after he was born. The doctor kept chuckling about this amazing fact all the way back to the truck.

When the doctor had gone, Isabel stood in the kitchen, rocking the now perfectly peaceful baby in her arms. She said to me that I probably thought it was strange, how she hadn't told the doctor the baby wasn't hers. She explained it was just easier that way. Then Isabel asked me if I would help her to keep it a secret. She made me swear I wouldn't utter a word about where the baby had come from. She just said it would 'complicate' things if people were to find out and so I never did. Of course, I told Malc and the kids, but only when it was absolutely necessary. Other than that I always kept your Mum's secret - always.'

Kitty sits back in her chair looking very pleased with herself. Her audience appear not to be quite so delighted with what they have just heard. I have to force myself to say, 'but Kitty - the baby, you haven't told us the name of the baby.'

'Didn't I dear? I'm so sorry, well, it was Michael of course, who else could it have been?'

## Chapter 31

When Kitty has finished her tale, she looks about ten years younger. After Colin signals for the nurse to escort his mother back inside, she turns and gives us a cheery wave, slowly making her way back up the garden towards the house. The four of us remain resolutely in our seats. I am hoping Colin will be able to answer at least some of the multitude of questions that are circling around inside my head.

As soon as Kitty is out of earshot, it is Allan who breaks the awkward silence. 'That can't be correct,' he says stubbornly. 'You cannot bring up a child as your own for all those years and simply get away with it. Michael and Imogen are so much alike - it just can't be true.'

'But so many things are starting to become clear to me Allan - things that had never really made sense before. I used to think Dad was so hard on Michael because he was his first born. Now I see it was because Michael didn't really belong at the farm, just like him. Dad wanted to prove that both of them had the right to a life at Lower Kilduggan and that Michael had the right to inherit that life. He wanted to prove it through sheer hard work, because that's what Dad's background had taught him.'

'But I can't believe,' Allan persists, 'that Mum had no blood ties to Michael whatsoever. He was her bloody *favourite* for God's sake.'

'It doesn't work like that,' Hugh interjects. 'Isabel fell in love with Michael as soon as she set eyes on him - *before* she had set eyes on him, even. Her love for him began when Angus read her the contents of that letter. She was prepared to do anything to keep him with her.'

'Allan, don't you remember how hard it was when Michael tried to go and study in the United States? Mum couldn't find his birth certificate. There was no record of it anywhere, so they had to go through a really complicated process to get a new one registered,' I say.

'So he wasn't even adopted or anything?' Allan says this in a slightly shrill voice as the truth slowly begins to sink in. 'Then Mum had no claim on him at all.'

This shocking fact hangs in the air between us for a little while before I turn to Colin and ask, 'what about Mary Galbraith, how does her death fit into all of this?'

'From what Mum and Dad told me, your parents didn't hear anything from Michael's real mother for years. They'd had every intention of taking the baby back to the mainland when he was better. But the longer it went on without them hearing anything, the older the boy got. Michael became a tall, strong and healthy lad quite quickly. Of course, by this time, both of your parents loved him.

During those years your mother had a baby of her own. Allan was born at the same time as my Mum had Sandra. They both suffered quite bad complications because it was a first labour for both of them. This experience brought my Mum and Isabel even closer together - along with the secret they both shared.

In fact, the first time your parents had any contact with Mary was in the early seventies. At this point she started writing your father letters. They enquired as to how Michael was keeping. Mary even sent your parents his birth certificate - the real one, that is. But Isabel told Mum there was something menacing in those letters, she read them as a threat that she might, at any time, come back for him.

Michael was getting older by this point and Isabel claimed they were always going to tell him the truth about his parentage when he turned eighteen. But then, on that summer's day in 1973, Mary showed up. She just walked down to the Kilduggan shore, as calm as you like, to see her son.

Your father spotted her before she reached Michael. He led Mary off somewhere to have it out with her. Mary told him that she was married now and had her own boys. It was time for her to take her son home. Angus told Isabel his sister was reeking of booze. He knew she didn't really mean it and was just toying with him.'

Colin pauses here and I take the opportunity to add, 'your Mum seemed to think that it was *Isabel* who was desperate to have Michael here on

Garansay with them. But in some ways, I think our father's desire would have been even greater. He knew what life was like in that flat in the Gorbals, with an alcoholic, good-for-nothing, violent father and a dreadful poverty that crushed their every dream and expectation. I bet Dad was determined that Michael would never be made to go back there.'

Colin nods his head in agreement. 'It certainly fits with what Dad told me, because that afternoon Angus offered Mary money - a lot of money, to clear off the Island and never come back. Mary jumped at the proposal, which suggests this was what she was really interested in the whole time. Your father had to get hold of some ready cash, so he called in at Loch Crannox Farm to see my Dad. The two of them scraped together what they thought would be enough to see her off.

Angus then left Mary with my father and asked him to make sure she definitely got on the boat. Sadly, my father was a weak man. As soon as Angus had gone, Mary started working on him. She took him into the bar at the Gilstone Hotel and plied him with drink. Dad said Mary was a very beautiful woman, tall and ebony haired with a pale, creamy skin and blood red lips - she looked just like you, Imogen.'

I gasp. It makes me feel deeply unsettled to think I resemble her so closely. But it certainly explains why I look so much like Michael too - Mary's son.

'But Dad did not accompany Mary up the hillside to Aoife's Chariot that evening. He was back at home with Mum well before midnight. There may have been some other fool who followed her up there on that night, but we will never know for certain. Personally, I always believed she had some kind of accident. She was swimming in the loch, slipped and banged her head. Because she was so drunk, she simply drowned,' Colin finishes.

'That's what Eddie Galbraith always thought - but then what happened to the money if that was the case?'

Colin simply shrugs his shoulders, providing me with no answer.

'Once Mary was dead, there was no one left who would be able to say who Michael really was - except your mother, Colin,' I supply.

'Mum always maintained that Angus and Isabel were determined to tell Michael the truth when he turned eighteen. But then your father had his accident and after that I think your mother was terrified of people finding out, because without Angus, she had no claim on Michael at all. She told Kitty once that folk would simply see her as a child-snatcher,' says Colin.

I suddenly have a thought. 'So for thirty years, Alison Dickson knew that Michael wasn't really our brother. I wonder if that was why she was so jealous of me - because she thought that Michael's affections could easily have turned into something else as we got older. What if that was one of the reasons why she never revealed the truth?'

'But that isn't how it works,' Allan says quietly. 'I'll never think of Mike as anything but my brother. This news will never change that fact.'

I nod and lay my hand over his.

'What is in those documents then?' asks Hugh, who has remained quiet up to now.

I carefully untie the string and straighten the papers out on the table. For the next few minutes we all select a document each and fall silent while we take the time to read through them all. The letters from Mary Galbraith are all here, as is Michael's real birth certificate which lists his father as 'unknown'. There is even the original letter from my grandmother to my father, Angus, in the pile. It is dog-eared and worn by time, but I can still clearly make out the date, scrawled in the top right hand corner, which reads: February 16th 1956.

## Chapter 32

There was another letter in Mum's bundle. Allan found it as he was sifting through the pile. Unlike the other documents, the letter remained unopened and the envelope bore the small and deliberate handwriting of my late father. Allan and I decided that it was our responsibility to deliver the letter personally. We felt this was the least we could do, considering it would be reaching its recipient about forty years too late.

Michael knows we are coming to see him, but we remained vague about the purpose of our visit. Allan and I have prepared no speech in advance but we fully expect to share with Michael everything we have learned. After setting foot onto the austere and stylish staircase that winds its way up to Michael's first floor flat, Allan suddenly takes hold of my hand. So as our elder brother lets us in through his elegant front door, we are presenting a strong and united front.

We allow Michael to prepare us afternoon tea before we shatter his neat and ordered existence with our revelation. Michael can tell we are behaving oddly and it is he who prompts the disclosure of our news. 'I sense this is some kind of deputation,' he says, as he finally sits back against the leather chair, with his cup and saucer balanced on his lap.

'Michael,' I venture. 'We found out quite a lot of things about the family while we were on Garansay.' I slide myself along the sofa so that I am closer to him and put my hand into the satchel to retrieve the letter.

Before I have a chance to hand it over, Allan interrupts, 'we have a letter for you, Mike. It was written by our father a very long time ago and it's about you. It probably explains everything a lot better than we ever could, but just the same, I think that you'd better hear all about it from us first.'

Unexpectedly, from this moment on, Allan takes charge of the proceedings. He positions himself opposite Michael and sensitively explains everything that we have found out about our family. It turns out that Allan is absolutely right. The news is far better coming from him, and he does the job surprisingly well. After Allan has finished, Michael is very still and quiet. For a few moments, I begin to feel quite concerned for him.

Then Michael looks up and says, 'I always knew.' And when Allan and I look surprised he explains, 'not the details, of course, I had no idea that Aunty Mary was my mother. What I mean is that I always knew I was different. I knew that I wasn't really accepted as one of the family. I always had to work for it, you see. Dad made me work hard for everything and, of course, now I can see why.'

'Would you like to read the letter?' I ask tentatively.

Michael says nothing at first, but he reaches out his hand and takes the envelope. 'From what you have told me, I believe that Angus wanted me to read this letter but Mum never did. She believed that the truth would have served no purpose and I agree.' Michael hands the unopened letter back to me and says, without a hint of malice, 'you keep it Imogen. You are the one who searches for the truth, and you've got a real gift for finding it. If you want to read it at some point in the future then you have my full blessing to do so. As far as I am concerned, I know enough.'

## Chapter 33

It is a beautiful sunny day. It feels as if I could not be happier as I stand on the Hythe Quay in Maldon with Hugh, Bridie and Ian to watch the magnificent Thames Barges begin their race along the River Blackwater. We send up a triumphant cheer as the boat that Bridie and Ian spent so long helping to decorate glides passed us, with the crew and a few select staff members and pupils from the Secondary School on board.

The Hythe is thronging with spectators, many of whom are clutching pints of beer purchased from 'The Queen's Head' and 'The Jolly Sailor'. There would be no hope of being able to drink them in the beer gardens themselves anymore, as they are filled to beyond capacity by the good-natured crowd. Hugh and I share a private joke as I point out to him that the theme for the School's barge this year is the 'Vikings' yet again. But the boat looks terrific and I know we shouldn't mock this town's wonderful heritage. We walk along the promenade, following the groups of spectators who are enjoying their locally made ice creams and waving their banners and flags. I put my arm around Bridie's shoulders and feel quite certain that I never want to go anywhere without my children ever again.

As it turned out, Hugh and I were hard pressed to get back home in time for today's event but we knew that we simply had to, for the sake of the kids. We ended up catching a flight from Prestwick in the early hours of this morning which cost an absolute fortune.

Yesterday's visit to Michael's flat had been very difficult but it ended in good humour. I'm not sure quite how I was expecting Michael to react to our news but he surprised me. I still have the letter in my bag and, for the time being at least, that is where it is going to stay. After Michael gave me back Dad's letter, for the first time since we found out the truth, I had cried. Michael automatically leaned forward to comfort me and during our embrace I could see, out of the corner of my eye, that Allan had placed a reassuring hand, squarely on his older brother's broad shoulders.

The first barges are now reaching the finishing line and we have to run to keep up with them. It is difficult to see which boat has crossed the line first but I think it must be one of the visiting barges, one that has made the trip down from Chatham, on the Medway, to join in this famous race.

As for Lower Kilduggan Farm, we have decided that it is no longer for sale. I absolutely forgive Colin, for the break-in and for not telling me the truth about Michael earlier, because I know that his intentions were good. But I cannot find it in my heart to sell the farm to him now, it just doesn't seem right. So we are going to take a little time to decide what we will do with the place instead. Surprisingly enough, Michael said yesterday that we should keep it. He said that he and Sarah could use the farmhouse at weekends and Allan and

Hugh and I for holidays. Michael even suggested that Sarah and Ross might want to get married there. But I just laughed and told him to take things one step at a time.

Abruptly, I am drawn away from my thoughts by Bridie, who tells me that their boat is about to cross the line. As it does so, a great shout goes up from the crowd. We join in the celebrations by holding onto each other as tightly as we can until the kids are too mortified to be seen hugging Hugh and me for even a second longer. We suddenly break apart and, still laughing, stride back towards the town, with the brilliant summer sunshine beating down on our heads.

*

Imogen and Hugh return in 'The Only Survivor', which is available now to download or order in paperback from amazon.

© 2013, Katherine Pathak, all rights reserved.

Books in the Imogen and Hugh Croft Mysteries Series:

Aoife's Chariot

The Only Survivor

Lawful Death

The Woman Who Vanished

Memorial For The Dead

**THE GARANSAY PRESS**

Acknowledgements:

Many people have given me great encouragement and support in the writing of this book. However, some individuals deserve a special mention. My parents, Bob and Sue have been superb proof readers, editors and historical advisors. My Dad's knowledge of the history and geography of western Scotland is second to none. My husband, Rakesh has also been a star by helping me to proof read the book and in summoning up the energy to read through sections for me at the end of a long, hard day. And, finally, to my sister, Anne, who has been extremely enthusiastic from the start of this project and who very kindly offered to design my front cover using her fantastic artwork - I couldn't have hoped for a better illustration for 'Aoife's Chariot' than one of Anne's original oil paintings. Just perfect, thanks.

K